WOLVES, BOYS, & OTHER THINGS that might KILL ME

WOLVES, BOYS, & OTHER THINGS that might KILL ME

kristen chandler

VIKING

An Imprint of Penguin Group (USA) Inc.

VIKING
Published by Penguin Group
Penguin Group (USA) Inc., 345 Hudson Street, New York, New York 10014, U.S.A.
Penguin Group (Canada), 90 Eglinton Avenue East, Suite 700, Toronto, Ontario, Canada M4P 2Y3
(a division of Pearson Penguin Canada Inc.)
Penguin Books Ltd, 80 Strand, London WC2R 0RL, England
Penguin Ireland, 25 St Stephen's Green, Dublin 2, Ireland (a division of Penguin Books Ltd)
Penguin Group (Australia), 250 Camberwell Road, Camberwell, Victoria 3124, Australia
(a division of Pearson Australia Group Pty Ltd)
Penguin Books India Pvt Ltd, 11 Community Centre, Panchsheel Park, New Delhi – 110 017, India
Penguin Group (NZ), 67 Apollo Drive, Rosedale, North Shore 0632, New Zealand
(a division of Pearson New Zealand Ltd)
Penguin Books (South Africa) (Pty) Ltd, 24 Sturdee Avenue, Rosebank, Johannesburg 2196, South Africa

Penguin Books Ltd, Registered Offices: 80 Strand, London WC2R 0RL, England

First published in the U.S.A. by Viking, a member of Penguin Group (USA) Inc., 2010

1   3   5   7   9   10   8   6   4   2

LIBRARY OF CONGRESS CATALOGING-IN-PUBLICATION DATA
Chandler, Kristen.
Wolves, boys, and other things that might kill me / by Kristen Chandler.
p. cm.
Summary: Two teenagers become close as the citizens of their town fight over the
packs of wolves that have been reintroduced into the nearby Yellowstone National Park.
ISBN 978-0-670-01142-1 (hardcover)
[1. Wolves—Fiction. 2. Interpersonal relations—Fiction. 3. Survival—Fiction. 4. Yellowstone
National Park—Fiction. 5. National parks and reserves—Fiction.] I. Title.
PZ7.C359625Wo 2010
[Fic]—dc22
2009030179

Printed in U.S.A.   Set in Sabon   Book design by Jim Hoover

For Brent and Gayle Chandler,

who taught me to treasure

what I can't tame

WOLVES,
BOYS, & OTHER THINGS
that might KILL ME

1

SUMMER SCHOOL

WOLVES DON'T ACTUALLY howl at the moon. Mostly they howl at each other. I'm a girl, so I get that.

When I hear the first howl, I'm standing knee-deep in Yellowstone meadow grass, loaded up like a packhorse, being assaulted by the first shards of an August hailstorm, listening to the couple we are guiding argue. Over the rumbling clouds and upperclass bickering I hear the wolf's howl. It is low and kind of whiny. The call of the bothered. I get that, too.

I'm out in front of our foursome. My dad calls from the back, "KJ, go left, to the trees." I take a few steps and then hear him call loudly, "Your *other* left."

I stop walking and let the couple pass me. Dad holds out his hand as he walks past. "How's that left doing? Maybe you should tie a string around your finger." This might be funny if I hadn't been hearing it my whole life. The man and his stuck-up wife turn and hear my dad's big joke. The woman looks down her pointy nose at me. I turn away and look out into Hayden Valley. I search the weather-bent grass. If I get to see a wolf today I can put up with some harassment.

I hear more howling. Competing wails. Then barks. The tourists, both doctors with advanced degrees in know-it-all-ness, freeze in their tracks.

"I heard something," says the woman.

"No kidding," says her husband.

"I thought these things only howled at night."

My dad clears his throat. "Canids howl when they need to. This sounds like a discussion about territory."

The afternoon sky has gone dark in that sullen, angry way it does in the Yellowstone caldera. The hail and the heavy sky make it difficult to see. But poor visibility usually means more wildlife. I don't use my binoculars so I can scan for movement.

After a moment I make out two coyotes. Then I see the wolf. The hail lessens and I see the wolf is three times the size of the coyotes, light gray to their tan and orange outlines. We are less than a hundred yards away. I whip out my binoculars and focus until they look like they are practically at my feet.

"What is it? Is it a wolf?" the woman says. Her two-hundred-dollar hat is soaked. She waves her manicured hand at me. "Get out the scope."

"Where do you see it?" her husband says, lifting his binoculars into the freezing hail. I stop watching the wolf so I can put up their scope. That is what I'm here for, after all. To be the Girly Sherpa. The maid in hiking boots.

The woman explained to me before we left the shop that she was "outdoorsy" and that she could handle her own equipment. Apparently her idea of outdoorsy means she takes a guided fishing trip once a year, and her idea of handling her own equipment is having my dad and me carry the cameras, the scope, the tackle, and the lunches so she can carry her featherweight, collapsible graphite rod without messing up her hair. The woman grabs her scope and starts swinging it around trying to sight the wolf.

Dad knows more about the wildlife in this country than most people know about their own children, but he says nothing.

We stand there like that for a minute and then the yapping of the coyotes fills the valley. I blow into my hands, listening, trying to keep warm. The sounds come from two places, one in the meadow and one higher up in the trees.

Finally Dad says, "They have a den."

I say, "But it's so late in the year."

"Yep," he says.

"Where?" the woman says, salivating. "Wolves or coyotes? I can't see a thing in this hail."

"If you'd be quiet maybe Samuel would tell us," her husband says.

"I'll be quiet when I want to be quiet."

"Let me know when that happens."

The wolf moves in and out of the coyotes' nips. I think for sure the wolf will tear into one of the little runts, but it doesn't. Instead the wolf spins and runs, reaching back with its teeth to defend itself, but not chasing the coyotes off.

I say, "How come it doesn't go after them?"

The woman snaps at me. "I'd like to know where the hell you're even looking."

Dad raises his eyebrows and then points for the woman. She goes obediently back to her scope.

The man follows Dad's finger with his binoculars. "Oh. Oh," he says. "He's huge. Can't you see him, honey? He's right there. And the coyotes are biting him. This is very exciting."

I guess doctors miss blood when they're away from the office.

The woman swings her scope more violently. "I still can't see them."

Dad's voice is low. "That's because you need to calm down."

Why can't my dad act like the rest of the guides and just suck up to his clients? His tip is in the toilet now for sure.

"I'm perfectly calm." Her head shakes when she says this.

Her husband looks like Dad just slapped his wife. "I think she can manage."

"Good," says Dad. "Now how about I line up that lens so you can both get a good look?"

I go back to watching the wolf and coyotes. My eyes strain to catch every detail of the animals. Through the spattering hail I see the coyotes working the tag team defense. The pups go silent, but their parents keep up the bursts of barking. I can't believe we're seeing this. People think it's so easy to see a wild wolf now that they've been back in the park a few years, like they're big fat grazing buffalo or something. But just because you can buy a T-shirt with a wolf on it doesn't mean I've seen many of them.

Then things happen fast. The hail stops, like someone has flipped a switch. The air seems to freeze and everything goes silent. Five other wolves appear out of the grass, like they just grew there. Without two seconds passing, the coyotes disappear into the trees, leaving the solitary wolf alone with the new pack. It seems to me that the wolves have saved their friend from harassment; maybe they have even come to help him kill the coyotes and rout the den. But that is not what happens.

The biggest wolf, black with huge feet, leads out to the solitary wolf. He stands out front for a few seconds without moving. I think they are locking into each other somehow, and then the solitary wolf steps backward and drops down on its back. The man whispers to his wife, "It's submitting to them. I've seen that on television."

I hear Dad breathe funny, and I know something bad is about to happen.

The man starts to say something else, and my dad holds up his hand and *shh*s him. The woman doesn't say anything for a change. The four other wolves step behind the big black. The big black lunges at the wolf lying down. I can't see what is happening except that the wolves swarm and make tearing sounds that I feel down in my stomach muscles. The wolf being killed yelps four times. In the emptiness left by the storm I can hear everything. I don't know how to describe the sound, except it's sharp and pitiful. We just stand there, staring. I think I'm going to throw up, but I don't.

Then the hail comes back like a wave, pelting us and the ground and the wolves. The pack stands erect in the weather, heads up. Then they just circle the dead wolf once in a line and trot off.

The woman grabs her husband's arm. "Oh, I can't believe it."

Her husband says, "That was disgusting."

I whirl around. "Dad, they killed him."

Dad's face is hard and flat. "Yes, they sure did. And don't you forget it."

Don't you forget it? I let that boil for about ten seconds.

I say, "Gee thanks, Dad. I'll just put some more string around my finger."

He eyeballs me. This look probably scares some people.

"That's not what I meant, KJ. The minute that wolf backed down it was all over."

Classic Samuel Manning Carson. It was the wolf's fault for being outnumbered, ambushed, and then ripped to Alpo. It's a dog-eat-dog world out there, little missy, and you better get used to it. Lessons from Life. Spare me.

We scowl at each other and then look away. The couple stays silent on the way back to the van. Dad needs to report the wolf death since Fish and Wildlife are out counting noses all the time. The hail has ruined the fishing for today. *So what,* I think. My tip was in the toilet anyway.

WELCOME BACK, WEST END WOLVES!

It's time for another school year to begin, and we look forward to seeing all two hundred and thirteen students, with their friends and family,* at the Meet and Greet Bonfire Friday at sundown to kick off the school year!

You've worked hard all summer, so come have some fun before the school year starts. Bring your blankets and marshmallows. See you there!

*Chuck Daniels saw a sow grizzly and a cub walking on the field last week, so we're asking everybody to keep tabs on their kids during the event.

2

THE FIRST DAY OF
THE END OF MY LIFE

IT TAKES ME twenty minutes to walk to school from our cabinesque house. Last week I read in the *West End News* that the average commute in town is six minutes. I guess they didn't survey anyone without a car. The paper said the town's year-round population is 947 strong, but I find this statistic hard to believe. Sometimes it feels like I could fit the whole town inside my head. Ever since kindergarten, it's been the same school, same kids, same me.

I guess I'm not exactly the same me. After sixteen years, I finally started to look like a girl this summer. Not a big deal. I had to buy a real bra and I grew my hair out. But Dad acts like it's a big deal, like I'm a felon until proven otherwise. All

I know is that if he says I've "bloomed" one more time I'm going run away from home and become a shrub.

I pass the Brandin' Iron Motel and then the Pony Express RV Park. The summer tourist season is still in full swing. At the RV park, a mom in yellow overalls yells at her pint-size son, "Get in the car, before I leave you."

The little boy wails. I hear car doors slamming. The air smells of diesel from motor homes lining up to get into the park.

I pass the High Country Fly Shop and Touring Company. Dad's inside, tying flies with Ruben, one of the guides. I'm not sure where the other three guys are this morning, probably out with clients. I am not a guide, I'm a flunky. But at least I stay around all year. They'll be gone before the snow sticks, leaving me and Dad to run the store, just like every year. I wave to Dad, but he doesn't see me.

A police truck passes me in the street. Officer Smith waves and yells, "Lookin' good, KJ."

The ornery half of the West End police force is right behind him in his truck going two miles an hour. Officer Farley yells, "Nice shirt, KJ."

Must be a big police meeting at the Quickie Mart.

I hurry along, picking at my stupid new shirt. Why did I think salmon would be a good color on me, and why is it suddenly so tight in all the wrong places? One of the many disadvantages of not having my mother around is that there is no one to tell me not to wear things like this shirt. There is no one to say, "Was the light off in the bathroom when you put on that makeup?" Most girls think they would love it if their mothers left them alone, but that's because they never had their dad do their hair on the first day of kindergarten.

I see my reflection in the bakery window. It still startles me. Mrs. Williams waves from behind the counter inside. She makes the worst doughnuts in three counties. I wave back and keep walking.

I guess it sounds superficial to complain about my clothes and hair when I'm talking about my mom being gone. Fashion advice isn't what I miss most about having a mom. It just sucks having to wear my momlessness every day.

Maybe one of the worst big things about having my mom gone is that it's like she never existed. She died in a car wreck when I was three. It happened about a year after my parents moved to West End. My mom's sister, Diane, told me that my mom and I were driving to Bozeman to stock up on groceries, and she hit some ice. We smashed into a telephone pole so hard it snapped in half. Diane said they found me tucked in my car seat, sucking my thumb. She didn't say what happened to my mom. I've just guessed about that part.

My dad doesn't talk about my mom, and I don't ask him to.

I walk through the door of the school just as the first bell rings. I am going to be late, as usual. I don't remember my schedule so I have to pull it out and read it for the fiftieth time: period 1—journalism.

This class will probably be a joke, since the journalism teacher is really the home economics teacher, Mrs. Brady, aka Mrs. Baby. She has had a baby every year for the last four years she has lived in West End. Everyone says she only teaches for the maternity benefits, but I think she comes to school to get away from all her crying kids.

When Mrs. Baby was my foods teacher last year, she suggested I take journalism. I think she likes me because I did an annotated recipe book for my class project entitled "Twenty-Five Uses for Leftover Elk Meat." Her favorite was Elk Shakes—The Real Man's Protein Drink.

Every other week the journalism class turns out a newspaper for the school. It's usually so boring even the seventh graders don't read it.

I walk as fast as I can through the Hall of Fame, our illustrious entry hall full of trophies and photographs of notable West Enders. Surprisingly my picture has not yet been selected for enshrinement.

Everyone is saying hello and pushing around in the hallways. I say hello to a few kids. A few kids say hi back, like always. But they're looking at me. The class pervert says, "What happened to you this summer?" when I pass him in the hallway. I am going to throw this shirt in a hole and set it on fire when I get home.

I open the classroom door just as the final bell rings. Mrs. Baby gives me an irritated look so I sit down quickly. I can't believe it—she's totally pregnant again.

"Glad you could make it, KJ."

"Thanks," I mumble.

When I finally stop gaping at Mrs. Baby's prolific belly I realize I'm sitting next to someone I have never seen before. Someone who is not from my corner of nowhere. Someone whose green flannel shirt is topped off with blond shaggy hair.

At the end of roll call, Mrs. Baby says, "Virgil Whitman." She pauses, stares at the name, and then looks at the shaggy head in front of me. "Um, Virgil . . . do you go by a nickname?"

Nice one Baby, I think. *Way to insult the new guy.*

"Virgil's fine." The voice from the hair cracks a little. He has some sort of faint accent but I can't place it. Then I think maybe it's just that he doesn't sound like everybody else around here. All the kids in the class stare at him.

"Well, that's fine. You're a junior? Where are you from?" says Mrs. Baby.

"Saint Paul, Minnesota." His voice stretches out the last syllable and makes it sound like *Min-e-sooda*.

"My dad's been there," says Addison. Addison is so lame. The only place her dad ever goes is the hardware store, and she's already got a prime hulk of a boyfriend, Kenner Martin, sitting next to her, as usual.

"Why'd you move?" says Kenner, sounding none too happy.

"My mom is doing some research here," says Virgil. "We're just here till June."

"What kind of research?" says Kenner. Kenner is smart but he likes to take swipes at anybody who admits they are, too. He comes from a long line of reflexively resentful ranchers. Plus he just likes to torment people.

Mrs. Baby jumps in. "I hope she's not here to study our strange customs."

Virgil says, "No, she's a wildlife biology professor. She's here to study the wolves."

"That is so sweet," says Kenner.

Virgil looks over at Kenner but doesn't take the bait. "And she wanted to be close to my aunt Jean."

"Jean Arrant is your aunt? It just keeps getting better," says Kenner and smirks at Addison. Addison smiles back at him. They're like married people.

Virgil nods. "Yeah, she's actually my great-aunt. Do you know her?"

Addison says, "Oh, everybody knows her."

Jean Arrant is like the Howard Hughes of West End. Rich but crazy. Supposedly eats cow brains and sculpts porn.

Clint, one of the requisite stoners taking the class, says, "Party at Virgil's." His friends Bret and Stewie nod in righteous agreement.

"Your mom studies wolves? Oh, that is so lucky," says Sondra Reese. Sondra is a genuine animal freak. Today she is wearing a purple T-shirt with a giant turquoise dolphin on the front. Last year she stood outside the Fourth of July Rodeo with a sign that said RODEOS ARE INHUMANE! EVERY TICKET CAUSES PAIN! The police asked her to leave after some kids started trying to rope her feet.

The shaggy head turns to Sondra, and I get the profile. His face is a little broken out, but his nose has a perfect Roman hook. His eyes are deep and surrounded by amazing long lashes. He looks embarrassed, which of course makes him devastatingly cute.

"So you must travel a lot then," says Mrs. Baby.

"A little. My mom brings me along to take pictures."

"You're a photographer?" says Dennis Welch, getting into the act. Dennis has more acne than the rest of the school put together. I've only heard him speak when he was using the words *Star Wars* or *computer* in the sentence. Either he has a crush on Virgil, too, or he's trying to get some points with the only guy in school who hasn't given him a wedgie.

"No," says Virgil. "I just do it for fun. But I could bring some stuff in tomorrow."

"That's a great idea," I say. I say it out loud . . . before my brain can control my mouth. I slide back into my seat but there is no place to hide.

Virgil turns around and looks at me. He has the sunniest

face I have ever seen. His skin is tan and rough except around his pale blue eyes. His whole face is curved up in a disturbingly unguarded smile. Even his bushy eyebrows smile. He's solar. I smile back, from my crouched position. He says, "I'll bring some pictures."

Mrs. Baby says, "Yes. Good. Well, as most of you probably know, this class puts out the school newspaper every two weeks. And newspapers need pictures. So, Virgil, bring your photos in. Friday we'll assign departments. Everyone needs to bring in a sample of their writing or photography, and we'll figure out what everyone wants to do."

"What about editor?" says Dennis. Last year's editor, Logan Kittredge, moved to a real city so his dad could make some real money doing a real job, or at least that's what Logan said.

"I won't assign that job for a few weeks, Dennis."

Kenner says, "Ease up, *Star Trek*."

Dennis pulls out his day planner and makes a note.

I would laugh at all my provincial inmates, but I'm too busy lusting. I'm not usually interested in a guy with "take a number" on his forehead, but this guy doesn't have a forehead—it's buried in messy blond hair. And he's not one of the twenty guys I've known my entire pubescent life. He smiles like the Fourth of July. What's a dumb girl to do but get in line with everyone else not in his league? I guess journalism just became my most beloved class.

I go to my Spanish and PE classes on autopilot. Then on to English. Mrs. Vandergraf, our teacher, is about four hundred years old and has been my English teacher twice already. She thinks *Beowulf* is edgy. But she lets us read in class, so I don't mind.

I sit with Joss Tanner and Mandy Wright at lunch. When I show up they just keep talking. This isn't surprising, because Joss and Mandy are arguing about the cosmic repercussions of grams and calories, and that's not a subject that should be interrupted mid-debate.

"That roll is like the worst thing you can eat," chirps Mandy.

Joss snorts. "How about that salad dressing you just flooded your lettuce downstream with?" Joss is two inches taller than any other girl at school and she doesn't like advice.

"We have to be serious or it won't work." Mandy has strawberry blonde hair that she styles in tight curls every morning. She has a patch of freckles on each cheek that make her look like a perturbed Cabbage Patch doll.

"Be serious?" says Joss. "You are a serious pain in the butt, Mandy."

"Fine. You look like this the rest of your life if you want to, but I'm on my way out of these stupid clothes."

"You're on your way out of your mind while you're at it. It's a roll. You need to breathe more."

Mandy starts forking her dressing-swamped salad to death. Joss puts half the roll in her mouth at once.

"Hi," I say for the second time.

"Hi," says Mandy in full pout. Joss looks at me like I'm an old newspaper.

I like Mandy and Joss, but it's always been clear that they are the pair and I'm the extra. So they call me to do stuff, but I don't have metabolism issues so I'm not inner-circle material.

Not a total loser, more like a free-floating oddball.

I inhale half my cheeseburger. Ketchup gets on my face about the same time I spot Virgil Whitman wandering around the lunchroom trying to find someplace to sit down. I nearly aspirate my food. I grab Joss's dirty napkin and clean off my chin. He sits down by himself and starts drinking his milk.

"Excuse me," says Joss. "Who is that?"

"His name is Virgil," I say. "He's a complete jerk. I'm sure you wouldn't like him. And he smells bad and is probably gay."

"Did you meet him?" says Mandy.

"Sort of," I say.

Joss snorts. "Have you spilled anything on him yet?"

I continue rubbing my chin. "Not yet. But thanks for asking."

"Did you say anything to him?" says Mandy.

"Not exactly," I say.

"Where's he from?" says Joss.

"Min-e-sooda," I say quietly, trying to look at him out of the corner of my eye. Dennis has migrated to his table and is talking his ear off. Lucky Dennis. "His mom's a wolf scientist."

Mandy takes her napkin out of my hand, "Whatever. Just because you got boobs and haircut. He's still way out of your league, sweetie."

Joss laughs with her mouth open. "KJ doesn't have a league."

I stop chewing. I know they're kidding. They're always kidding. But it's not exactly cracking me up today. "What's that supposed to mean?"

"Nothing," says Joss. "Don't be so conceited."

"I'm conceited? About what?"

"Sooo defensive," says Mandy.

"Sooo true," says Joss.

"I've got to go," I say. My lunch doesn't taste good any-more.

Mandy pats my hand like I'm lost in the grocery store. "We're not trying to make you feel bad. . . . We totally love your new look, don't we, Joss?"

"What?" I say.

Joss opens her mouth again. "At least you don't look like a Peppermint Patty anymore, right?"

"Well, not totally, anyway," says Mandy.

I say, "I'm going to the library."

"There's a shocker," says Joss. "Don't worry, he's probably gay. Look at that hair."

I pick up my tray and take it to the trash can, trying not to look at Virgil, and walk straight into Kenner and Addison. Walking into Kenner is sort of like walking into a moving van. I nearly fall on my face trying to get out of his way.

Kenner says, "What's new in Dorkville?"

Same old Kenner.

"Be quiet, Kenner," says Addison. "You look so cute today, KJ. I love your new look."

I didn't know I had a look. And if I have one I'm getting kind of tired of it.

Kenner says, "Geez, Addie, KJ doesn't care about that stuff. She's a tree hugger. She wears bark for underwear, right?"

"Oh, be quiet," says Addison.

"*You* be quiet," says Kenner.

"*You* be quiet," says Addison.

The happy couple walks toward their waiting minions.

My next class is Algebra II, the second installment of last year's nightmare. Even stoners are better at math than I am. And this is West End High—not exactly the Harvard of the West.

I do well in most of my classes. Partly because my dad is a

gale-force freak about my grades. And partly because, much to my shame, I like school. Some of it, anyway. But anything involving numbers, spelling, or a foreign language . . . is like a foreign language to me.

The only semi-bright spot in the algebraic abyss is my teacher, Mr. Muir. He owns a knife and gems store called Sticks and Stones. He's pretty cool for somebody that teaches math and sells weapons to bikers. Last year he figured out I have dyslexia, and I became his pet project. I studied my guts out and he gifted me a C-minus. But I still can't do math.

I sit in the back as usual. Mr. Muir looks up from his table and gives me a little wink. He's trying to be nice, but it makes me feel like I need a special parking space.

Kenner and Addie come in and are followed by three other guys from the football team. The Algebra II text must be preferred reading for the jock book club this semester. Addie waves at me like she hasn't seen me all year and I wave back. A minute later Mandy and Joss walk in, followed by the new guy. He sits down right in front of me, again, and pulls out a book a foot deep.

Addie says, "Hi, Virgil." She's practically panting.

Virgil looks up, smiles, then goes back to his book. He reads in class more than I do, poor guy.

"That's a pretty big book," says Kenner. Two of Kenner's brick-brained friends laugh. They're like a walking sound track, especially Road Work Reynolds, who seems to have donated his brain to science. Kenner has a look on his face that doesn't bode well for Virgil. "Mr. Minnesota must be a bodybuilder. I bet his boyfriends like that."

Virgil keeps reading. He looks relaxed, at least from behind. But why not? He's from the real world.

I stare at Virgil's head with impunity. I can't help it. The blond mess, slightly lopsided and honey colored, makes me momentarily immune to my own typically incapacitating inhibitions.

"Whatcha readin' Vir-gil?" asks Kenner in his best Addie voice.

"Oh, shut up," says Addie.

"Don't tell me to shut up," says Kenner.

Mr. Muir says, "Both of you shut up. Welcome to class, Virgil. Now let's get to work everyone, and see what you remember from last year."

Mr. Muir gets busy writing things on the board. I get busy remembering I'm a math idiot. I also remember I'll have to stay in this town for the rest of my life being harassed by people like Kenner if I don't pull a decent grade. My dad will disown me. I'll end up working the night shift at the gas station, living on the edge of town in a camper. I've got things to think about other than the gorgeous freak of nature sitting in front of me.

Right. From where I'm sitting I can smell the wool in his shirt. The blinking fluorescent tube on the ceiling above him makes little dents of light in his hair.

Mr. Muir leans forward. I realize he has just asked me a question.

"KJ, remind the class what the difference is between a conditional and unconditional inequality."

What? I'm supposed to be listening to math theory when I have Sexy Hair sitting in front of me? My face floods with traitorous red color.

"Unconditional inequality is . . . um . . ."

"Yes?" says Mr. Muir, pointing at something he has obviously just explained on the board. He turns to me and gives me the Special Ed. smile. I feel around in the darkness of my brain. . . .

Kenner whistles faintly through his teeth making the sound of a crashing airplane. Road Work adds the laugh track.

Mr. Muir turns back to the board. "Mr. Reynolds, you have a lot of energy today. . . . What is unconditional inequality?"

Kenner twists in his seat and hands Road Work the algebra book with the page open. Road Work says, "Unconditional inequality is . . . when things can't ever be the same?"

I hate Kenner. I hate Road Work. I hate algebra.

"Exactly," says Mr. Muir and continues writing. "And conditional inequality?"

Road Work looks quickly at his book and draws a blank. Kenner whispers to him. "The opposite?"

Mr. Muir looks back at him skeptically, sees the book, and says, "Virgil? How about you?"

Virgil's warm Minnesota voice floats out in front of me. "When the value of variables changes, when the values can be reversed or destroyed it changes the inequality."

"Exactly," says Mr. Muir "If the variables can change it makes different outcomes possible. Yes, class?"

Yes, class. Sometimes things can change. Exactly.

A Poem about Numbers

If I put it in my head
It just goes out my ear instead.

A Poem about Math

Why is this so hard?
I hate it.

3

HOME AGAIN, HOME AGAIN, JIGGITY JIG

THE GOOD THING about the first day of school is that eventually it ends. The bad thing is that this means I have to go to work. The other good thing is that Virgil Whitman is in almost every one of my classes. My goal tomorrow is to avoid talking to him. Guys seem to like me better that way.

On my way walking to work, I figure I have earned fifteen minutes of hooky. I head for the tree house.

The "house" is a pie slice of plywood wedged in between four lodgepole pines and buttressed up by other scrawny lodgepoles hammered underneath. It doesn't exactly meet building codes.

This castle was built by someone else's dad, but I took it

over when I was about seven. It's on the edge of national forest property, so it's really anybody's tree house, and I know from the cigarette butts and beer cans that other kids occasionally come here. Luckily it's in bad enough shape that most of the burnouts have better places to get wasted.

From the uneven plywood perch I can see the trees that stand next to our house and a few signs from town, but I never look that direction. The other view is mostly just the tops of lodgepole pine and lots of sky. Not a calendar shot, but restful, especially when the wind is blowing. The pines really do whisper around here.

One thing I love about the tree house is that this section of the forest is full of old men trees, piney giants that have lived through enough fires and bug infestations to tower over me and make me feel like they are watching. I don't mind being watched by trees. It's everyone else that makes me feel like the stupid-smart–intermittently-imploding girl.

I think about the wolf I saw killed and my dad's little speech afterward. "The minute that wolf backed down it was all over."

All over. I should be so lucky.

I lie flat and cogitate about Virgil Whitman. Solar smile. Naked hair. Floating voice. It almost makes me want to go back to school tomorrow. I drift until a raven circles over me and squawks irritably. I look at my watch. My dad is going to kill me.

◇   ◇   ◇

My dad lifts his head to look at me as I walk in. He's with a customer so he gives me a quick glare, which I pretend not to see.

I say, "Hi, Dad."

He furrows his brow slightly and ignores me. This is how it goes. People come from all over the world just to fish with my dad and have the pleasure of his company, but he only speaks Nod and Gesture to me.

I recognize the fisherman my dad is talking to from last fall. I remember chatting him up when he bought his licenses; he sells townhouses in Utah. Has a daughter about my age that won't fish. Bob Andrews or Anderson. He triple sneezes as I come closer. He did that last year. His name rhymes with "achews." I walk up and say, "Welcome back, Mr. Andrews."

He looks at Dad. I love it when people give that look to my dad. "It's good to be back, dear. How are you?"

"Well, I started school today."

"That's a shame," says Mr. Andrews.

I shed my ghastly day like a bad shirt. In the shop I'm just me. No freak show explosions. "How's your daughter Melinda doing?"

Mr. Andrews winks at Dad. "Impressive . . . Wish my daughter paid that much attention to what I said." He turns to me. "She just started her senior year. Total nutcase. Wants to be an astronaut."

"Way cool," I say.

"I guess," Mr. Andrews says. "But I'd just as soon she was a doctor or lawyer or something that involved staying on this planet."

"Don't let her be a lawyer then," Dad says.

"Yeah, lawyers definitely live in their own little world," I say.

Mr. Andrews smiles at Dad. "Got a law degree in the closet, Samuel?"

"Back with the mothballs," says Dad.

"Is that right? Before you got religion, huh?"

"Yep," says Dad. "Now I'm a Born Again Fisherman."

Mr. Andrew fingers the small salmon fly in his hand. "Hey, what's the difference between a dead cat on the road and a dead lawyer on the road?" Mr. Andrews isn't looking at Dad when he says this. I freeze a little but it hits me slower than my dad. "A dead cat has skid marks around it." He looks up for the laugh but he doesn't get one.

I try to smile a little and distract Mr. Andrews from my dad's face. I say, "Does your daughter like yoga? We have new yoga pants in the back."

Mr. Andrews looks confused. Maybe he thinks we don't have a sense of humor about Dad being a lawyer. He has no way of knowing my mother was an attorney, too. He probably doesn't even know she's dead, let alone that they had to pull her out of her car with a crowbar. "Yoga? No. I don't think so."

"They're really comfortable," I say. "You can even sleep in them."

Mr. Andrews tips his head at Dad and frowns. "No offense, Samuel. I just thought . . ."

Dad doesn't say anything.

The phone rings and Dad says he'll take it in the back room. I sell Mr. Andrews some yoga pants for his astronaut daughter and tell him not to worry, my dad's just tired.

No skid marks. It's a dead mom joke. It's the start of a whole new brand of sick humor.

When Ruben comes in to help me close I tell him about Mr. Andrews' bad joke. Ruben smiles and then frowns. He always does that. He says, "Make him something good for dinner and he'll be fine tomorrow."

I like Ruben. His accent makes his words float a little before they land. Some of our clients are jerks and don't respect him as much because he's from Mexico. Like he doesn't know how to catch American trout if he wasn't raised on American cheeseburgers or something. If Dad gets wind that somebody's mouthed off about Ruben, that's the last time my dad will take that person fishing.

I say, "I'll close up if you want to go home."

Ruben says, "I'm in no hurry. You go home and make a salad for your Dad. He needs more roughage."

"He always looks that way," I say.

"He's lucky to have you," says Ruben. "Go home and remind him."

"That would take one amazing salad," I say. I feel bad because I know Ruben misses his two boys and his wife. I also feel bad because he's leaving soon, with all the other guides. Then, just like every year, it will just be me and Dad in the store. At least I can talk to the customers.

I walk home fast and hope that there is something edible in the fridge I can make for my dad. It's been a long day for both of us. I know he won't eat, but at least if I cook something we can both pick at our food and pretend that we are fine. We're good at that.

KJ's Super Deluxe Recipe for Roughage * †

A big thing of Romaine lettuce, or whatever
1 tomato—if they have them at the store
4 carrots—carved with dad's hunting knife so they curl
2 peppers from my jalapeño plant
Elk strips, fried with those little onions and butter
Ranch dressing

*Gets you moving, one way or another

†Best served with a cold beer and no talking

4

BLACK AND WHITE
AND READ ALL OVER

MRS. BABY CALLS the roll every day, even though there are only nine kids in the class. I think with so many of her own kids, she can't remember who we are unless she can read our names at the start of class.

Virgil comes in and sits behind me. He looks at me as he passes, raises his eyebrows and says, "Hey."

A week into the semester and I am still a loaded geek gun around this guy. After avoiding saying a word to him all day yesterday, I have a spasm of congeniality. I spin around and say, "We have a lot of classes together."

"I noticed that," says Virgil. "I mean, I noticed you. You're pretty."

I'm pretty? You can't just say that to a girl in casual conversation. Is he from Minnesota or the moon? I'm so surprised I go blank.

"Do you want to see the pictures I brought?" He digs out an envelope, and Dennis and Sondra swoop over.

"More vermin babies?" says Kenner.

"Hush, Cro-Magnon," says Sondra.

Mrs. Baby says, "Virgil, would you like to share something with the class or can I finish calling the roll?"

"Sorry for the interruption, Mrs. Brady," he says.

I think Mrs. Baby wants to adopt him.

Mrs. B. directs us to an ancient table in the back of the room to read our ideas for the first issue. "Let's go, team! Remember our motto: 'Fair, fun, and friendly.'"

I'm not sure where Mrs. Baby learned about journalism, but I don't think it was in college.

Addison reads a groundbreaking article she's written about "Fabulous Fall Fashion Trends." Kenner hands in the football team's schedule. The JV stoners, Bret and Stewie, read two fart jokes. Clint, the varsity stoner, shows pictures he took of his friends jumping off a cliff into a river. All blurry, "'cause he was freakin' wasted." Dennis has a two-page story about a new D&D video game. Sondra reads her exposé on the evils of pet stores, which turns out to be interesting in a depressing sort of way. I read something I wrote at eleven P.M. last night about whirling disease in western fisheries, mostly because my dad has enough articles about it to pad a mattress.

Virgil, on the other hand, has an entire portfolio of wildlife photographs. He's photographed badgers eating, elk jumping, and sandhill cranes in flight. But mostly he has wolves. Wolves hunting, wolves licking each other, wolves with pups, and wolves with Virgil's mom holding them.

"How did you get these shots?" I say.

"Maybe he's a wolf whisperer," says Dennis.

"Oh, look at that," says Sondra. "You got that little one smiling at your mom." Sondra needs a pet.

"Look again, Bambi," says Kenner. "It's baring its teeth."

"Really?" says Addison, scooting closer to Kenner.

When they kidnapped the wolves from Canada and put them in the park a few years ago, some forest rangers came in their uniforms to our school. They told us all about the Endangered Species Act, and how wolves used to live here and then they were all killed and how that messed with the balance of things so the government brought the wolves back. Then they showed us a movie about how wolves don't really kill people, and our teachers put on their happy faces and had us make wolf packs out of macaroni.

But outside of school I heard people talking about how wolves would slaughter the cattle and sheep, wipe out the elk, wreck the park—all so bureaucrats in Washington could impress people that don't live here. Everyone talked about how the program was being instigated by "outsiders."

One night, over burnt spaghetti, I asked my dad if the wolves were going to wreck Yellowstone and eat all the cattle. My dad told me that was the rancher's job, and he thought we'd be in business a long time.

"On the other hand," he said with a deep frown, "I'm not a rancher. Those guys have got their hands full."

"Those are some impressive photographs, Virgil," says Mrs. B. "You capture the wild nature of the animals well."

Virgil half smiles. "Actually, a lot of these pictures are canned."

"Canned?" said Mrs. Brady.

"My mom helped me set them up, at the university lab." Virgil looks embarrassed by this information, but I don't know why. All he did was take the picture.

"Those wolves are captive?" says Sondra.

Kenner says, "If that wolf was wild, it would have ripped his mom's head off."

"Wolves are the greatest, most noble predator in the American West. They should not be used as lab rats," says Sondra. "Your mother should be ashamed of herself."

"That's enough, Sondra," says Mrs. Baby.

"Yeah. It's for research, right?" says Dennis passionately.

I think he's actually trying to protect someone besides himself. It's kind of cute.

Sondra scowls at all of us.

"I hate wolves," says Stewie. "They kill all the elk so there's nothin' left to hunt."

"You couldn't shoot an elk if it fell on you," says Bret.

Stewie shoves Bret. "Screw you, man."

Kenner says, "Wolves kill more than elk. They're butchers."

Sondra chirps up, "What do you call what your family does? Babysitting?"

Kenner focuses in for the kill. "Honest work. Which is more than I can say for your money-mooching family."

Sondra nearly shouts, "You get more government welfare to run that death ranch than my mother ever dreamed of. You're nothing but a bunch of greedy flesh-gouging—"

Mrs. Baby suddenly seems to realize her "team" is in trouble. She stands up fast so her belly shoots out like a canopy from her body. "That's enough," she says. She straightens her dress over her protruding stomach. "Now, I know that there are strong feelings on this subject. But let's not get rude."

Virgil puts his pictures away. I can only imagine what he thinks of our little class now. I wish I wasn't from Redneck, USA. I want to say something . . . redemptive. I want to be from a smart small town. A sanctuary of intelligence augmented with real-life proficiency. Plus I want Virgil to like me.

"Mrs. Brady," I say. "I have an idea."

"Yes," says Mrs. Baby, clearly ready to have someone else in charge of this moment.

"Maybe Virgil could do a thing for the paper. You know, about the wolves. Since everybody has so many ideas about what wolves are like, maybe he could take pictures of them when his mom studies them and then one of us could write about the pictures and do updates about what's happening with the wolves. You know, like a column. Then everybody could decide for themselves."

I'm totally making this up.

"That's a very interesting idea, KJ. What do you think, Virgil?" says Mrs. Baby. "Would you like to do some pictures of the wolves here? They're a little harder to get to smile."

I look at Virgil and I realize he is looking at me, not Mrs. Baby. He quietly says, "If KJ will write the column."

Kenner groans, "Oh, like KJ will be fair . . ."

Mrs. Baby glares at Kenner and then at me. Mrs. Baby never glares. Her idea of discipline is one less cookie. She says with a huff, "For heaven's sake. KJ, doesn't your dad shoot animals?"

"He's a guide."

"Does he kill things?"

"He hunts."

"So you'll be fair, won't you? Tell both sides of the story?"

"I guess so," I say. I'm not following her logic, but I'm not going to mess with an angry pregnant woman.

"Well, there you go, Kenner." She claps her hands to-gether. "I think Virgil and KJ will be a great team. Kind of a random look at what's happening with the wolves since they put them back in the park and how people feel about it. What should we call it, class?'"

"'The Wonder of Wolves,'" says Sondra.

Kenner says, "If KJ's doing it, maybe it should be 'Trips with Wolves.'"

The class laughs, even Mrs. Baby.

"No. No," says Mrs. Baby, swallowing a chubby chuckle. "What about something like 'Wolf Notes'? That sounds nice and neutral." If Mrs. Baby looked any more pleased with this idea she'd go into premature labor. "I'll want something for next week. We'll put you on the front page."

"Sure," says Virgil.

Virgil? Front page? I suddenly feel violently conspicuous. The class is looking at me. Virgil is looking at me. This is bad because when I get embarrassed my neck turns red and starts to itch.

"Are you feeling all right, KJ?" says Mrs. Baby. "Your neck is turning red."

I keep my chin down and look away from Virgil. "I think I'm dehydrated," I say.

"De-hy-drated?" says Clint. "You look like you have a giant hickey."

I stand up to go outside and accidentally fling my pen-cil off the desk with my hand. It rolls under Virgil's chair.

I lean over and say, "I dropped my writing utensil."

Stewie and Bret burst out laughing. Bret says, "Writing utensil? Nice one, KJ."

Kenner says, "I need a u-ten-sil."

Addison shoves his shoulder, but she is laughing, too.

Dennis says, "Is that really a hickey?"

Everyone is vomiting laughter. I'm hilarious.

Virgil hands me my pencil. He doesn't say anything. It's eerie.

Clint says, "Do you remember in fourth grade when she said she had to *urinate* and then she peed her pants anyway?"

"So totally gross."

"Now . . ." says Mrs. Baby.

"In Driver's Ed . . . last year . . . I thought Mr. Moonie was going to drop a brick when she dented the test car."

"Omigosh, how about when she hurled at . . ."

I walk out of the room and close the door behind me as the class finishes reliving my greatest hits.

5

JUST GOOD TO GET OUT

I LIKE THE WEEKEND, even if it means work, because it doesn't mean school. I clean the store, prep trip supplies, and stand around trying to sell gear. I also get to play Sherpa a fair bit. And all that is fine, but what I really love is to row.

I don't usually get to row because I'm not a guide. Fishing guides must be masters at mixing pointers with stories and keeping their clients entertained in between success with gullible fish. They pull out knots in people's lines and suggest flies and philosophies of presentation. "Try that little riffle, Hank, it's a dandy. Watch your drag, now."

I just like to row. But if I row I take up a seat, so if it's more than one client we usually have to take the four-man

(-person) inflatable raft. And most people like the wooden drift boat. Honestly they just look better.

So mostly I store-sit on fall weekends. But every so often, every blue moon or red dawn or whatever, I'm allowed to row. And although I am an abysmal fisherman and rotten storyteller, I can row. Dad likes to say I'm hell on oars.

Along with all the other inconsistencies of my life, even though I am uncoordinated and scrawny, I'm also freaky strong for my size. Last year Dad bought a rowing machine so he could use it during the winter. He didn't use it more than twice, but I did. By spring, I could do fifteen pull-ups from the tree in my backyard. Dad could only do four.

He got so excited he took me out on the Madison River the next day. We put in at the McAtee Bridge and by the time we hit Ennis Bridge he said I was worthy to row anything in the shop. That was one of the best days I can remember.

The only problem is that most men don't like having a five-foot-four Pop-Tart row like a sailor while they do their manly fishing, so Dad usually saves me for women's groups, who think I'm the best thing since the sports bra.

This morning Dad is guiding a couple of female lunatics from Colorado, and I'm up. He says he wants me to row because his shoulder is bothering him, but we both know he wants me on board for protection. Last year these two got drunk before lunch. My dad said he thought for sure at least one of them would fall out of the boat, but they just kept catching fish. When they came back into the shop, one of the women kept putting her arm around my dad like they were great buddies. I'm guessing they tip well or my dad wouldn't put up with this twice.

Dad's recovered from the Mr. Andrew's joke fiasco and seems like he's almost in a good mood today. On the way over I say, "If they pinch your rear end I'm tipping them out of the boat."

He looks at me and actually smiles. "I'm more worried about them throwing up in my boat."

"I don't see why people come on the raft to get drunk when they've paid to have you show them how to fish."

Silence. I am a connoisseur of silence and its various connotations. In this case, I interpret Dad's silence as friendly because my dad is:

(1) not scowling, rolling his eyes, or clenching anything on his face.

(2) allowing the radio to be on.

(3) tapping the steering wheel to the music.

I say, "People should just sit in a bar if they want get drunk."

"Let them worry about it," says my dad. Another long pause. "It's just good to get out."

This is the phrase Dad uses to put a positive spin on unmet expectations. If he drives all day to try a new place and gets skunked (catches no fish) then he says, "Just good to get out." If he goes out guiding for wildlife and they don't see anything but blue sky and lodgepole, or if he comes home from a hunting trip with nothing to show for himself but a red face and a sore back . . . well, "It's just good to get out." I like this about Dad but I also find it mildly annoying.

We pick up the lunches from Gus's Deli and meet the Denver Duo out front. One woman is skinny with a sunburn. She has on an expensive fishing vest, a hat from another fly shop, and some gigantic sunglasses. She's the one who likes to hug my dad. The other has short blonde hair that she combs back wet. She's wearing baggy safari shorts and striped wool socks and Birkenstocks. She looks to me like a woman who wears what she wants.

Dad reintroduces everyone. "Carol and Becca, this is KJ."

"Well, love," says Carol, the sunburned one, "you don't look quite thick enough to row that boat."

"Don't listen to her," says Becca. "She hasn't had coffee."

"Well, if you get tired, I brought something in my fishing vest to perk you right up," says Carol. Her voice is edgy and I look at my dad to see how he's taking the news that she's packing pharmaceuticals.

He looks nonchalantly at Carol and nods. "You just make sure you have a license for everything you do on my boat and we'll all be fine." He chuckles a little to smooth it over and everybody makes nice.

Carol talks gear with Dad and she seems to know a fair amount about fishing. Apparently all three of her ex-husbands had this hobby in common.

We go out in our Avon raft twelve-and-a-half-foot self-bailer. Not the McKenzie, but steady and built to fish. Today we put in at the Greyling Arm, on the northeast side of Hebgen Lake, to fish for rainbows and browns. The lake is mirror quiet. We see two fishing boats moving slowly on the north side of the lake, but other than that it's just us and the grebes.

The mist is burning off and the air is tepid. Bugs have started moving, so the fish are waking up. I don't see any rises, but the women say that they want to dry fly instead of nymph. Fishing with nymphs is better when the fish are eating underwater, but it doesn't look as flashy. We pull out the dries.

Dad starts the ladies on Callibaetis. The fish this time of year have lived through the summer and are ready to go into spawning mode. That means they are big and smart and fight like miniature pit bulls—it takes a good fisherman to get one on the line but it takes a great fisherman to get one in the raft. I'm not counting on seeing a lot of either happen today.

They fish for forty or so minutes then switch to Woolly Buggers. Then suddenly we are in fish up to our armpits, and I'm just trying to stay out of everybody's way with the oars. The sound of line stripping fills the air. I never get tired of

that sound. Carol hauls in a brown that Dad thinks is four pounds. I stop rowing and pull out our little water camera. I get Carol, Dad, and the gorgeous fish right before the fish starts flopping. Dad puts him back in the water while Carol curses for joy about ten times and then breaks out the hard stuff to celebrate.

"I take a drink for every fish I catch, and every fish Becca catches, too," she says to me.

Becca is reeling in a fish, too, but she stops to frown at Carol, then goes back to her rainbow.

"Nice one," says Dad. His face is lit and happy as he nets Becca's catch. I take more pictures.

When Becca gets the fish off the hook and back into the water she sits down. She looks cheery but tuckered out.

"Well, it isn't fair," she says. The air moves hard from her lips as she talks. "That bit about her drinking for me."

"Becca can't drink anymore," says Carol. "Her doctor says her liver's grounded. . . . So I drink for her. I think it's pretty generous of me."

We row along for a few minutes talking about the fish and Becca's liver. We pass two other fisherman: Ray White-head from the gas station and Kenner's older brother William, in William's beat-up two-seater. Regulars. We wave as we pass.

Dad says, "Any luck?"

William nods politely. "Fresh out of luck. You?"

"A couple."

"Big ones," says Carol, holding up her hands like she caught a marlin.

William says, "I've always said this lake is partial to women." Unlike his brother Kenner, William has manners. I had a big crush on William when I was an eighth grader, like every other girl in the school. One of the best basketball players to ever come out of West End. They called him Sure Shot.

"See you have short stuff doing the rowing today," says William.

"She's little but she packs a punch," says my dad.

I instantly forget how to row. Luckily Carol is being obnoxious while I bobble the oars and bump myself in the chin. She says, "They say luck is contagious. Maybe we should rub some off on you."

"I wouldn't know about that, ma'am," says William. William's fishing buddy snorts at that one.

Becca and Carol crack up as we row away. Carol turns to my dad. "Oh, he's adorable. Are the men around here catch and release, too?"

My dad says, "'Fraid so."

"Then I'm definitely going to need that second beer," says Carol.

I'm starting two good blisters on my hand and sweating in spite of the slight wind that has picked up in the last few minutes. Dad suggests we stop and eat something. It's half an hour before the usual lunchtime so I wonder if Dad is worried about how I'm rowing or about how much Carol's drinking on an empty stomach.

I pull out the enormous sandwiches we get at Gus's Deli, complete with six-inch pickles, kettle chips, and homemade oatmeal cookies. I eat my entire lunch and drink two bottles of water before I realize Dad is grinning at me.

"Hungry?" he says softly.

"I guess," I say.

"Did you bring some gloves?"

"I forgot," I say, feeling stupid and sore.

"You want to take a break?"

"I'm good," I say.

The two women are eating happily on the other end of the raft. Dad scoots closer to me and pulls out his first-aid kit. He washes my hands with some bottled water, spreads something smelly on the blisters, and wraps my hands with two big Ace bandages. The bandages look melodramatic, but my hands feel better.

"Now you watch this wind," he says.

I look around. Even if I could see wind I wouldn't be looking at much. The water ripples gently in front of me. The sky is tinged with gray, but the air is still filled with sun and bugs. Just the same, I listen to Dad because I've never rowed for a group on the lake before. Normally I'm on the river, and there are a lot less options when you're floating down-stream.

"If we start to get that storm, we're off. You don't even wait to ask. I'll explain it to Carol and Becca. You just lay your back into it and head for the dock. Got it?"

I look at the shore. I can't see the dock anymore, but I know where it is because of the tree line and the mountains. We aren't in the center of the lake, but we are farther out than Dad usually comes. A good thirty minutes of hard row-ing with no headwind.

We finish our oatmeal cookies and start to fish again, with no luck. The streak is over. I get bored, so I start think-ing about Virgil. I think about how his voice hums and how his hair smells like baby shampoo. There's an endless list of things to think about.

A few more boats move in lazy circles on the water. A water-skier sends us a small wake and then disappears around the bend. After an hour my dad nets in two more rainbows for Carol and one little scrawny brown for Becca.

I'm thinking about how Virgil smiles with his eyebrows when I realize the sky has changed color and the ducks are gone. I look up at my dad and see he is waiting for me. Why does he do that? Why can't he just say, "Hey, KJ! Big storm! Let's go!"

I twist the oars and shift my back. The shore is even far-ther than it was at lunch. I've taken us too far out. The wind is pushing the water in the opposite direction but we have to get back where we put in if we want to get to the truck. The current pushes away my oars as I try to aim toward the dock. I look over at my dad, but he is explaining something to Carol.

I put my whole body into it, but I can't get the angle that I need. We are heading toward shore but we're too far down. My hands ache and sting under the bandages. The wind makes the water lap against the raft so it is difficult to hear. The lake is deserted from all other life. My shoulders feel like they are going to twist off. I suddenly feel massively uncoordinated, and I know I look it.

Carol has pulled in her rod and is watching me. "Sam, I think Tiger Lily needs some assistance."

Dad nods, "How you doing, KJ?"

Why does he ask me questions like that? What am I supposed to say?

He says, "Put a little more weight on that left oar. Straighten out."

I look down at my oars. I feel that tickle inside my head when everything is shutting down. Left? Left? Which one is left?

"Your other left," says Dad.

They are all staring at me now. My chest is tight and I know my dad expects me to keep going. It's one thing for me to be masochistic, but I can't stand it when he expects me to be. It starts to rain.

Carol says, "This is ridiculous, Samuel. Her hands are sore and I'm freezing."

Becca says, "Would you like me to take a turn, hon?"

Dad's voice is calm and all business. "She's fine . . . aren't you, Katherine Jean?"

Katherine Jean. I feel the familiar heat in my face, the pinch in my neck, the itch beneath my skin. I aim for the tiny, faraway dock, I just don't row that way. Every sweep of the oars takes us farther toward shore but farther from where we need to go. If I try to turn into the current, to muscle my way back on track, the hesitation in rowing makes the raft drift even more.

The water is choppy and high. It splashes onto our feet. I know this raft is sturdy, but it is definitely capsizable and in this lake, we would all be in big trouble if that happened.

I see myself tipping the raft with every stroke, falling into the freezing water with my dad and two unhealthy women. I look behind me and see Dad hunching a little in the wind, face calm and steady. He has given waterproof blankets to the women. Carol is emptying another flask. I look ahead. Even Becca is drinking now.

He is watching. I am the point he is proving, but why? He knows I can't do it. He sits watching me fail. It takes a sadistic person to sit idly by while your daughter tries to drown four people.

He calls to me over the wind, "You've got it, KJ. Just

don't get sideways. You've got to compensate for the wind. Keep going. You've got it."

I've got it, I've got it, I mutter inside my fuzzy head. I've got blisters burning holes in my hands. I've got a butt so sore my toes are cramping. I've got a dad so starved for a son he's willing to kill me off to prove he has one. I've got a head so messed up I keep going along with him.

The clouds settle in like a bad cold. I can't make out the shore anymore. The rain is whipping into the raft, so I keep my head down and just row. I don't look at Becca because I know she thinks it is all my fault, which it is. *We should be there in ten minutes,* I tell myself. Either that or drown, so either way it will be over.

Then I remember the Thurstons, the retired couple that drowned last year. They lived on the other side of town but they came into the shop all the time. The man, Garry, was a good fisherman. He and Edie stayed out just thirty minutes too long on Henry's Lake and that was it. They found the boat the next morning, but it took them a week to find the bodies floating like blue logs in a slough.

Everything speeds up. Everything swells inside my head until there is not room for anything but fear. I have to get out of this situation. This is how it always happens. I panic and then I fail.

I look at Dad. "I can't do it."

He sits down and faces me. "Stop rowing like girl." Most days when he says this he's kidding.

"I am a girl," I say. I'm not kidding today either.

He takes the oars. He doesn't say another word. I know his disgust will manifest itself later, in small precise ways. The women make ridiculous small talk about some life-threatening experience involving pack mules.

When we finally see a piece of shore, there is no place to take the raft up. He rows along the bank, and I jump out and pull the raft onto the sand. The women climb off in a flurry of blankets and cursing, grabbing branches and soaking themselves. Some of Carol's expletives are variations of words I've never even heard before. I couldn't agree more.

I let Dad beach and secure the raft alone. I head for a big tree and then I unwrap my hands. The bandages are soaked red. My fingers are covered with exploded blisters.

After a few minutes Dad comes up and puts his hand on my shoulder. "You could have made it."

I shrug at him. He doesn't even look at my hands.

"How can I put you at the oars if you act like this?"

"Like what?" I say, hissing mad. "Like my hands are bleeding off? Why does everything have to be a great big test to you?"

He says, "I'm going to walk the women back to the truck."

"I'm sure they'll like that," I say.

"I expect you to help."

My teeth chatter all the way back to the truck. I carry my own coat and two rods. I'm done working today. I let them walk ahead. These women can bellyache all they want. I'm done.

I stand by the car as Dad loads things up.

"You're dad's a tough guy," Becca says as she gets in the truck.

"Yep," I say.

"My dad was like that, too," says Becca. "Old beast got me through my chemo when everyone else quit, including me."

Honestly. Does everybody think they have to have a teaching moment with me today? Is there a law somewhere that all adults think they know everything?

"Thanks," I say with as much sarcasm as is possible to interject into a single syllable. "I'll try to remember that."

"You'll remember," says Becca. "Some things you can't forget, even when you want to."

"You have no idea," I say quietly.

"Yes, I do," she says.

Adults, I think. *Spare me.*

Younger pack members are continually subjected to the dominance of the adults. This feature of the wolf pack helps keep order in the group and ensures that the alpha pair retains its privileges. . . . Of course, younger pack members do not always follow the pack. . . . Like teenagers they practice independence.

L. David Mech, *The Way of the Wolf*

6

GOLDILOCKS AND
THE BEAR'S DEN

I SIT IN the corner of the Bear's Den bookstore, "browsing." The owner, Arlene, is eyeing me, and I know I've got about five minutes before she comes over to ask me if I'm going to buy anything.

The first real wolf column is due in two days, so I'm scrambling for research. Our city library is about as current as a card catalog, and our school library is only slightly bigger than a bread box—and everything in it is stale. I've been surfing the Net, but I need something that isn't a travel log, eco-rant, or redneck spew.

The Bear's Den is jammed with great books, and everything is coated with the smell of coffee and cinnamon from the bakery in the back of the store. Unfortunately the price of the books I've found is roughly equivalent to a car payment. I'm trying to skim, but reading fast isn't my specialty.

I look up. Arlene closes the register drawer. She's coming for me.

Suddenly the bell on the door shakes. In walks a middle-aged woman with wild curly hair. I mean there's windswept, and then there's I-keep-a-bird's-nest-in-here hair. The woman heads immediately to the counter to talk to Arlene, which is perfect for me. Arlene loves fringy women. And this one looks like she took a wrong turn in San Francisco and just kept goin'. I settle back into my chapter on "Territorial Battles and Pack Relations."

My head burrows into the details of pack life. It seems that although being an alpha has the most perks, being a beta can be decent, too, if you're with the right crowd. They hunt; they sometimes sneak in a little mating; they bide their time. Omega wolves are the lowest wolves in the pack hierarchy. Their lives pretty much consist of being harassed or expelled. It would be nice if I didn't relate quite so much to the omega wolves.

"KJ," says a raspy voice I don't recognize.

I look up. The woman with the crazy hair is talking to me. Arlene is looking at me, too. I freeze. The woman smiles big and starts walking toward me. She walks fast. "You must be KJ. My son has told me about you."

I'm mute.

"I'm Eloise Whitman."

I am subterranean in my silence.

"You are KJ, aren't you? The girl that's on the school newspaper with Virgil? He told me you were pretty . . . but good grief, you're like a little patch of lupine sitting over here buried in books." The woman puts out her big tan hand to me.

Virgil's wolf-chasing, supersmart, cooler-than-Elvis mother! I fold up the book and stand up right into her hand. I step backward and almost fall over when the chair cuts into my legs. I stand up again to the side.

"Easy there," she says, putting her hand out to steady me. She smells like citrus.

I breathe out and try to imagine I'm normal. "I'm KJ."

She smiles big again. "I understand you're interested in wolves."

"Sorta," I say. I lean on the stack of books I'm wrecking, but they move with my hand and I nearly fall over again. "Yeah." My neck must be as bright as a rope burn by now, but I try not to think about it.

Eloise says, "Looks like you've picked up a little reading material."

Arlene hoots from the counter. "Picked it up is about right. Or lifted it, maybe."

"Sorry, Arlene," I say.

Eloise says, "Don't be sorry, life's too short to be sorry. Don't mind Arlene here, menopause is a terrible thing. If you need books, I've got some you can borrow. Why don't you come over right now, and I can hook you up with some good stuff, not this Red Riding Hood malarkey." She smiles over at Arlene.

Arlene shakes her head and drinks more coffee. "Good stuff. You out-of-towners think you invented this place."

Eloise says, "That's the trouble, isn't it? Do you think we could grab a few of those bear claws before we go, KJ? I need a little self-love today, if you know what I mean."

I have no idea what she means by self-love, but a chocolate-covered bear claw sounds good to me.

She puts her arm around me. "We should get one for Virgil, too, although he rarely indulges himself. Not only is he a vegetarian, he's also deluded by the idea that sugar is bad for you, poor kid."

In spite of the fact that I am completely terrified of Virgil's mom and going to Virgil's house will provide endless opportunities for me to demonstrate my epic awkwardness, I also know Eloise can give me two things I want: books on wolves and more time with the mysterious Virgil. I put away my stack of pilfered print and follow the smell of chocolate and citrus out of the Bear's Den.

We walk to Jean Arrant's house. It's a long walk, even at Eloise's pace. Maybe Eloise is poor. No adults willingly walk anywhere in this town except to the refrigerator and the bathroom.

Eloise talks like she walks, fast. "So I'm here to study predation patterns. You learned much about that yet?"

"You mean the way a wolf goes after its prey?"

"That's what I mean."

I try to think of something impressive to say to the professor who is also Virgil's mom, but my brain is filled with intimidation static. I say, "They eat the weak elk first."

"That's the theory. Doesn't always work out like that though. I'm mostly focusing on how predation patterns interact with climate change to result in ungulate decline."

"Ungulates are elk, right?"

She glances backward at me. "You have some work to do."

The road to the house has an iron gate at the entrance with carved totem poles on both sides. Eloise punches a code into a security pad next to one of the poles and the gate opens. I've never actually been farther than the gate.

The rambling two-story house is built in the old log-and-shingle style like the lodge at Old Faithful. In the entryway to the house, we pass some deranged bronze sculptures of girls praying. One of them isn't wearing a shirt. Their heads are smashed in the middle and their eyes look like they've been carved out with scissors. "Aunt Jean did those herself."

"Interesting," I say.

"She calls them *Young Love*."

"Nice," I say.

We find Virgil sitting at the kitchen table. The table is the only furniture visible that isn't covered in books, clothes, and papers. Eloise says, "Hey, kiddo. I brought you home dessert."

He looks up at me and blinks.

She puts the bag of pastries on the table. "Not her. The bear claws, for heaven's sake."

"Hey," he says, and kind of laughs. When Virgil laughs he closes his eyes and tilts his head. I've watched him do it a few times. "What are you doing here?"

"I don't know," I say, and for a split second I have no idea what I'm doing here except for gawking at Virgil. "I mean, your mom says I can borrow some wolf books."

"I run a loose ship around here," says Eloise. "Make yourself comfy while I find something for you to read, KJ."

She turns to go. "Where's Jean?"

"Sleeping. As usual."

Eloise strides out saying something I don't hear.

I sit down next to Virgil at the kitchen table. Somehow it makes me feel less nervous, even though normally it makes me a wreck to be next to him. "I ran into your mom at the bookstore."

"She probably grabbed you by the ears, huh?"

"Sort of . . ."

"She adopts people. It's weird."

"Am I adopted?"

"Do you like chocolate?"

"Yep."

"Welcome to the family."

Virgil pulls a bear claw out of the bag and hands it to me. "My mom could live on these things."

"My dad likes bacon."

"What?" says Virgil.

"I mean my dad eats unhealthy stuff, too. He eats bacon all the time, so our kitchen always smells like breakfast."

"I'm a vegetarian."

"Wow," I say. "At my house it isn't dinner if there isn't something dead on the table."

"I don't like blood."

"Oh." I feel so stupid I start to eat my bloodless pastry. It also strikes me that I am not all the way comfortable with a teenage guy who is a vegetarian. I don't know which makes me feel more uncomfortable, Virgil or me.

"How's the article?"

"Not good," I say. "Have you decided which pictures you want to use? I could use some direction."

Virgil motions me to follow him. We walk down a long musty hallway that ends in a bedroom. He walks into the room and then walks out again. "Are you coming?"

"In there?"

He smiles with his eyebrows. "That's where my pictures are."

My romantic experiences are meager, but I'm sure there's a rule somewhere about boys and bedrooms. I can't pin down the rule, so I go in.

Virgil's room is so amazing I almost forget about Virgil. Unlike the rest of the house, it has giant windows that fill the room with sunshine. Where there are not windows, he has plastered his walls into an animal encyclopedia: siberian tigers, humpbacks, lemurs, flying squirrels, iguanas, piglets, eagles, octopi, javelinas, and of course, wolves.

"So you hate animals then," I say.

"I did it last week. Weird, huh?"

"No, it's great. These are all yours? You've been all these places?"

"The rhino and tiger shots aren't mine. My dad took them."

"He's a photographer?"

Virgil doesn't look so sunny anymore. "No, he's a surgeon. He goes to Africa a lot. They're divorced."

"I'm sorry."

"It's fine," he says. "Do you want to sit down?"

When he says this, I stare at him. This makes me dizzy. I sit on his bed, the part that's made. He sits on the part that isn't, then he lies back and looks at his work.

"So how do you like school here?" I say, trying to remain calm.

He closes his eyes. "It's kind of a bizarre."

I feel a twinge of protectiveness for my little patch of no-where. "I like to think of it as unique."

"Speaking of which . . . what was that thing in class? Where you turned colors?"

I dig my hands into my pockets. "I get nervous."

He sits up and looks at me. "About what?"

Virgil staring at me makes bad things happen. I can't think. I don't know how to explain to someone who's been to wherever you go to take pictures of lemurs what it's like to be intermittently embarrassing in West End. "I don't know. I'm the *Mission Impossible* message—give me thirty seconds and I self-destruct."

Virgil talks to the ceiling. "I don't get it."

"I just do stuff. Like in fifth grade. I wrote a ten-page book report on *Island of the Blue Dolphins*, which was about nine pages longer than every other kid's, but the teacher failed it because I spelled everything wrong, including the title."

"D-o-l-f-i-n-s?"

"Kenner couldn't decide what to make fun of me for first."

"I don't get Kenner either. He's a dick and everybody treats him like he's the king."

"Just us redneck losers, I guess." Back to protecting my school.

Virgil sits up. "Sorry, I didn't mean to be rude. I'm just not used to this. . . ."

"No, it's true. This is a small town. When we aren't working our butts off, there's nothing to do but get drunk, wasted, or pregnant."

"You really believe that?" he says.

"No."

"So why do you say it?"

"Everybody says it." My voice is rising. I feel awkward sitting on his bed next to him. I feel defensive, freaked out, and attracted to him at the same time. I'm not even sure what I'm doing here. His sheets have dolphins on them. He's practically old enough to vote, and he has dolphin sheets. He's put more time into decorating his bedroom than my dad's put into stocking his shop.

He says, "I like your cowboy boots."

"Thanks," I say.

"No, really. They're great."

For a split second I'm thinking that these boots must be better looking than I'd realized. Then I have a terrible realization. Of course. I've read about this just a few weeks ago. Guys compliment girls' shoes to tell them they're gay. It was a three-page article in *Seventeen* on "gaydar detection." But it suddenly all makes sense. The perfect hair. The perfect room. Hanging out with me.

All repressed gay guys have homely, insecure girl friends. I'm the neurotic sidekick. He's gorgeous and I'm the village idiot. How could I have been so stupid? But then the sidekicks never know. That's why they always get shot instead of the main character.

Virgil looks at me funny and then puts his hand on my elbow. "Are you all right, KJ?"

"I'm fine," I say, choking a little. I have to test the water. "Do you show all the girls your bedroom?"

Virgil does the shy smile thing, still holding on to my elbow. "No girls. I did show it to Dennis though. He's going to help me do a Web page with some of my stuff."

I knew it. No girls. Dennis and Virgil. He's holding my elbow because I'm the homely sidekick. I could cry.

Virgil lets go and scoots backward. "You don't have to worry about me attacking you or anything."

"Oh," I say. Of course I don't. Outside, I laugh, like a complete idiot. Inside, I gasp, like a complete idiot. He's going to tell me now and I can't stand it.

Then Virgil does something else I don't get and have no cultural preparation for: he takes my hand. His hand is surprisingly big and warm. I'm totally confused. I grab my hand back. We stare at each other.

"Okay," he says. "Not a good idea. I'll get my pictures."

"No. I mean . . . It's just . . . my dad doesn't like me to be in guys' rooms. Even if they're . . ."

Virgil raises his eyebrows at me. They disappear into his hair. Gay guys always have the best hair. The article said so. He says, "Even if they're what?"

I go into bolting mode. How am I supposed to know what to do now? I say, "Even if they don't like girls like that."

Virgil stares and shakes his head. "Like girls like what?"

If my mouth were a faucet I would definitely need a plumber. "Don't get mad."

"Like what? Do you think I'm gay or something?"

"You're not?" My eyes wander around the room. Maybe I could pretend to be having a seizure.

Virgil stands up, twisted off to one side with his hand on his hip. He looks like he's dropped something on the floor. "No. I'm not."

"I'm sorry." I feel like my head is going to burst. "I'd better go."

I run to the door and practically fling it open. Through the darkness Eloise's voice bellows, "Don't forget your books." I don't know where her voice is even coming from, but when I get to the kitchen I look down and see three books on a chair. I spin backward and Virgil is right behind me.

We stare at each other again.

"Whatever," he says.

I gather up the books. I can't get out fast enough. I say, "I'm sorry."

"Life's too short to be sorry."

He escorts me past his great-aunt's demonic sculptures. He opens the door and holds it open, but not in a nice way. I rush out the door and don't look back. I should have tried the seizure.

Ten Cool Things about Wolves

1. A wolf can use its hair to tell other wolves it's going to beat them up.

2. A wolf can run at speeds of between 28 and 40 miles per hour for up to 20 minutes, can jog almost indefinitely, and may cover distances of up to 125 miles in a day. That's what I call endurance.

3. A wolf's teeth and jaw strength could pop a monster truck tire.

4. The wolf pack could have its choice of elk victims but it chooses the sick, old, or weak. I think that's so ecologically polite.

5. Wolf pups are low on the pecking order but they still get to wrestle with the alpha without getting their head ripped off.

6. A wolf's sense of smell is practically bionic. It's more than a hundred times better than humans.

7. Wolves pee with form and function: they can mark territory, show dominance, and leave little love scents. They can even tell their family what's for dinner.

8. Wolves like to sing on family vacations. And they harmonize.

9. Wolves are the most popular villain in European fairy tales, but they are really the least likely of the major predators to eat you or your grandma.

10. Wolves never worry about yesterday or tomorrow.

7

TAKING INVENTORY

DAD GETS ME up early to help with inventory. "How are things?" he says over reel boxes.

"Things?" I say.

"School."

"A's except for math."

"How bad?"

"Not good."

We unpack boxes for a minute. I rip. He stacks. Then I try again. "I took a review test I probably bombed. I can never tell. It's starting to sound familiar to me though."

He takes a bag out of my hand. "You've gotta have decent math grades, KJ."

"I'm pretty sure I know that," I say.

"Don't back off just because it's hard. You can't back off."

We both stop talking now. This is old, ugly ground.

Dad goes through his checklist. He hands me a box of fishing line. I hand him a set of waders that are in the wrong stack. He says, "What I meant is, how are other things at school?"

"*Other* things?"

He stacks the waders. I know he'll wait me out.

"I like the newspaper. I'm supposed to write a column about the wolves."

"Wolves?" Dad looks amused. "That ought to make you some enemies."

"Yeah, Kenner and his friends. I'm brilliant at making enemies."

He stops stacking. "Oh yeah?"

"Mandy and Joss told me I'm conceited."

"I can't say I'm surprised."

"You think I'm conceited?"

"You don't look like their little brother anymore."

"Geez. That's what they said."

I rip off some packing and hand him two reels. That was almost a compliment. I say, "Plus there's this new guy who is really great who I've thoroughly offended."

Dad looks the reels over in the light. "Teenage boys don't listen enough to be offended."

"I said I thought he was gay."

"They listen to that. You really like him?"

I unpack another reel.

He says, "Well, keep your shirt on."

I hand Dad the reel. "Not every guy is like that."

He nods. "I thought you said he wasn't gay."

We work for another twenty minutes without talking.

Finally he says, "So the year's off to a good start then."

"It's like this every year, only worse. It's my pattern."

Dad unwraps a flannel shirt with a pseudo-Indian design on it and shakes it at me. Maybe the ugliest shirt I've ever seen. "A pattern is only a pattern if you follow it."

"What if I *am* that pattern, Dad? Well, not *that* pattern. What were you thinking when you ordered that beast?"

"I like it."

"I'm the pathetic random pattern. I'm a nonsequential but recurring loser. I'm fluid stupidity."

Dad smashes plastic wrap in the trash can. "You love a good bellyache, don't you, Katherine Jean? Do you think you're the only kid who ever had a bad day or got a bad grade? If you don't like your life, change it."

As long as I can remember, this is how it goes. My dad can only listen for so long before he has to judge, criticize, or give advice that involves telling me to "buck up" because "life isn't fair." That's his pattern.

I take the box openers and split open a box of fishing

socks and somehow manage to slice myself. Blood jumps out of my finger onto the box and the socks inside. I step back and blood escapes to the floor.

Dad barks at me, "You're bleeding!"

"Sorry!" I bark back. Scaring my dad scares me a lot more than blood. I run to the sink in the back room and run my finger through the water. Outside the room, I can hear my dad cursing.

Sometimes I wonder if my dad wishes that I had died with my mom. He could have remarried and started a new family. The cold numbs the deep slit in my skin. I wish I knew how to change my patterns—all of them. But it's like the blood in my finger. I screw up and there it is, just the stuff I'm made of, making a mess again.

After work I head over to the tree house with the books Eloise gave me. I've wrapped them in a special bag to keep them nice. They feel heavy and important in my arms. I pick my way slowly through the dying grass and fallen trees that cover my path. Overhead ravens argue and the changed light of fall shifts in the branches of the trees.

When I get to the house I find someone has ripped three of the supporting logs out from under the platform. I stand and stare at its dismembered remains. There are beer cans in a heap by a nearby burned-out circle. Why would someone wreck a tree house? At least wolves destroy things they can eat.

I climb the rope ladder to see if the platform can still hold my weight. It creaks and tips but I don't drop to the ground. I look at the swaying treetops, and my brain rambles around to thinking about what my dad said in the shop. But how can I change? How do I stop being what I am?

I open up the book and look at all the pictures of dead wolves and wonder what got into people to do such a thing. Then I look at the pictures of dead livestock and I remember.

I hear four-wheelers out in the trees, coming straight for me. I wonder if I'm about to meet the creeps who wrecked the tree house. Or hunters. The bow hunt has started but nobody hunts this close to town. Either way I'm going to feel ridiculous up here. I lie flat on my stomach and think camouflage thoughts.

When they get closer I realize it's three machines. I see a red flag flying through the lodgepole, which I recognize as Road Work's. I see the heads of the other riders, but I can't get high enough to see who they are.

I put my head down flat against the boards of the tree house. I hear yelling, a guy's voice. The engines whine and grind in a wide circle around the tree house, slowing only slightly. Then I hear a sudden pause in one engine and a muted crashing sound. The other machine stops and Kenner's unmistakable laugh opens up the ground beneath me.

Kenner. I will seriously die if he sees me up here.

"You shouldn't drive like that." I don't recognize the guy's voice. It's not loud, but it has an edge.

Kenner says, "Whatever, *Mom*."

Road Work's thick words tumble out, "It's okay. My folks don't care."

The softer voice says, "They make their living off these things, and if Golden Boy cracks one of them open then you can guess who's going to pay for it."

"What do you care?" says Kenner.

"Maybe because you don't."

"Geez, Will. You're like an old woman."

So it's William. Of course it's William, being responsible, unlike his little brother Golden Boy.

I hear branches snapping and movement, then shoving. I hear the sudden crack of wood on skin. Kenner whelps, "Hey! Knock it off."

I hear more branches snapping. And a hard slap of skin.

"Hey," says Road Work, laughing. "Stop it."

"Is that your best shot?" Kenner says.

"You'd know if that was my best shot. Forget it. We've got a lot of ground to cover before we have to be back at the ranch. That guy said he saw 'em clear back on the river-front."

"This is stupid, there's nothing this close to town," says Kenner. An engine starts.

The voice calls back cheerfully, "And that's why I'm the

brains and you're the little brother. We turn at the tree house and head along the ridge."

I'm not sure about William's brains, but in high school he ran the basketball team. He would drive down the court like there was nothing else in the world. When the team was jammed up, he was always there to shoot them out of a hole.

I've heard he went away after graduation to play ball but got hurt and lost his scholarship. Now he works for his dad.

The second machine starts as the first screeches away. I look up enough to see the outline of three heads bolting through the forest. William is in the lead, followed by Kenner and Road Work. Branches jut everywhere but neither Kenner or William veer or slow down. Road Work is so square he has to duck at everything.

I stay quiet on the platform until I can't hear their engines anymore. I wonder what they were looking for. I doubt it's anything good. That said, it's nice to know that even Kenner gets the cocky kicked out of him sometimes.

"You're only pretending to be a sheep," said the shepherd.

"How do you know?" asked the wolf. "I look like a sheep."

"You say you are a sheep," said the shepherd, "but you act like a wolf."

Aesop's Fables

8

NO MORE MR. NICE GUY

MRS. BABY'S EYES are bloodshot and her voice is hoarse. She sends us all to our workstations and tells us to "brainstorm" for an hour. After a short nap on her desk she scans my article like a grocery bill.

She calls me over. "This reads like you took it straight out of a book."

I look at the floor. Ever since Eloise gave me the books I have been reading like crazy but not writing. It was late when I finished cleaning up the store last night, and I had a doomed math assignment to wallow in. I didn't think Mrs. B. would notice as long as words filled the page.

Mrs. B. looks as serious as she can with another human

being swelling her to three times her normal size. "It's plagiarism if you don't cite your sources."

"How am I supposed to report on wolves when they mostly live on the other side of the park? I work in my dad's store."

"Anyone in this town old enough to carry a plate has a job, honey. Virgil brought in these pictures this morning." She holds up an eye-popping photograph of two wolves running. "Why don't you drive over to the park with him and learn something."

Of course I've screwed this up. My head spins. I'm being fired.

Mrs. Baby skewers my thought bubble. "Can you do this or not?"

Virgil is in the bathroom at the moment, but I still lean into Mrs. Baby and whisper, "Virgil and I aren't really getting along."

She doesn't whisper back. "If you don't have something better for next week we'll cancel the column. You can cover the girl's sports for Addison. I'm giving her a new job."

"What's that?"

"An advice column. 'Dear Addie.' I thought of it myself. Maybe you can write to her and find out how to get along with Virgil."

Because I have nearly all my classes with Virgil, it takes work to avoid him. Fortunately he is an expert at acting like I don't exist. I brainstorm with Sondra in journalism—which means we talk about her writing an article on vegetarian recipes for an hour. In Spanish we have conversation day, so nobody talks except the three Hispanic kids. In PE, I tell Mrs. Coleman I have endometriosis. She looks concerned and I feel guilty. In English I just sit in the corner and pretend to care.

I sit alone at lunch. Joss and Mandy glare at me once and go back to their salads. I should feel bad but this way I can read my book about wolf extermination in peace. Halfway through I come across a picture of wolves strung up on a barn. I dump my food in the trash and head for the halls. This objectivity thing is going to be harder than I thought.

I go to the hallway where Virgil comes after lunch. I'm not really a stalker, but my school is so small it's hard not to notice a person's schedule if you have a compound crush and guilt complex about them.

He rounds the corner talking to Dennis. Dennis is explaining something with the words "X-wing" and "*Death Star*" involved. Virgil barely looks at me even though I am standing right next to his locker. Dennis is so wound up explaining the implications of galactic warfare that he ignores me, too.

I interrupt.

"Can I talk to you, Virgil?"

Virgil looks at me. "Dennis is telling me about something."

Dennis looks exulted.

"Okay," I say.

Dennis takes a breath and keeps talking at light speed. Virgil nods and switches books. I float away in my cloud of nothingness. I have learned the secret to being invisible. All you need is a knack for making people wish you would disappear and then you really do.

After school I see Virgil walking home with Dennis. Dennis is waving his arms around, and Virgil looks caught up in whatever Dennis is telling him.

I walk slowly so I won't catch up to them. At the corner Virgil waves to Dennis, and Dennis takes off down the street alone. Virgil leans against the streetlight and waits for me. I force myself to walk the same pace all the way to the light.

"Hey," he says. "I wasn't trying to be rude. I just didn't want to talk to you today."

Two can play at this whole say-what-you-are-actually-thinking game. I say, "I don't need help feeling stupid."

"No, probably not."

I take a step back. "When did you get so mean?"

"You feel stupid. That isn't my fault."

I feel something foul forming in my throat.

He says, "It also isn't true."

I swallow the scatological analogies I'm about to spew and try to keep up with what he's saying.

"KJ, you assumed something about me. . . ."

I growl back, "I know . . . and I'm sorry. I'm an idiot."

Virgil looks at everything but me. His hands fold and drop in front of him. I can't tell if he's furious or just bothered by having to talk to me. "But here's the thing . . . you aren't the first person to think that about me. I got that in my old school."

"You did?"

"And your buddy Kenner had some nice names for me today, too. He's a gem."

The thought of being aligned on Kenner's side of anything makes me ashamed. "I'm so sorry."

His voice goes flat. "I have even wondered about it. Like maybe I'm in denial or something."

I consider this. "How do you know you aren't?"

"Well, you know . . ." he says. His face is slightly sunny, like the first day, but with a chance of showers. "You're with someone, and you just know."

"Oh," I say.

I'm not entirely sure I know what Virgil is saying, but if he's felt the way I feel about him, about a girl, any girl, I get why he's so confident about his preferences. We stand there watching the tourists for a minute. A couple that collectively weighs five hundred pounds eats ice cream at the Dairy Queen.

Virgil says, "Mrs. Brady told me to take you wolf watching. How about me and my mom pick you up at four o'clock on Saturday?"

"P.M.?"

"A.M. I thought you fishing guides were up at three."

"We don't actually sleep after our twelfth birthday."

"You bring the bear claws," said Virgil. "I'll bring my mom."

"That's really nice of you," I say.

"Mrs. Brady's right; you can't write about wolves by copying stuff out of an encyclopedia."

I can't believe Mrs. B. told him that. I'm so mortified I just stand there with my arms folded across my chest.

"Later then," he says, and jogs across the street against the light.

The truth is we know little about the wolf. What we know a good deal more about is what we imagine the wolf to be.

Barry Holstun Lopez, *Of Wolves and Men*

9

CINDERELLA WOLF

THE BAD PART about a car ride with Eloise is she never stops feeding you. The good part is that she never stops talking. Virgil is polite, but it's obvious that this trip is not his way of saying he likes hanging out with me.

Eloise says, "Nobody messes with the alpha female in the Druid Peak pack, Number Forty. That's probably the pack we'll see today, if we see anything. She's fast, mean, and doesn't take sass from her lessers, which is everyone, including Number Twenty-One, the alpha male."

"How come everybody is so interested in the Druids?" I say. I know from my reading that each pack has a name but the individual wolves have numbers so the people won't get attached to them. Some of the packs, like the Druids, have real celebrity status.

Eloise says, "Most of the people that come out here to watch the wolves for more than a week are avid Druid or Rose Creek watchers. They are the packs you can see with a scope from the road, and they're always feuding so they're the best soap opera in town right now, next to you and Virgil."

"You eat too much sugar," says Virgil.

"You need a little protein," says Eloise. "You're looking pale all of a sudden."

Starting in Mammoth Hot Springs we listen to Eloise's two-way radio. It's not even light yet and her radio is buzzing with commentary from the Wolf Mafia. She narrates in between their dialogue. The Wolf Mafia, as they have been called by some of the locals, aren't criminals, but they are a little zealous. They are not official park rangers or scientists. They are the volunteer keepers of the flame. They watch out for the wolves and record their activity. They range from groupies to gurus.

"As with any tight-knit group, you need to be mindful of your place out here," says Eloise.

"Which is where?" I ask.

Eloise chuckles. "Next to me."

The season of car access into Yellowstone is coming to a quick conclusion. Fall can disappear on the first day of

September around here, but we usually make it into the end of October before winter really comes to stay.

September is brilliant in the park. The colors change and a mist settles on the valley like a giant sigh of relief after three months of RV rush hour. But this morning the road is still lined with cars. We stop at the biggest cluster.

"Doggone it. I hope we're not too late." Eloise parks her truck on the lip of the road. For most people it's not even breakfast time yet, but campers and trucks jam the tiny pull-out. Eloise gathers her gear and goes to greet a circle of parkas. She is chatty and generous with each cluster of observers while she navigates a prime position and sets up her scope. I watch with jealousy as she both gets what she wants and ingratiates herself with everyone in her wake.

Virgil and I throw on our jackets and strap on our equipment. If he knew how much time I spent picking out this cornflower-blue-water-resistant-non-pilling fleece to wear, I'd die. My dad humored me with a new T-shirt, too. Luckily my dad doesn't have as big of a mouth as Mrs. Baby.

We wonder into the crowd. Two women with matching tan stocking caps and green snowsuits talk in hushed tones with Eloise. It's thirty degrees. That's practically swimsuit weather for locals.

Virgil whispers, "They're up here from Florida."

I whisper back, "They look like zucchinis."

Virgil shoots me a reproving look and starts setting up his stuff.

The first zucchini says, "She's beating her up again."

"I don't know how much more of this that little sweetie can stand."

"Her sister is a true leader. She gets the job done."

"Well, she beats the daylight out of everyone, that's for sure. But can't keep her man happy."

"Oh, he's just as much to blame for the way things are and you know it."

I step in close to Virgil so my back is to the zucchinis. "Who are they talking about?"

Virgil whispers, "Druids."

"They're talking about wolves?"

Eloise's voice carries over the buzzing crowd. "Just below the tree line."

Everyone quiets down and goes to their scopes, including Virgil. He focuses and takes a dozen shots. I try to find movement with my binoculars, but all I see are trees and brush. I feel like a tourist.

"What's going on?"

Virgil steps back and pulls me in front of him, so I can see into his camera scope. I try to look more interested in what's in front of me than what's behind me. He says, "Forty-Two's hating it. Can you see her?"

I sort through the colors and shapes of the mountain but draw a blank. "I'm blind," I say.

I feel Virgil's breath on my neck. "She's in front of that juniper, just below the big rock."

My eyes focus in, and I see a dark shadow that turns into a head after I stare at it for a second. Then I see the hunched line of her back.

One of the zucchinis says, "I saw her limping right before you got here, Eloise. She's been through the ringer. Do you think she'll stay?"

Eloise nods and speaks softly to the woman. "It will be unusual if she sticks around with so much abuse. Especially if Forty killed her pups and lover boy doesn't seem to change his ways any time soon."

"But she's been through so much already."

"You can never tell with a situation like this one. To be honest, this pack is just another reason why I tell people you can generalize about wolf behavior, but you can't make rules about it."

I turn to Virgil. "Her sister killed her pups?"

"No one actually saw Forty-Two's pups. But last year Forty-Two dug a den and then Forty, the über alpha, showed up and let Forty-Two have it. Not the usual harassment, but a real beating. Forty-Two didn't even fight back. Afterward, Forty-Two abandoned the den. The theory goes that the pups were killed as part of the punishment."

"That's horrible," I say.

"Forty's famous for her brutality. Even for wolves, Forty's brutal. I saw her rip a coyote to shreds a few weeks ago just for wandering a hundred yards from a kill. I think she enjoys her work."

"But why did Forty-Two even have pups? I thought only the alphas got breeding rights."

"In this pack they think there have been as many as three litters at a time."

"Is that alpha male crazy?" I say.

"That's why people love the Druids. They're very dramatic and easy to romanticize. Especially Forty-Two. She's an impressive hunter, and she has clearly identifiable dark circles around her eyes that give her a neurotic look. She does the work and takes the beatings. They've started calling her the Cinderella wolf."

"Cinderella wolf?"

"Everybody loves a fairy tale."

"It doesn't sound like a fairy tale to me."

Eloise joins in, "This Cinderella will probably have to splinter off like the mom and the sister. It'll be a shame though. She's a great hunter."

"What will she do?" I say.

"The other packs around here are highly territorial. She'll probably have to head out alone for a while until she gets to the perimeter of the park and then look around for a new pack that will take her."

"Can she make it alone?"

Eloise writes a few things in her notes and then remembers we are talking. "A lone wolf is usually a dead wolf if the isolation goes on for long. They can't hunt big game alone and they wear themselves down."

"If Forty-Two's such a good hunter, what's the point of driving her out?"

"Breeding competition."

"So it's like a girl fight?"

Eloise gets an annoyed look on her face. She says, "Wolves are like people, but they aren't people."

Virgil says, "Deep thoughts, Mom,"

"I know. I scare myself sometimes," says Eloise.

Eloise goes to work, and I stand aside so Virgil can take pictures.

"I don't think Forty-Two's going anywhere today," says Virgil.

"Why?" I say.

"Take a look."

I stare into the lens and see Forty-Two's legs and head above the grass. Forty-Two is sprawled out in full submission, licking at Forty's legs. Forty looks straight ahead, indifferent. I have to look away. It's one thing to relate to the things I read in Eloise's books; it's another to see the behavior played out at the end of my binoculars.

I know that wolves' survival depends on their hierarchical system, but this feels all wrong. Why does Forty-Two take it? The memory of the wolf I saw killed crawls in my insides like a poisonous spider. "I saw a wolf pack kill another wolf this summer for doing the same thing. The Nez Perce pack, I think. The wolf was submitting like that and they shredded it."

Eloise says, "We always say 'survival of the fittest,' but I think with wolves it's more 'survival of the most aggressive.' Physically there's no reason for Number Forty-Two to be the kicking bag, except that she's not willing to fight Forty to be anything else."

"Are wolves just born alphas, betas, and omegas?"

"We used to think that, but what we've found by living so close to wolves is that there is a fair amount of transition. Age, injury, pups, offspring all impact a wolf's social position. Wolves can actually take all those roles in a lifetime."

"So what makes the difference between Forty and Forty-Two?"

Eloise looks off at the Specimen Ridge. "The thing about an alpha, male or female, is that they can lead. When things get desperate they attack instead of retreat."

It occurs to me that I'm the luckiest student Eloise has ever had. I get to have the professor all to myself and skip the tests.

"Why do you study wolves?" I say.

"I've wondered about that myself, KJ. I didn't start out to study them, that's for sure. But the more I learned about them the more I was fascinated. They are tenacious killers, but they also sing and play and live in families. They go hard and go home. I respect that in an animal, any animal."

"Do you think it's going to work, having them here?"

"I hope so. For Yellowstone's sake. Having them back in the food web gets the elk off the aspen. More aspen means more beaver habitat, which means more streambeds holding together and more fish. When there are more fish and the streams are healthier everything is healthier."

"You talk too much, Mom," says Virgil.

Shortly after the licking episode the entire pack breaks camp. We sit in the turnout, glued to the scopes, hoping they'll come back, but they don't. I lose track of time. We go back to the car and eat an early lunch, then wander around to a few other pullouts with no sign of activity. I start looking for other wildlife, watching the water, wondering what the fishing is like today.

We move up to Dave's Hill by Slough Creek. I spot a badger in the field below, so Virgil and I leave Eloise and scurry down through the rocks.

A trumpeter swan circles over our heads. Its thick call echoes in the valley. The swan's honking is joined by the clickety-clack of a sandhill crane and the trilling of the meadowlarks. In the pond below we can see cinnamon teal and loons circling on the water. All but the swan will be gone in a few days. The trees and grasses are coated in the fall light. The ground has that worn gray look it gets right before it snows. I see fish rising in the pond as the sun starts to set. This would be romantic if Virgil didn't think of me as a homophobic bumpkin.

He's fixated on the badger. "I got a shot of him but it's no good. He went underground."

"Sorry," I say.

"Life's too short," he says, smiling.

"I *am* sorry, Virgil."

Virgil puts the cap on his lens. "I'm going to run down and see if I can get a shot of those teal."

I find a rock to sit on while Virgil entertains himself. Eloise is nowhere to be seen. I let the slanted sunlight move across as I work on my article. I keep seeing Number Forty-Two licking Number Forty. It makes my skin crawl.

What is the story here? If the wolf I saw die this summer was killed for backing down, why is Forty-Two allowed to stay with her pack for the same behavior? And if the outnumbered wolf I saw this summer had resisted, would things have been any different?

We move to a hill near Tower Junction. Virgil gets a great shot of a beaver on the river. The Wolf Mafia is out in full force this evening, along with a few locals. Everybody's looking for a show.

We stand on the hill watching a meadow across the road that Eloise says has been popular this fall with the elk. She stands patiently assessing everything in her field of vision. I watch her percolate with understanding. In a weird way, she reminds me of my dad. I shudder.

After twenty or so minutes, she says "Rose Creek pack, dead ahead."

I see five wolves in my scope, but the fading light makes it difficult to see them in detail. Three of the wolves duck into the grass then reappear at the edge of the elk herd. The leader runs at one of the smaller elk and the others follow in a flanking formation. Their running is smooth, connected, and tight. Invisible rhythm.

The leader lunges at the elk's hindquarters, and the elk bucks and kicks. The wolf holds on for an instant and then is thrown to the ground. The other wolves jump to replace the alpha, but they're not fast enough to get their dinner. The injured elk moves to the center of the herd and the herd jogs to safer grazing. It's all over in a few seconds. The wolves head up into the trees away from the elk with the leader galloping full steam.

Eloise says, "Did you see that? That alpha got kicked square in the chest and he just popped up like toast. That's fast food the hard way."

"Doesn't that hurt him?" I ask.

"Absolutely," says Eloise. "Most wolves don't live past their sixth birthday."

I fade to the back of the crowd while people in front of me start to put away their scopes. I feel someone watching me from behind so I turn around. There on the ridge above me, less than thirty feet away, are six magnificent wolves standing in a row. They are watching us watch them.

I hear someone behind me say, "Oh."

In the center of the wolves, two great gold eyes stare into mine. He's huge. Too big to be a female. The other wolves drop back quickly as people turn and see them, but the black wolf stands his ground.

His eyes are incandescent yellow. I stare at those glaring eyes and they stare back at me. I am not afraid. He is not afraid. Something lights inside of me, ignites. I am not afraid. There is nothing to be afraid of. Then he spins and lopes straight up the rock, his tail sweeping the air behind him.

Virgil, Eloise, and I follow the pack with our scopes. We see more wolves traveling above, but we're losing light so spotting is difficult. The pack appears and disappears as they traverse the steep ridge. Eloise says they are working down to get to the other wolves across the highway.

We run along the road with our hi-tech binoculars. It gets colder and harder to see. Everyone else is gone. We are alone with the howling shadows. We follow in the dark. Then the howling stops and the show is over.

When we get back to Eloise's car she climbs inside to make notes. Virgil and I stand outside in the dark. We listen to the echo of snipes. Virgil looks through his telescope at the stars. He shows me Venus and Jupiter and its six moons. In spite of what Virgil thinks of me, I am sparkling from the inside. I want to yelp with the wolves, but the wolves are quiet, so I am, too.

"Did you get something to write about?" says Virgil.

I don't know if he's making fun of me, but it doesn't matter. "Could you believe that? The way he looked at us."

"You mean the way he looked at *you*," says Virgil. "He looked like he was out for blood."

"I didn't feel scared."

"What did you feel?" says Virgil.

"I don't know," I say, wondering myself. "I felt, I feel, *different*."

Virgil stands next to me in the dark, close but far away. He laughs softly. "So, what, you're Wolf Girl now?"

I laugh, too. "Shut up, Virgil."

But I do feel different.

My mind hums. The spell of the day is wrapped around and inside of me. Eloise says wolves aren't people, but I wonder if people can be like wolves.

"I'm talking wolf! I'm talking wolf!"

Jean Craighead George, *Julie of the Wolves*

10

ANTHROPOMORPHISMS

I LOOK AS haggard as Mrs. Baby, minus the water retention. I have been working on my wolf article in between school, homework, and the shop. Late last night I took the article to Virgil's house. I read it out loud to the whole family in the kitchen.

Virgil snorted in his hot chocolate. Not sure that was a good thing.

Eloise said, "What's with all the anthropomorphism? You know better than that."

"Mrs. Brady says I write like a textbook. She wants me to punch it up," I said.

Aunt Jean said, "Mrs. Brady is a dingbat."

Eloise sighed. "All right, dear. Get their attention. But

shorten it a bit. And then grow up and never write like that again."

I went home, fretted about artistic integrity, and then made the article half as long and twice as punchy. At three I cracked my math book to get ready for the quiz. I finished right before my morning alarm went off.

I put my article on Mrs. Baby's desk next to Virgil's shot of Forty-Two licking up to Forty. The detail in the picture is astounding. It could be the cover shot for *National Geographic.*

"You look a little rough this morning, KJ."

"I didn't copy it out of a book this time."

"Glad to hear it, dear," she says.

I watch each student walk up and dump their stories on top of mine. She takes Virgil's photo and holds it up so everyone can see it. "You all see this? Virgil has outdone himself with this shot."

Virgil the perfect. Virgil the brilliant. But she's right.

I look over at Virgil. His ears are pink.

Mrs. Baby says, "It's such a sweet shot. Look how much these two wolves love each other."

Virgil says nothing. I can't stand it.

I say, "It's not really love. That one is licking the other one to keep from getting thrashed. You can't tell from the picture, but the one standing is ruthless. The one on the ground is the one they call the Cinderella wolf."

"Cinderella wolf? That's the biggest load of crap I ever

heard in my life," says Kenner. "Nature boy's done his job dressing up a cold-blooded killer."

"Well," says Mrs. Baby, "he certainly has. I think it's a lovely picture. How did you get it?"

Virgil shrugs. "I guess it's all about the angle."

"Well, it's nice to have quality photography for a change," Mrs. Baby says. "Now, everyone gather round the team table." We groan. I love Baby, but she should really teach kindergarten.

"Remember . . ."

Dennis says, "Fair, fun, and friendly!"

I feel my eyes rolling out of my head. I wish she would just make him editor and get it over with. I sit next to Kenner and Addison. I come out of my stupor enough to notice that Kenner's hand is wrapped in a bandage. Addison is hovering.

"What happened to your hand?" I say.

Kenner glares at me and then at Virgil.

Addison leans forward and says, almost in a whisper, "They had some stock get out last night. They think a wolf pack spooked them. Kenner was helping and cut his hand."

Sondra sits down next to me. She says to Kenner, "Are you okay?"

Kenner ignores her. Addison leans forward and whispers, "His dog is missing."

"I had a dog like that," says Sondra. "But he always came back when I put treats out for him."

Addison purses her lips at Sondra. "Cow dogs don't just run off."

Mrs. Baby says, "Kenner, I don't see your article on the football game."

Addison says, "He got hurt . . . working."

Mrs. Baby puts her hand where her hip used to be, "Is he unable to speak, too?"

Kenner shoots a look of disgust at Mrs. Baby.

She flutters her hands in the air. "Well, whatever. Addie, how is the column going?"

"Good! I have three people that sent something in for this issue."

"Great. We can use that to fill up most of Kenner's space. But we need some mention of the game. Dennis can you write a quick paragraph?"

"Sure thing, Mrs. Brady," says Dennis.

Kenner doesn't say anything about being replaced by Dennis, but I think he's going to get a cramp in his face if he doesn't relax his jaw a little. When class is over I notice that Kenner is limping, too.

I follow him out. "I'd like to interview you for the paper."

He keeps walking. I can see from Addison's reaction that he heard me. I see the wolves, running straight at the elks' feet. I step a little faster. "Hey, Kenner, I'd like to interview you about what happened."

He stops and looks at me. "Why? So you can make me look like a bloodthirsty redneck?"

"No," I say. I have the feeling I should back off. That's what I would normally do. "I want to interview you so I can tell the rancher's side of the story. I need someone to tell me about that."

"I'll pass," says Kenner. Kenner's a big guy, but there is something beat up, even defeated, in the way he's holding himself steady. Maybe I smell blood. Probably I'm just a jerk.

"I'd only write what you tell me to," I say. "Just your words, as long as they're printable."

"Well, they ain't." Kenner never says "ain't."

I say, "Addie, what happened?"

Addie looks flushed and uncertain, but she answers me anyway. "When they found the animals loose, he and Will went out and it got dark. First he cut his hand on a wire gate and then his dog went missing. Kenner stayed up all night looking with his hand wrapped in a shirt. He raised that dog from a puppy."

"I'm so sorry, Kenner."

Kenner doesn't look at me as he shuffles off. "Like hell you are."

Virgil steps into the hallway behind me. "It's too bad about his dog."

I write a few words in my notebook. "Holy smack. It

really is. And I know I need to hear his side of it. But if his dog had been nabbed by a cougar or bitten by a snake everybody would just call it bad luck."

"I guess it's all about the angle," says Virgil.

At three past three I hide behind my locker door and go over my math quiz one more time. It says five out of five answers are correct. If I were alone I'd sing Christmas carols. Even if this wolf-stare thing is all in my head, I don't care. Where else is something if it isn't in your head? I've been possessed, and I like it.

It sounds silly, even to me. But writers, biologists, and regular people say basically the same thing. Exchanging stares at close range with a wild wolf can hook you up to something "other." Or at least make you think so.

Aldo Leopold, the naturalist, got up next to a wolf when he was about my age. He was actually shooting at the wolf at the time, but when he rode in to inspect his dying trophy he saw its eyes had "a fierce green fire." He never got over it. As an adult, not only did he develop the country's wildlife management program, he gambled his career to initiate the reintroduction of wolves to the west, beginning with Yellowstone.

I look at the math quiz again. We take these quizzes nearly every day, but in two years I have never had more than three answers right at a time. Addison graded my paper. She put a smiley face at the top and wrote, "You are so smart!!!"

I studied and then I performed. No second-guessing. No panic. Just a perfect five.

I reach in my locker and start to load up my books for the walk home. I'm startled to see Mrs. B. standing behind me when I turn around.

"We need to talk." She's holding my paper.

"Is something wrong?" I say.

"Did Virgil's mom write this for you?"

"She says it's anthropomorphic."

"How nice. I like it, too."

"Thanks," I say. "I guess."

"Listen, KJ, would you like to be editor?"

I'm too surprised to answer.

She says, "I know you have a lot to do, but it's mostly proofreading and helping me organize everything on the page. It will look good on your college application."

I feel the stare because I am staring. Having a lupine transfiguration is one thing, but I'm dyslexic. I can barely proofread my own name. No one puts me in charge of anything. I say, "I'd love to do it."

"You start tomorrow. Come an hour early."

"Sure," I say, like I have the slightest idea of what I'm getting myself into.

I watch Baby waddle away. I'm in a daze. I'm going to be the editor. The sleepless night and the good news collide. I have to sit down. I walk toward the wall heaters in the front of the school.

Dennis is already sitting there. "Made you editor, didn't she?" he says. He looks like he's going to cry.

"I guess so."

Dennis says, "You can't even spell."

He stomps to his feet and strides away before I can think of what to say. Apparently my wolf stare isn't useful for everything.

WOLF NOTES
The Cinderella Wolf

Here's a story for you, a Cinderella story. But in this story, Cinderella is a wolf.

The story of wolf Number Forty-Two, or Cinderella as her fans like to call her, began when she was wolf-napped from Canada, along with her mother and two sisters. They were plunked down in Yellowstone as part of the Wolf Reintroduction Project. Once they settled in, Cinderella's mean and nasty sister, Number Forty, chased off Cindy's mother and third sister. Cinderella stayed with the pack, but you guessed it, she was forced to be the lowest-ranking wolf. Let's just say her sister liked to chew her out.

But did that get her down? Wolf no.

Of course things got a whole lot worse when a guy got involved. Usually the king and queen (aka alpha) wolves, are the only ones that get to make more wolves. But the king wolf has a thing for Cinderella. Last year it looked like Cinderella had pups in her den but then the queen came to call. Sure enough, Cinderella got a royal thrashing and none of her pups survived.

But did Cinderella turn tail and run? Wolf no.

Instead she hunts for the pack like a champion. She pampers the pups and howls up a storm. She's even been seen dropping sticks at a buffalo's feet as if she wants to play. Some say she's got to stand up for herself or leave the pack. We'll have to wait and see.

Maybe it's not happily ever after, but we humans could learn a thing or two about life from a wolf like Cinderella.

11

ONE IN EVERY FAMILY

I LOPE THROUGH the sidewalks of town. I know Dad's taking some California moneybags for a weekend bow hunt as soon as I get to the store. Talking to Mrs. Baby has made me late.

"Dad," I gasp as I run through the door. Three men are standing around him. They're all camo'd out, and they have that look on their faces. They're ready to shoot something.

"Hey," Dad says nonchalantly.

I know it's unprofessional but I can't help it. "Guess what?"

Dad and his buddies all kind of lean back and watch me do this, act young and female and stupid as sticks. "I'm going to be the editor. Mrs. Brady loved my wolf article."

It takes Dad a minute to register my words since they broke the sound barrier. "Good for you, honey. That's great."

"Uh-oh," says the man with the fanciest bow. "Samuel, you got a storyteller in your family?"

The man next to him says, "Your dad tells stories, too, but they're about the buck he got last year." They share a man laugh.

"What kind of wolf story? Is it a fairy tale?" says Fancy Bow. He must make a lot of money. He thinks he's hilarious.

"Well, kind of," I say, trying to play along. "I wrote a story this week about the Cinderella wolf."

Dad purses his lips. He wants me to do the same.

Fancy Bow is having none of it. "Does she get the prince or eat him?"

"There's not really a prince in this story. It's about a real wolf."

A short man with a red complexion says, "You got a wolf lover for a daughter?" His voice tilts up like he's kidding, but he isn't as cheerful as Fancy Bow.

Dad gathers up a small pack filled with drinks and snacks for the front seat. "We'll be back Sunday night, KJ. You know how to get a hold of me."

The short man says sympathetically, "Well, there's one in every family these days."

Fancy Bow smiles over at Dad, "Just as long as there aren't two, right, Samuel?"

Dad gives back an easy smile, "Let's go get some elk, gentlemen. See you Sunday, KJ."

"Good luck," I say.

He nods to me and heads out the door. His face gives nothing away. If this were a fairy tale Dad would settle this conversation with these men. But he won't. In a fairy tale he wouldn't even have to go with them, if he didn't want to. I wouldn't have to sit in this dumb store alone all weekend, waiting for a handful of people to come in and not buy anything. But in the real world, we're heading into the slow season, and we need every dollar we can get. So we both do what we have to.

Wolves and people aren't so different, I think. *In the real world, they both have to eat.*

The only way I can get through a beautiful October day caged inside the store is to spend the early morning hours outside. I pull on my jeans at six and walk through the dark to a stream that flanks the south of town. I take my fishing gear and an orange hunting vest—so no one will shoot me.

The mist is still heavy on the stream when I get there, but there is enough dawn to tie on a fly. The meadow grass is bent with dew. Mud clings to my boots. I watch the water for a minute to see what to fish with, but I'm not thinking very hard about fish. I have the feeling I'm being watched.

I could be wrong. But I still listen for twigs snapping or

hunter's voices. I look into the trees for the shadow of movement. I sing a little in case it's a bear.

An osprey startles me with its cry. It circles twice and heads off toward the lake. I hear a branch swish. I hold my steel rod case across me like a quarter staff. I'm going to feel ridiculous if this turns out to be deer.

Then the silence is broken by a high-pitched sound and a crash. I drop to a crouch, then lose my footing. I tip halfway to the ground, just in time to see a brown blur, and roll to the left in the mud. A young moose bolts past me into the trees.

I lurch up from the freezing-wet ground and shake myself. Thankfully my case and rod aren't broken, but I am covered in mud.

"What are you doing here?"

I nearly jump out of my wet skin at the sound of a human voice, especially Virgil's human voice.

"What are you doing here?" I say.

"Taking a picture of that moose, at least I was trying to, before you showed up."

"That moose nearly killed me," I say.

He eyeballs my orange jacket and my rod case. He says, "He must have thought you had it coming."

"Geez, Virgil," I sputter. "I'm not hunting. I'm fishing."

Virgil says, "Mud looks good on you." He takes a picture.

I lift up a muddy boot and flick it. "You, too."

He caps his lens. "Dennis said Baby put you in charge of the paper."

"Is he still mad?"

"Let's just say we watched every episode of Star Wars last night."

"He's right. I can't even spell."

Virgil shrugs and steps closer to me. "Sometimes greatness is thrust upon you."

I feel a shiver. "And sometimes it's just mud."

We stand in awkward silence. I hear another branch snap. "What's that?"

Virgil says, "The moose?"

I resist the urge to make fun of Virgil for being a city kid. A moose breaks a lot more than twigs when it's on the move, but I'm the one wearing the puddle.

"Maybe it's the mud in your ears," he says.

I scan the trees one more time. "Or maybe it's the sound of the birds falling out of their trees laughing at me."

Virgil smiles. "Or that."

We walk back to my house together, almost like we're friends. I smell like the creek bed. Virgil doesn't seem to mind. He tells me about how they filmed the first Star Wars using tiny models and paper with pinholes. He offers to hold my gear. Nobody has ever offered to hold my gear.

I refold the T-shirts to keep from losing my mind. There are no customers. My homework is done, mostly. Through the front windows of the shop I see occasional cars pass on Geyser. I couldn't care less about what's going on in town today. The town is nothing. I know flecks of slanted light are shimmering off the rivers. Elk are rutting. Bears are eating everything not nailed to the forest floor. The air is cool. The meadow grasses have dried the color of bone and the willows on the river's edge have deepened to burgundy. Virgil is out there somewhere, taking pictures. And here I stand, folding.

At noon I eat a bacon, tomato, and onion sandwich.

At twelve twenty I regret the onion.

At twelve fifty I open the medicine cabinet and discover my dad buys antacids in bulk. For all my dad's silence, I know he worries about stuff even more than I do.

At two o'clock in the afternoon I have dusted everything in the shop including the inside of my own eyelids. We have had exactly nine customers all day and two of them were twin toddlers that destroyed my water bottle pyramid and then wiped their ice-cream-covered paws on the glass case at the register. Of course their mom was "just looking," and didn't buy a thing.

At five ten I discover a Louis L'Amour in the back room. *Dark Canyon.* It could be worse.

When the store door opens at five twenty I have started reading the part where the perky girl lets down her guard.

The door sucks the air from the store and Mr. Martin, Kenner's dad, walks in. Mr. Martin isn't a fisherman, but he comes into the store every so often to swap pheasant and grouse information. Dad says he's a crack shot with anything long and loaded.

Mr. Martin is built to last, like Kenner, plus forty pounds. I can't say I'm happy to see him amble through the store door; he looks like he's in a bad mood, and he's carrying a skinny gray paper in his hand that looks a lot like the school newspaper.

"Hello, KJ," he says in his barbwire baritone. "Your father around?"

"He's hunting," I say. "May I help you, Mr. Martin?"

He nods. "I'd like to think so."

A little nerve in my neck tightens, but I keep my trap closed. He drops the strangled school newspaper on the counter. "I'm afraid I don't appreciate this."

"The paper?" I've only been editor for one day, and there are already complaints?

"Cinderella wolf. Did you write that?"

"Yes, sir."

"What is the point of this garbage?"

"Excuse me, sir?"

"Do you know what a wolf does to a calf or a lamb? You ever seen a dog that's been attacked by a wolf?"

"No, sir." I am scared, for sure, but more than a little

freaked out that Mr. Martin cares, or even reads, what's in our paper. My dad hasn't read it and I'm the editor.

"No need to make this more than it is. I'd like to ask you to rethink the way you're depicting these animals. They aren't pets, and they sure aren't fairy princesses. They hurt people."

"People?" I say.

"They most certainly do, young lady."

I just stand there.

"I suggest you do your homework a little better."

"Uh-huh," I murmur.

He looks around the store. "So you're dad's off hunting, eh? Good man. No reason for him to get messed up in this, is there?"

Mr. Martin walks out before I can reply.

When my dad gets home on Sunday he is dirty, hairy, and ebullient. They got a six-point bull. The men tipped him double what he was expecting.

I have a good dinner waiting because I know my dad hardly eats when he's working. After his third biscuit he asks me, "How was business?"

I say, "Not much." I don't want to talk about business, or Kenner's dad, or Virgil, but I've sure been thinking about them.

"A few more hunts like today and we'll be in good shape."

I nod and clear the dishes. My dad turns on the TV to a legal show. My dad says he didn't like being a lawyer, but he must have liked part of it because he loves to figure out the killer by the first commercial, which used to annoy me but doesn't anymore because I do it, too.

The other thing he loves to do is bust the shows that get their legal facts wrong. Tonight I'm sure he's going to start griping about the guy who gets off after he robs someone's safe, just because he confesses. "That's so stupid," I say, trying to beat Dad to the punch. "It's not like you can just confess and it all goes away."

"If you've got a good lawyer you can sometimes plead down nonviolent felonies to fines and probation."

"That doesn't seem fair."

"Fair is someplace you go to see prize-winning pigs, KJ. In the real world it doesn't exist."

When I go to bed that night I think about what my dad said. I think about Mr. Martin. Maybe I haven't been fair about the wolves because in the real world fair doesn't exist. On the other hand, maybe it should.

I am glad I shall never be young without wild country to be young in. Of what avail are forty freedoms without a blank spot on the map?

Aldo Leopold, "The Green Lagoons"

12

DEAR ADDIE

WE PUT THE paper out every other Thursday. For the first time in the paper's history, kids actually seem interested in what they're reading. They come to the classroom and ask for more. But the paper's popularity has nothing to do with me being editor, or a writer . . . it's all about Addie. Dear Addie.

For the last two weeks I have been coming in early to work. Mrs. Brady isn't doing so well with this pregnancy, so she hardly ever makes it to school before the first bell. Barney, the janitor, lets me in. I like being the first one to work on the paper each day.

This morning, I'm supposed to work on format. I start with Kenner's "anonymous" article about the football team.

> The five-man football team only has two subs this year, but the kids on the team make up for it. Team captain, Kenner Martin, says, "Even if we lose, we make the other team sorry they came."
> We lost to Mountain Ridge last Friday, seven to three.

Clint took pictures at the game, but they're so blurry it looks like it was raining. I'll have to use one anyway. I wonder if it's my job to ask Clint to wait to get drunk until after he's taken his pictures.

Sondra wrote a companion piece to Kenner's. It's an editorial poem on using a skin-free football.

> The tradition of a ball of skin
> Is just another redneck sin.
> Let's use a ball that is synthetic.
> Animal cruelty is not genetic.

I have to give it to Sondra—she has consistency.

I lean my head on my desk to rest for a minute and listen to my stomach growl. I forgot breakfast again. I need my cheat sheet for layout, so I turn to the first edition of Addison's advice column:

Dear Addie,
    My best friend started a rumor about me.
What should I do?
    Stabbed in the Back

Dear Stabbed,
    If people can't say something nice
they shouldn't say anything at all. You
should share your true feelings with
your friend. Friends love that.
    Addie

My stomach makes another noise. I'm not sure it's hunger or nausea from Addie's letter. I read the second letter.

Dear Addie,
    My teachers are always giving me home-
work. I never have time to hang out with
my friends and play video games.
    School Suxs

Dear School Suxs,
    Homework is kinda part of school. But

if you feel that your teachers are being unfair, you should talk to them and
tell them your true feelings. Teachers
love that.

    Addie

Dear Addie,

    There's this guy that I totally like,
but he doesn't seem to know I exist. What
should I do?

    Got the Hots

Dear Hots,

    Sometimes boys are sorta shy. If you
really want him to notice you, you should
try flirting with him when you see him
around. Also, it might help to wear more
makeup and call him at surprising times.
That really gets guys' attention.

    Addie

I didn't understand why Mrs. Baby assigned Addie to
write an advice column, but it's a hit. I hear kids talking
about it in the halls. She gets more letters every week. I love
Addie, but I mean, what if people really take her advice?

I reread my article on the volleyball team and Dennis's

article on the fund-raiser for the senior trip. I insert Virgil's amazing picture of a moose standing in the mist at Duck Creek. I try not to think about how he looked at me when he walked me back from the stream, because it turns me into a well-cooked marshmallow.

Virgil walks through the door of the classroom. Our eyes do that crash thing where you try not to look at someone, so you have to.

Mrs. Baby actually shows up before the bell rings. Her clothes are hanging the right way, and her hair is held down in militant barrettes. "Today we are going to discuss the *W*'s of journalism. Can anyone guess what they might be?"

"Who cares?" says Stewie.

"Very good, Stewie," says Mrs. Baby, and writes *who* on the board. Stewie looks shocked.

I'm a little shocked that Mrs. Baby is trying to actually teach us something.

She says, "Who is involved and who reads about the story?" She keeps writing on the board as if we might take notes. "The magic *W*'s. Who, what, when, where, why, and how."

"*How* starts with an *h*," says Dennis.

"Very good, Dennis," says Mrs. Brady. "Which brings us to the next rule: Rules are made to be broken, if you have good reason. In this case, how a story comes to be is often at the heart of all the other *W*'s put together. And how is always an important general question."

"We have to answer all those questions in every article we write?" I ask.

"Yes," says Mrs. Baby. "To be a true journalist you should always be thinking of these questions and applying them correctly to get to the truth."

"Doesn't that get boring?" says Clint, who seems to be listening for the first time all year.

"The truth, well told, is not boring," Mrs. Baby says in her listen-to-your-mother voice.

Addie chirps in, "The Bible says, 'Ye shall know the truth, and the truth shall make you free.'"

Kenner says, "The Bible wasn't written by reporters." Addie and Kenner frown at each other. It looks like the honeymoon is over.

Sondra says, "It was written by men who treated women like a piece of property."

"The truth hurts," says Kenner.

Stewie and Bret laugh but Addie doesn't.

"Who decides what the truth is?" says Virgil.

Kenner says, "What's the truth about you, Vergee?"

"I think we're talking about reporting the news, Kenny," says Virgil. The best part of this comment is that Virgil smiles so sweetly when he says it.

Sondra stands up in her chair and hits her desk, "Reporting the truth is a journalist's sacred duty."

"Reporters don't care about that crap," says Kenner.

"And you base this opinion on what?" says Addie.

Kenner glares at his girlfriend and then turns to Bret and Stewie as if they were the only ones in the room. "Some of us read the paper for more than the fashion section. . . . News flash, match your socks."

Snickering.

I say, "Yeah, Kenner, I bet you get all the way to the sports column. . . . News flash, the West End football team lost."

This time Bret and Stewie laugh at Kenner.

Kenner stands up and faces me. "There you go again. Shooting off your spastic mouth. You wouldn't know real news if it bit you in the—"

"As I was saying," says Mrs. Baby. "Yes. What was I saying? I had a whole lesson today." She runs her hands over her dress, but she still looks ruffled. "Kenner, would you please sit down so I could remember what I was saying?"

Kenner doesn't sit down. He steps toward Addie. His voice is quiet and raw. "I took this stupid class for you, and now you're as bad as them."

"So leave," whispers Addie.

For a split second Addie and Kenner seem paralyzed. It's horrible to watch something so personal become everyone's business. I want to make them stop. I look at Virgil. He's reading.

"He'll do no such thing," says Mrs. Baby. "You two just need to calm down. . . . Sit down, Kenner. Right this minute."

Kenner grabs his backpack and walks to the front of the classroom. "You're all the saddest sack of freaks and losers I've ever seen," he says, and then he kicks open the class door and storms out.

More snickering.

Clint says, "Dude. He's pissed."

Addie rubs her eyes and says, "What were you saying, Mrs. Brady? About questions or something?"

Mrs. Baby pouts and walks out the door after Kenner. I feel bad for her. She had a real lecture. She did her hair.

Sondra leans out of her chair and forces a sideways hug on Addie. "You go, girl. You go."

"Oh, stuff it, Sondra," says Addie, and breaks out in a big fat sob.

Later that day the entire news staff eats lunch together. We have finally found something we have in common: we all feel sorry for Addie. Across the lunchroom Kenner sits with his friends. He's talking and laughing like any other it's-good-to-be-Kenner day. Some of the girls at the table are Addie's friends, too, but none of them are coming over to talk to her. They're talking to Kenner, and he looks happy about it.

"I can't believe it," Addie keeps saying into her hands.

It's common knowledge they planned to get married out of high school. Which is gross, but not as gross as it sounds, when you see them together.

I put my arm on her shoulder. Hugging people is not my best thing, and Addie still gives me a sucrose imbalance, but I hate to see her cry. "Maybe you should talk to him?"

"Are you kidding?" says Sondra. "He called her a sad-sack freak."

Addie puts her face into her hands again.

"Maybe you could tell him how this makes you feel," I say, before I realize who I'm quoting.

"Oh, like that would work," says Addie bitterly.

I wish I could say I'm just trying to be nice, but there is guilt factor here, too. I know Kenner's dad hates the paper, and that can't make anything easy for Kenner. On the other hand, he *did* call us all sad-sack freaks.

Meanwhile Virgil sits at the end of the table, reading *Slaughterhouse-Five*, eating his lettuce and tomato sandwich. Like nothing has happened. Peace, love, and vegetables.

"I'm not talking to Kenner, ever," Addie sniffles.

"Really?" says Sondra. "I thought you guys were, like, married."

Dennis says, "Haven't you guys been together since you were in sixth grade?"

"Fifth, if you count summers," Addie says, rubbing her

running nose on the back of her hand. "I made him a . . . quilt with our names on it."

"Wow, that's so depressing," says Sondra. "It's like Romeo and Juliet, if Romeo dumped Juliet and called her a . . ."

"Yeah . . . okay," I jump in. "I know you've got a lot going on, Addie, but I could really use a few more letters for the paper if you have time to answer them for the next edition."

Addie's puffy face lights up. "Really?"

"Totally," I say, handing her a dinner napkin.

She sniffles bravely, and wipes off her face. "How about tomorrow morning?"

"Perfect." I pull out another napkin and wipe a tiny snot streak off her cheek.

Virgil peers out from behind his copy of his book. His bushy eyebrows are raised into his hair. He grins at me and I nearly lose my train of thought.

Stewie says, "I've heard, like, five people talking about that Dear Addie thing. You're, like, famous."

Addie smiles at Stewie. "Really?"

Sondra says, "You're like the West End Oprah."

"Oh, you're just saying that to cheer me up," says Addie, beaming now.

Bret says, "I could tell you another fart joke . . ."

Addie says, "I'll pass."

"I think I just did," says Stewie, groaning. Then we all groan.

When I stop writhing from the smell, I say, "Seriously Addie, don't worry about Kenner. It'll all work out. People just say stuff. I mean how could he live without you, right? You made him a quilt. Guys are just like that. They show off a little and then get over it. The good guys anyway."

"Do you think so?"

I see Virgil tilting his head out from behind his book. He dips it back in but it's too late, I saw his smirk. I stare down at my lunch and cover my happily blotching neck with my hair.

Dear Addie,

This girl keeps calling my house late at night. My mom gets way mad at me. The girl acts like I like her but I don't. It's like she's stalking me.

Bugged

Dear Bugged,

That's totally weird. Everybody needs their space. That girl needs to respect your personal bubble.

Addie

I finally get some mail:

Dear Wolf Notes,

    The way you write about wolves makes me laugh. You might as well write a column on skunks. They're more "endangered" in the park than wolves but maybe the people in Washington like wolves because they make them feel more at home when they come to visit.

    Save the Skunk!

Dear Save the Skunk,

    I don't know about the people in Washington, but I agree with you about skunks. They are more endangered in the park than wolves. The rangers killed them by the hundreds back in the 1870s, along with wolves, cougars, and wolverines. A Skunk Reintroduction Program? Why the smell not?

    Wolf Notes

13

PRETTY IS AS PRETTY DOES

ADDIE SHOWS UP twenty minutes before class wearing white cords and a cream sweater. She could sell toothpaste.

"Sorry, I would have come sooner but have you ever tried to do three little girls' hair? It's like braiding porcupines. And Riley and Landon are getting toilet trained, so it's just one big poo fest around my house."

"You get your brothers and sisters ready for school every morning?" This kind of thing has never occurred to me. "Is it fun? Having such a big family?"

"Sisters whine and brothers smell. Guess I'd miss 'em if I got the chance, but not this morning. What are we working on?"

"I'm editing your column. Do you want to look at mine? I just wrote a short wolf update."

Addie sits down next to me, looking affectionately at her letters. "My parents told me to stay out of the political stuff."

I'm dumbfounded. "My articles aren't political . . . they're informative."

"KJ, you write about wolves."

"I'm writing about what they're doing; that's not politics."

Addie scoots over into the chair next to me to get a better view of her letter. She says, "Like, do you put in all the bad stuff they do?"

"*Like* what bad stuff?" I say, scooting off the chair.

"Well, you know, like, eating people's cattle and dogs and kids and stuff. You haven't done any articles on that."

"They don't eat people's kids. And Kenner wouldn't talk to me about his dog."

Addie looks up patiently, through her perfectly curled eyelashes. "Whatever, KJ. Why do you get so into it? I mean you're pretty now."

I am seriously regretting inviting Addie to come early to school. "What does being pretty have to do with anything?"

"Well, I'm just saying that writing about wolves makes you seem hostile, and guys don't normally like hostile girls."

"Who says I'm hostile?"

"It's just that wolves bother people," she says. "I don't see the point."

I chew on my pen. "The point is they belong here. When they're gone the elk eat everything to a nub, streams erode, and then the whole place starts to fall apart."

She smiles. "Did you know it takes more than seventy-two more muscles to frown than to smile?"

I frown. "That's a myth."

Addie holds up her finger like she's actually doing the toothpaste commercial, "Do you feel relaxed right now?"

I slump down in a chair across the room to start work on Stewie's stickman comic strip about a killer toilet. I guess we all write about what we love. "Your letter about avoiding onions on a date is done," I say. "I'm sure Mrs. Baby will want it on the front page."

"Oh, good," says Addie. "I know exactly who wrote that one and I don't want them to miss my answer. Stink-er-roo if you know what I mean."

I look at Addie. She's undeniably beautiful, and smart about a lot of things I'm not. She helps her family, and she writes a column that everyone loves. I say, "So you're telling me that if I would write about something besides wolves, people would like me more?"

"I'm just saying that if you would just ease up a little . . . Now's your chance, you know. And if you want to come over to the house some night I bet I could fix you all up. A little petal pink blush might even soften your frown muscles."

"That's nice, Addie. But I'm okay."

"Maybe I'll write a column about that, 'Pretty Is as Pretty Does.' What do you think?"

I think I'd rather write about wolves than onions.

Mr. Muir hands back the quizzes in math. Two out of five. I'm going to have to study more, but at least I feel like it might do some good. He writes a note at the bottom, "Love the wolf column. Do your math homework."

During class Joss and Mandy pass notes. Ten minutes before the bell Mandy tosses one of the notes to me. The letters are big and curly. "The newspaper sucks butt."

Joss and Mandy hate me. I tuck the letter into my binder. It's important to savor life's small pleasures.

After school Virgil is waiting for me by my locker.

"We need some more wolf pics this weekend. I'm going out with my mom right now. Do you want to come?"

"Now?" Even if they left right now it will be dark by the time they get to Lamar Valley. "Where are you going to sleep?"

"My mom met a guy with a camper who said it was fine. He's cool."

I imagine this story going into my dad's ears. "I have to work. Inventory."

"So meet us in the morning. Slough Creek. Maybe we can find Cinderella."

"I'll figure something out," I say.

Even Cinderella didn't have to borrow the car from her dad.

When I get home, Dad is finishing on the phone. "That was your math teacher."

"What did I do?"

"He wanted me to let me know you currently have a B in the class."

"He called you to tell you I'm *not* bombing math?" I feel antigravitational devices moving under my feet.

"Well, I asked him to . . . periodically," says my dad calmly. "Just in case."

"In case of what?"

"KJ, knock it off. How should we celebrate? You name it."

"Anything?" I say.

"Anything that costs less than twenty dollars and won't get me arrested."

Sometimes you just have to roll the dice when you're feeling lucky. "How about letting me take the car to the Lamar tomorrow?"

Dad eyebrows pinch together. "That's a long drive."

We both know how I drive.

He says, "You could get snow."

We both know how he feels about bad roads. I may as well start folding T-shirts, but I don't.

"I need a new wolf article."

"Mr. Muir says you're doing a good job with that, too. Says it's about time kids hear both sides of this thing. Guess I should actually read what you're doing."

Visions of Mr. Martin dance in my wee little head.

He says, "How about I drive? I'll hang a sign on the door."

"You're going to take off work just because you don't trust me to drive?" I say.

"Pretty much." He smiles, but he's not kidding.

Q: Why did the Yellowstone wolf cross the road?

A: She was ready for her close-up.

14

THE LEADER OF THE PACK

IN OCTOBER THE tourists are long gone, and if we're lucky, like today, we still have a few red and gold mornings before the snow locks up the roads in the park. The light softens, and the air is crisp and fresh with the promise of storms. We hear elk bugling in the meadows below Mount Haynes. We see their outline in the meadows between Madison and Norris Junction but it has been warm, so the elk are more sparse than usual for this time of year. Just below the Chocolate Pots, right up next to the road, we see two bull elk fighting. We pull over and listen to the clap of their horns thrusting against each other.

I like to drive with my dad. I can sleep. With other people

I feel like I have to watch the road, so they will be careful. I know my dad will be careful. I like to think my apprehensive attitude is left over from my mom's accident. I'd like to think I remember something about her, even something bad.

On the other hand, I wish Dad didn't worry so much. He has good memories of Mom to remember her by. At least I think he does.

The pink light of the sunrise makes its entrance at Slough Creek right as we do. Dad pulls in and parks right next to Virgil getting out of Eloise's car. Virgil waves. I sort of forgot to mention Virgil. I sort of forgot to think this through.

"Friend of yours?"

"That's Virgil."

"Virgil?"

"You know . . . the guy . . ."

"*The* guy?" my dad says with drama.

I can feel my skin changing color already. "No . . . Don't, okay?"

Dad bounces out of the car and introduces himself to Virgil while I sit in the car and hyperventilate. Then he comes back and tells me to get my lazy butt out of the car and find a wolf.

"Nice," I sneer.

Dad smiles. "He seems perfectly manly to me."

"You know, Dad," I say with utter sincerity, "I really hate it when you take an interest in me."

I get out of the car, and Virgil walks over and takes a picture of me telling my dad I don't need a coat. "I love family portraits," he says.

We all walk up the hill to the viewpoint. Eloise is already in position with a half dozen other people. Everyone in this crowd has a thermos, a scope, and a handheld radio. We reverently join the faithful.

Eloise looks from her scope just long enough to whisper, "Two wolves and a griz. The wolves think it's their kill, but they're about to lose breakfast."

"Hi, Eloise," I say. I'm amazed at how much I've missed her. She looks so perfectly Eloise today. Her cheeks and lips are pink from the cold air, and her straw-colored hair is tossed around her head.

She says, "Hey, honey, thought you'd never get here."

"This is Eloise Whitman, Virgil's mom. She's a wolf biologist," I say to Dad. He gets a funny look on his face. Maybe he's not used to seeing women over forty that look like they're a roadie.

"Are you here guiding today, Mr. Carson?" says Virgil.

"No," says Dad cheerfully. "Today is strictly pleasure."

Eloise looks up annoyed. "Virgil, you're missing it!"

Virgil goes back to his scope quickly and starts snapping off shots. Dad sets up for us so I get to watch all three people disappear into their work like water into sand.

"Nice views," whispers my dad.

After a few seconds he lets me look. I see a good-size grizzly swatting at two adult wolves. There's not a chance that these wolves are going to get back breakfast, but they seem to be making a point about the bear's manners.

Dad touches my arm. "My turn." He's as excited as I am. This cracks me up, since he's old. Well, he's not that old. But he's my dad, so that's old to me.

I hold my binoculars up to try to get an outline. I can see the grizzly lean back without moving his body away from the carcass. The wolves circle, one darting while the other distracts, but the bear is having none of it. He lets out some snorts and then a real roar. The bear lunges across the carcass and nearly gets a piece of the darting wolf. The wolves retreat. The bear is slower than the wolves but not too slow to chase them for a good hundred yards. The wolves disappear into the trees, and the bear plods back to his breakfast. It occurs to me that it was the wolves' breakfast, too. And they have expended a lot of energy, twice, for nothing. Being a predator isn't for wimps.

"Cutting it close," says Virgil.

"It's what they do best," says Eloise. "Now who is this guy, KJ?" She smiles at my dad like he's a new car.

Dad straightens up ever so slightly. "Glad to meet you, Eloise. Samuel Carson."

I don't like this posture-adjusting one bit. I've seen as many old movies as any other sixteen-year-old girl in America, but chemistry is not allowed between Eloise and Samuel. I saw Virgil first, and I don't double with parents.

What I have going for me is that Eloise isn't really my dad's type. If he ever dates, which is never, he goes out with skinny women with tidy hair who think he is the smartest person on Earth, because they definitely aren't. Eloise probably knows more about wolves than wolves do. And she's not exactly a supermodel under all that flannel.

"Samuel Carson. That sounds like a pretty serious name. Are you serious, Mr. Carson? Because your daughter is downright morbid."

"Just because she talks about killing Virgil all the time doesn't make her morbid," says my dad.

At this point I feel it's important for our parents to stop getting to know each other. "Dad, do you think that grizzly has cubs?"

"Do you see cubs?" he says, looking back in his scope.

"No, but I just thought . . ."

Eloise jumps in, "Looks like a male to me. About three, don't you think, Sam?"

"Maybe four," he says. "Looks like he's in good shape."

"Better than those wolves, I'd guess," says Eloise. "The older one of them was limping to start with. Hard to get much action if you're starting to fall apart."

"You can say that again," says Dad and laughs.

Okay. Teatime's over. I'm bringing the heat. "Boy, Dad,

it's sure nice of you to give up bow hunting to bring me out here," I say. "I know how you look forward to this season."

"This is a great way to enjoy my season, honey. Glad I could take a day off and come. Maybe I'm getting sentimental, but sometimes I'd a lot rather watch a wolf or a grizzly get an elk than get one myself."

"We're glad you could make it, too," says Eloise. "Always nice to meet another aficionado of the predator experience."

I'm out of ammo. I look at Virgil.

"I'd like to go down and get some more shots from a different angle. Anyone else? Mr. Carson?"

Virgil is amazing.

After Virgil and Dad leave, Eloise gives me the eye. "Are you setting me up with your dad?"

"No," I nearly shout. "He snores and never talks, and he always thinks he's right."

"So he's male then."

"Yeah, really, really male."

Eloise chuckles at me. "They all are, honey. Even Virgil. But don't worry. I'm not looking to take extra luggage home from Montana."

"Good. No. I mean . . . I mean I talk too much."

"I like how you talk, but you need to relax. Let's talk about something depressing for your little newspaper article. That ought to set you back to rights."

"I'd like that," I say.

"Did you hear there's a group in Park County raising a

stir because elk hunters aren't doing as well this year? They say the wolves are hunting the northern range herd to extinction. It's hard for me to believe they're serious. Every fool with an orange vest knows when there's no snow the elk stay up higher. And you could suntan this October."

"What are they going to do?"

"Who knows? Every time you turn around there is some bonehead trying to blame the wolves for something else. Next thing you know they'll be the cause of love handles and tooth decay. All joking aside, I believe something's brewing. These extreme anti-wolf groups are drawing crowds. And there's always somebody that thinks they can get the bad old days back again."

"I don't think people in town are like that. Not most of them anyway. Besides, I read a report that says wolves are good for business."

"That depends entirely on your business, honey."

We go back to watching the bear. After devouring a few more slabs of elk, the bear stashes his loot in a marshy part of the pond and moves off for a morning stroll. The guys come back and we all make awkward small talk until Eloise moves out into the crowd to visit with some of the wolf watchers. One woman has traveled here from Denmark. Her husband passed away a year ago, and she is finally doing some things she has always wanted to do. I hate it when old people say things like that.

"Do you like it here?" I ask.

"The wolves I like," she says. "Americans, not as much."

"Now, that's funny," says Eloise. "I always think of us as kind of the same deal. Except Americans eat more salads."

Suddenly there's a gust of surprise from the retired couple from Snowflake, Arizona. The man turns to Eloise and whispers, "It's her."

"Nine-F?" asks Eloise.

Virgil clicks into his scope and starts snapping shots off like crazy. My dad hogs his scope but doesn't say a word.

"Who?" I say to Virgil softly.

Eloise whispers over to me, "Nine. The Rose Creek alpha female."

I try to remember my homework. "The famous one who had pups after her mate got shot to pieces outside the park?"

"The very one. She's a dandy. But it looks like she may have lost her niche."

"Her pack kicked her out? Why?"

"Competition. In this case we think it's her daughter's doing."

"That's pretty heartless."

"Survival of the fittest," says Eloise.

Everyone is quiet for a minute. My dad finally gives me a peek through the scope. I watch Number Nine tear off some of the bear's stash. She drags an entire leg off to eat nervously under a tree. She's gray and thin but most wolves are thin.

She looks fine to me except she's alone. After she's gulped a few bites she lifts her head and jogs off with the leg dangling from her mouth.

After another stretch of nothing but ducks to look at, we head into Cooke City for lunch. We find a diner and order everything on the menu. Eloise and my dad hit it off like old college roommates. When my dad, the tightwad, orders dessert, I can't take it anymore and tell everyone I'm going out to look around town.

"Don't get lost," Dad says.

Right. Cooke City is about the size of most people's driveways, with about as many people living there, especially this time of year. My dad likes to say the only people that live in Cooke City year-round are the types that like to get naked and drive their Harleys up and down Main Street shooting a gun.

I get to the first gift shop before I feel Virgil standing behind me. "Looking for a T-shirt? That one with the pink Indian girl is nice."

I don't turn around. "You think they like each other?"

"They're just wildlife geeks."

"Really?" I say hopefully.

"My mom has been divorced a long time. She doesn't seem to mind it all that much."

I don't say anything. I feel a cloud settle in my chest. What if Virgil becomes my stepbrother?

"You worry too much," says Virgil.

"How do you know?" I say.

"Your face twists up like a wet rag."

"No, it doesn't," I say, and try to untwist.

"We're only here for the school year anyway. You'll have your dad to yourself in no time."

I hadn't thought of that. "When do you leave?"

"When school gets out. My mom has to get back to her job at the university. It's been fun to live with Aunt Jean though. She's really weird." Virgil raises his eyebrows and looks side to side like a lunatic.

"Do you want to see the town?" I say.

"I thought the diner was the town," says Virgil.

"Such a snob. They have a hotel with a bar."

"Impressive."

"And two blackjack machines."

"Can't get more excitement than that."

We walk out onto the abandoned street. A small storm is looming over the top of Pilot Peak. A drizzle starts before we get a block up the street and by the time we get to the Mine Road we are drenched. A giant crack of light splits open the sky and booms through the town. I don't see exactly where the lightning hits, but the air feels electric. We turn around and run for the diner. The sound of the rain slaps the puddles that fill the muddy road. A jacked-up truck drives past and sloshes us from a pothole.

The lightning flashes again and the thunder rattles a tin roof nearby. Virgil pulls me toward a stand of trees and shouts, "Here." He looks upset.

"What's wrong?" I say.

His shaggy hair drips into his face. "That lightning is right on top of us."

I suppress a smirk. "Don't you get lightning back in Minnesota?"

"We prefer depressing drizzles. It builds character." Virgil hugs himself and shakes. "I can't believe how fast that came on."

"You know what they say around here. You don't like the weather, just wait fifteen minutes."

My teeth start to chatter loudly. Virgil looks me over for a second and then puts both his arms around my arms and squeezes. "Your head's going to fall off if you keep doing that."

My teeth keep chattering, but Virgil warms me up in a hurry. I'm not good at this, but I figure Virgil isn't either. I look up. I can feel mud on my cheeks and forehead. He has a big clod by his mouth. I slip my arm out to clean it off and he plants one on me. Not a dweeby high school kiss. A real kiss. A Montana rainstorm kiss. My teeth stop chattering.

Virgil is a good kisser. Disturbingly good.

"Had a few girlfriends back in Minnesota?" I want to hit myself as soon as I say it. It just pops out.

"A couple."

Yeah, I'll bet a couple.

"You?" says Virgil, smiling wickedly.

I shake my wet head. "You've seen the selection."

"Good point."

He kisses me again. I can taste mud in my mouth and something else I'm not altogether sure about. Then the lightning fractures out in the street next to us. We both jump and fall away from each other.

Virgil grabs my arm and says, "Let's run."

We jog through the mud and rain together but stop at the entrance to the diner. Even diners in Cooke City draw the line at mud-caked teenagers. My dad and Eloise are drinking coffee and laughing. They don't even see until we knock on the glass.

Virgil is holding my hand. I wonder if my dad will care. It's fine with me if he does. Everything's fine with me, including the mud and the cold and the stuff at school. Even if Virgil is going home in six months, and even if my dad is having lunch with Eloise. If it got me to this place, right now, it's all fine.

So I smile at Dad though the window and wave a muddy hand. He waves quickly and then goes back to talking to Eloise. He's like a dog on point. How can he do this to me?

Eloise turns and waves to us, too. Her smile is light and airy. All the pucker has gone out of her face. There is a soft light from the kitchen that shines across the two of them. Virgil looks at me and smiles and then lets go of my hand. Lets it drop like a rock in water. He says to me, "You never know, do you?"

"Know what?" I say, rubbing my arms in the cold.

"What the weather's going to do next around here."

Thanksgiving Turkey

INGREDIENTS:

My Dad

Eloise

INSTRUCTIONS:

Stuff with Gross Middle-Age Flirting

Roast until Dead

Thanksgiving Side Dish

Mashed relationship with Virgil

Thanksgiving Dessert

Aunt Jean said she thought my dad was
too young for Eloise. Delicious.

15

THE PERSONALS

IT'S THE DAY after Thanksgiving. I sit at my computer in my flannel train pajamas and Elmo slippers. The snow has finally come, and the west entrance is closed to cars until spring. It's a long drive around, about four hours one way. I could do it alone if I could wiggle out of work I guess, but I can't handle doing the drive as a blended family. So today I settle for tracking the wolves on the Internet.

In the next room Dad is getting ready for his date with Eloise. He's singing. I might as well pick out my bridesmaid dress.

I read, "The wolves are beginning to disperse. The battle for territory and pack alignments will heat up in the coming cold until at last the rituals of winter culminate in the breed-ing and denning of the deep winter months." The battle for breeding territory. I could add a few paragraphs on that sub-ject from personal experience.

Eloise was right when she said there was trouble brew-ing though. People are talking about the elk numbers. And they aren't happy. Some are talking about getting the whole Endangered Species Act listing overturned and wiping the wolves out again. I found one Web site with a wolf-killing ammo ad and a detailed recipe for poison meatballs.

The whole thing makes me sick. Or maybe that's the stale smell of Eloise's turkey that still fills the house.

She brought over everything for dinner but her wedding china. And she brushed her hair back. And she wore perfume! Virgil spent most of his time talking to Dad about tracking wildlife and then sat in the corner and read *Zen and the Art of Motorcycle Maintenance*. Aunt Jean and I talked about her cat's digestive issues. One big happy potentially incestuous family.

Dad knocks on my door. "Anybody home?"

He comes in and stands with his hands in his pockets. He is pressed and combed. His teeth even shine. Finally he says, "How's the homework?"

"Fine," I say.

"Is this shirt presentable?"

Dad never asks my advice about anything. He certainly never asked me if he could date Virgil's mom. I say, "It's fine."

"Thanks," he says, and then just stands there. "I should be back around . . . hmm . . . not really sure."

I repeat one of his standbys, "Nothing good happens after midnight."

Dad actually blushes. I want to kill myself.

I look at the last edition of the school newspaper. Virgil's photos of the bear and the two wolves sparring are brilliant. I drift. If my dad and Eloise get married where will we live? Will I have to move to Min-e-sooda *and* live platonically in the same house with Virgil? Isn't that child abuse?

I have Cap'n Crunch for dinner. I try to do a math work sheet, but I end up watching the snow falling outside the kitchen window. I wonder what Virgil is doing.

I type:

```
Dear Addie,
    My father's love life is ruining mine.
I met the perfect guy and then my dad
came along and developed a midlife crush
on his mom. Now my Mr. Perfect treats
me like I have the bubonic plague. What
should I do?
    The Miserable Girl Next Door
```

Delete.

I nod to the houseplant and say, "Just tell him your feelings. Boys love that."

I walk around my room and look at different editions of the paper I've posted up. Virgil's pictures make our column look impressive, but Addie's column is the hit of the year. How can un-extirpated wolves compete with bad breath?

I read more entries from the wolf watchers. There's a buzz about the Crystal Creek pack's invasion of the Druid's territory. The mighty Druids got stomped. Outnumbered and outmaneuvered, the Druid Peak pack was chased off Specimen Ridge like a bunch of rank puppies. One report says, "Druids tucked their tails and ran."

I imagine mean old Number Forty barking the retreat to her pack. I turn to my plant. "You just never know, do you?"

I'm eating my third bowl of Cap'n Crunch when there's a knock at the door. I jump to my feet. I look through the kitchen window at the front door and see a dark hood. I take a kitchen knife out of the drawer. The hood is creepy.

"Hello?" I say through the door.

"It's Virgil. . . . I want to talk to you . . . about the newspaper."

I open the door. He's covered in two inches of snow. "You came over at ten thirty at night to talk to me about the newspaper?"

He smiles. "I don't know which is scarier, the knife or the train pj's."

"Do you want to come in?"

He sits on my tiny couch. I put away the knife and turn on the TV set because I don't know what else to do. I sit on the floor. When I'm alone with him everything inside me purrs like a giant cat. I have to actually control the impulse to rub my back against his leg. We look at the TV and listen to a man talk about killing his wife.

After a minute he says, "Do you like this sort of thing?"

"No," I say. "But it gives me and my dad something to talk about."

"You talk about killing people?"

"He was a trial attorney before he moved here. It's like watching football with an old jock."

Virgil drags his wet hair back with his fingers. If I didn't know better I'd think he was nervous. He says, "Can you come up here? I can't talk to the top of your head."

There isn't room on the couch for both of us. When I sit down I'm sandwiched in so tight I have to twist into his side to face him. His clothes are wet and cold.

He looks into my eyes and says, "I really love my mom."

"That's nice. . . ." I say, totally grossed out.

He sighs. "But this isn't working."

"What isn't working?"

"Trying to make just *her* happy. I want to make *everybody* happy."

"Everybody?" I say. "That's a whole lot of happy."

He looks at the floor and then takes my hand. He rubs my palm and fingers with his thumbs. It's weird but I'm a cat so I really, really, like it. I don't talk because I know it would come out *meow*.

Finally after my hand is about to fall off from happiness, Virgil looks up and kisses me. He touches my shoulder. And then I scoot up out of the torture couch halfway into his lap. He puts his arms around me. His shirt is soaking. A shiver runs up his back. We seem to have a thing about weather and making out.

I say, "How long were you standing out there?"

"I don't know. Forty-three minutes."

"You must be freezing. And a stalker."

"No, I'm fine. But this couch is impressively uncomfortable."

"My dad doesn't believe in furniture that encourages laziness."

"Smart guy," says Virgil, and pulls me to the floor. We start kissing again, but Virgil keeps shivering. I go to my dad's bedroom and get Virgil a T-shirt and then to my bedroom and get a blanket. He changes his shirt in front of me. His skin is paper white, but for a guy who never picks up anything heavier than a tripod, he's ripped.

"Holy smack," I say.

"What?"

"You have, like . . . muscles."

He grins stupidly. "I do Tai Chi."

"Yeah," I say, wishing I hadn't given him an extra shirt.

"I used to be big into Tae Kwon Do and that stuff," he says.

"Were you good?" I say, fascinated.

"I got my brown belt when I was thirteen."

"Why'd you stop?"

"Umm . . . I shattered my best friend's nose at a tournament."

Virgil's face is quiet, gentle. I can't see a trace of what he's talking about. "But it was an accident, right?"

"No . . . I was hurt and I was angry. I wanted to keep hitting him after he went down. The blood just made me angrier."

"Wow," I say. "You don't seem like that."

"I think everybody's like that. You just have to push the right buttons." He smiles weakly and a shiver runs through him. "So I don't push those buttons anymore."

I put my hand on his arm. "You're ice."

"Do you mind if I try on your blanket?"

He gets under the blanket and pulls it up around his wet head. "Nope. Still cold."

I get under the blanket with him. Nothing crazy happens. It doesn't have to. Just being next to Virgil, having him want to be next to me, makes me feel delirious. Of course the whole kissing thing is good, too. It takes a while, but eventually he stops shivering.

I don't hear my dad and Eloise come in until the front

door closes. I peek out of the blanket. They're standing in front of us.

"Hey," says Virgil calmly.

Dad says, "What the hell do you think you're doing with my daughter?"

Eloise steps between us and Dad. "Looks like pretty much the same thing we've been doing."

I've never seen my dad look so furious.

"It's not the same and you know it, Eloise."

"I think you're overreacting."

"Overreacting?" repeats Dad.

Eloise says, "Virgil, do you have your clothes on under there?"

"Sort of," says Virgil. "I borrowed Mr. Carson's shirt."

"How about you, honey?" says Eloise.

I nod my head and stand up. I realize too late what I'm wearing. I shuffle in my Elmo slippers. Virgil stands up, too.

"Wow, trains," says Eloise, laughing. "I need to get you some new things."

"Do you think this is funny?" says Dad.

"Samuel, of course I do. It is funny."

"I'm sorry to hear that."

"Virgil, we'd better go," says Eloise.

"Yes, I think you'd better," says Dad. "And I want my shirt back."

Virgil looks at me sadly and then strips off the shirt. I'm

so mortified at this point I'm covered in welts. Virgil, on the other hand, is bizarrely dignified for someone half naked, and just busted by a girl's father. He's like Gandhi with hormones.

Virgil folds the shirt neatly and puts it in Dad's hand. He looks at me again and then at my dad and says, "I'm sorry."

"Life's too short," says Eloise, and walks out the door into the cold, dragging her shirtless son behind her.

WOLF NOTES
Elk Incognito

The elk herds are down at the elk reserve in Wyoming. Which has people wondering if the wolves have eaten them all. Some scientists say the drought is changing the elk's migration habits. I personally think there's a big elk party somewhere and the humans just aren't invited.

16

MAN OF MYSTERY

MONDAY VIRGIL COMES to school in a good mood, which really hacks me off since I'm been scooting around on my belly thinking about how I'm grounded from him for the rest of my life. Plus Baby has assigned me to do a story on creative dating. Holy smack. In this town creative dating is wiping the dog hair off the seat before your date climbs in your truck.

"You're chipper," I say.

"I'm working on something, a new project."

I wonder if Baby asked him to write about dating, too. Maybe he can talk about being busted warming up with your date under a blanket. Not creative, but has a recognizable story line. I say, "What kind of a project?"

"A you'll-have-to-wait-and-see project."

"Are you building my dad a new brain? I'd like that."

Baby waddles over and taps my desk with her pen. She's in a foul mood this morning. "I didn't say you should start your date right now, KJ. Work, please."

Virgil gives Baby the kilowatt smile. "That's a great dress, Mrs. Brady. Blue's a beautiful color on you."

She smiles back. "Oh, for heaven's sake."

Virgil waits until Baby goes back to her desk and whispers, "Dennis is helping me. And Aunt Jean."

I pretend to be writing my story, when actually I'm writing my name backward. It relaxes me. "No offense, but I don't really want Dennis and your aunt Jean working on my dad's brain. He's already angry Spock."

"Your dad is just trying to protect you. You two are big on safety."

"What's that supposed to mean?"

"I'm a man of mystery," says Virgil.

He's got that right, but what man isn't?

All week long Virgil keeps his secret with Dennis. And since I'm grounded, I can't see him or call him after school. Friday he misses class altogether. I'm experiencing Virgil withdrawal.

During lunch break Kenner bumps me in the hall. "You part of Vergee's secret mission, too?"

"What?" I say.

"Dennis semi-squealed. Virgil and Dennis are doing something—besides each other, I mean."

Great. Even Kenner knows more about this than I do. "Got me," I say.

"Yeah," says Kenner. "I heard about that, too."

I hurry out of the hall so I can blush in the bathroom. I should never have told Sondra and Addie. I hate small towns.

After school I head over to the bookstore to see if they've got the book I ordered for my dad for Christmas. They don't, and Eloise is in my spot.

"What's up?" I say. We haven't talked since the blanket incident.

She raises an eyebrow. Apparently Virgil gets that from her. "You tell me, hon."

"What can I say? My dad's crazy."

She sighs and puts her coffee cup down. "He's not crazy. He's protective. If I had a beautiful girl like you in my house I'd be protective, too. I should be more protective of Virgil, but he's seems to be turning out all right. At least I think so anyway. How's he doing in school?"

"Why?" I say. Mostly I want to know why she's asking me.

"Because all of the sudden he and Dennis are doing an awful lot of homework. It's not like him. Even Aunt Jean seems to be in on it. But nobody wants to say what's going on. You don't know, I guess?"

"It's a mystery," I say, doing an impression of Virgil.

"My grant advisor is in Bozeman this week so this isn't a real good time for mysteries. I'll get it out of Jean when I get back. That boy has pulled a few stunts in his life. I feel stunt in the air and I don't like it."

She looks me over, from my boots to my beanie, and smiles. It makes me feel as warm as coffee. I wonder if my mom would have looked at me like that. She says, "Virgil told me some kids are giving you a hard time about this wolf column."

"No big deal."

"Hang in there, kid. If you don't have a few enemies, you aren't doing your job."

Ode to West End Christmas Decor

At Christmastime we freeze and quake.
Homemade presents oft we make.
We deck our halls, but not with holly.
We find that moose heads look more jolly!

17

THE CHRISTMAS STROLL

EVERY YEAR THAT I can remember I have gathered with my town on the second weekend in December to light the town tree, share some cider and doughnuts, and have a parade. It's always below freezing, so it's kind of a celebration of who we are. If you're standing on that street corner with a red face, stoically freezing your fingers off, you're a resident. Everyone's invited. Everyone belongs.

I meet Sondra and Addie in front of Mr. Muir's Sticks and Stones store. He has a festive wreath of knives in one window and new sculpture of a wolf pack playing in the snow in the other.

"I love this parade," says Addie with a sigh. "It always makes me feel like singing Christmas carols."

"Oh, me, too," says Sondra. "Deck the halls with gratuitous consumption. Fa la la la la."

Addie pouts.

"Sondra," I say in my jolly voice, "how about some peace on earth tonight?"

Three blocks of Canyon Street are decked out for the festivities with red flashing lights, plastic gold stars, and tinsel streamers. Everything sparkles in the falling snow.

"They wouldn't accept my entry," says Sondra.

"What was it?" says Addie.

"I was going to call it 'Rudolph's Revenge.'" Sondra rubs her nose.

"Festive," I say.

Sondra nods at me enthusiastically. "I was going to take a blow-up doll in fatigues and tie it onto the top of my mom's truck and then drive up and down the street dressed up like a drunk elk."

Addie whines, "Oh, Sondra!"

I say, "I'm really surprised they didn't let you do it."

Sondra says, "I even made papier-mâché antlers."

"And I'll bet you looked great," says Addie.

Sondra nods seriously. "This whole town is full of fascists."

Everybody migrates to the park. It's about twenty below and dropping fast. A thin mist of snow is falling. People are pulling out their flasks and six-packs to keep themselves warm. It's cold even for West End and people are drinking hard.

We are all waiting for the mayor. He and his wife dress up as Mr. and Mrs. Claus. The party can't start until "Santa" makes his big entrance on a horse-drawn sleigh and throws a premade snowball that is supposed to hit the tree and magically turn on its lights. The problem is that our mayor tends to warm up with a little too much Season's Greetings before the show. I hope his aim is better than last year.

We don't talk now because we have scarves over our faces, and it's too cold to move anything that's optional. Finally we hear the jingle of the sleigh, and the frozen people standing next to me cheer out of sheer relief. Parents take a layer off their kids' faces so they can see the sleigh, and a few little kids start to cry.

Addie starts singing "Here Comes Santa Claus." Sondra and I join her, even though our lips are frozen. Mr. Ashton makes a speech about "the joy of living with people you know and love," then throws the magic snowball. He misses the tree but everybody cheers, and they turn the tree on anyway.

I see Eloise across the park with Aunt Jean. I wave and they wave back. No sign of Virgil. I can't believe Eloise got Aunt Jean out in this cold. I wonder if Eloise is trying to kill Jean for her money after all.

We mill back over to Canyon Street, and two trucks covered in Christmas lights start off the parade. One has a sign on the grille that says THE SANTA CLAWS PARADE, and one behind it says BEARRY CHRISTMAS. I see Dad up the street with some of his hunting buddies. I wave, and they start making their way toward us.

A hay wagon full of frozen Presbyterians comes next in the parade, singing "O Come All Ye Faithful." They hurl frozen saltwater taffy bullets into the crowd. The kids not maimed by this treat dive into the snow up to their eyeballs to dig out the candy.

I look down the street, and I see Eloise and Aunt Jean walking toward us. Aunt Jean is hunched over like a candy cane. I look up the street and see my dad coming toward me from the other direction. Even though I'm the one grounded from Virgil, it's really our parents who aren't speaking.

"This is awkward," I mumble.

"I know. Did you see how they're looking at me?" says Addie.

I look across the street and see Kenner's drones standing together shooting hate stares at Addie. "Where's Kenner?"

"He's in the parade, I think. Look at them. I wish those idiots would just leave me alone," says Addie. "I can date other guys if I want to."

"Who are you dating?" says Sondra in an excited voice.

"Oh . . . I didn't tell you? William Martin. He's helping with the parade right now, but we're going out after it's over."

"His brother?" says Sondra. "You're going out with Kenner's brother? He's like twenty."

"Yep," says Addie. "But it's all a mess out there today."

"Oh, yeah?" I say. "I can't imagine why." I think of the two brothers fighting that day in the forest. William's good to look at, but Addie must be out of her mind.

"It's not me. Another wolf came right down into their yard last night. Right down to the pens. He said it wasn't even afraid of him until he fired a shot."

"I don't believe it," I say. "I didn't read about that on any of the wolf pages today."

Addie sighs. "KJ, geez. Do you think ranchers report that kind of stuff?"

I can't think clearly to answer. Eloise and my dad are closing in. Eloise gets to me first. She locks her arms around me and says, "Have you seen Virgil anywhere? I haven't seen him all day. And Aunt Jean here is a big liar."

Aunt Jean smiles triumphantly. "Yes I am."

"I haven't seen him," I say as I feel Dad step to my side.

"Hello, Samuel," says Eloise.

"Hello, Eloise, Jean," says Dad. "How are you?"

At least Dad is a gentleman. Which is more than I can say for Kenner's friends, who are currently giving Addie the finger from across the street.

"Oh, can you believe this?" says Addie. "So immature."

Eloise looks curiously at Addie but continues, "We're fine, thank you, Samuel. We're looking for Virgil."

"Haven't seen him since school got out yesterday," I say.

My dad looks at me suspiciously. "He was with Dennis."

Sondra nods. "They were completely not in school today."

Addie says, "Oh, who even cares what they do?"

Eloise shoots Addie another perturbed look. "Well, I do. I'm telling you anything can happen with this kid."

"You seem kind of serious, Eloise," says Dad. He may be a gentlemen, but that doesn't mean he's above sarcasm.

Aunt Jean says, "He should be along pretty soon."

"He's in the parade?" says Eloise. "Oh, heaven helps us."

Aunt Jean smiles. "He's using my Cadillac. Pulls like an ox."

"Oh, look, it's Stewie's family," says Addie, pointing to the parade.

In front of us there is a flatbed trailer with the manger scene. Stewie is sporting a shepherd's tunic, a wool blanket pulled over his head, and ski mask. Nestled down in the hay, his sister is wearing an enormous parka draped in a lacy shawl. Jesus is a doll so he only has on a towel. Stewie's dad is driving their hotel truck. On the side of the trailer there's a banner that says THERE'S ALWAYS ROOM AT OUR INN.

Four more "floats" come and go. I can hardly wait to bolt from Dad and Eloise.

I don't really see the last scheduled "float" until it's right in front of us. I'm too busy watching Jeff Dewey's dog relieve himself in the street. Then I hear whistles and look up to see a truck full of men in camouflage, holding guns.

On the side of the truck are banners that say WHERE ARE THE ELK? Men are holding signs that say WOLVES ATE MY SHEEP. WHAT SHOULD I EAT? PUT WOLVES BACK IN WASHINGTON WHERE THEY BELONG! SAVE A RANCHER. KILL A WOLF. And THE ONLY GOOD WOLF IS A DEAD ONE.

Kenner has labeled himself THE EXTERMINATOR.

I turn to Dad and Eloise. Dad is stone-faced, but his buddies are clapping and yelling, "That's right." Eloise looks like she's ready to draw blood. Suddenly I am surrounded by people cheering.

Kenner's friends go ballistic, chanting, "Ex-ter-min-ator! Ex-ter-min-ator!" Kenner raises his sign over his head and yells, "Ye-ah!"

It's like a dead wolf pep assembly.

Addie says, "He looks ridiculous."

I can barely bring myself to look around, I'm afraid I'm going to hate my whole town. The float moves on and is met with loud cheers. No one has cheered this loudly for any other floats, not even for the frozen Presbyterians.

Sondra is openmouthed. "Could this town be any more backward?"

"They could stone women who wear pants, but they're too damn busy painting their necks red," shouts Eloise.

Dad's friends go quiet. I put my head down. I feel trapped and ashamed of everyone. Then I hear jeering. Someone shouts, "Get 'em off the road."

I jerk my head up hopefully, but quickly realize the people aren't yelling at the truck of hunters. People are booing at a car following the truck. Then I recognize Jean's Cadillac. Across the top of the car is a billboard that says WOLVES FOR A BETTER YELLOWSTONE. On the bumper is a billboard that says THEY WERE HERE FIRST.

Aunt Jean shouts, "There they are!"

Inside Aunt Jean's gold Cadillac I see Dennis's glasses, attached to Dennis's grinning face. Next to him, also grinning, is Virgil. The windows are down and they are waving at the booing crowd like they just won Miss West End. Behind the Cadillac is a flatbed trailer covered in sculpted snow and ice. The project.

I turn and face Eloise, then Dad. Both look petrified. Only Aunt Jean is amused. I hear a few isolated cheers from the crowd. It's hard to see, but I can make out Mr. Muir and his wife clapping wildly not far up the street. Next to them, the town librarian, Ellen Stevens, is politely applauding. And I see Gary and Deena Harper, the hippies who run the bike shop, cheering and holding up their lighters. Mostly I hear booing.

A bar of car spotlights rigged over the top of the trailer shine onto the most elaborate snow sculpture I have ever seen. There is a mountain ridge swooping down to a riverbed. Elk the size of cats graze next to a buffalo. There are ducks in the riverbed. There is an eagle on top of a giant icicle, so it looks like it's flying. And in the center of the sculpture, dyed bright orange, are two wolves. They must have used a backhoe to get all that snow on there.

He's out of his mind to drive this thing through the heart of town. But it's brilliant.

Like an anthem, the wail of wolves comes booming from the car. The prerecorded howls fill the street and drown out the jeering crowd. I think everyone is finally looking at what Virgil has done. It's so beautiful it can't be real. The trailer glistens. Sondra and I go crazy. Even Addie cheers. A few other people cheer and clap. Then a few more. Then a few more.

Eloise shouts, "Virgil!" I don't know if she is barking his name out of terror or pride.

Virgil waves at her, and then at me, as he passes.

I yell, "Go, Virgil! Go, Dennis!"

Then, in this perfect moment, where everything seems brilliant and possible, a shotgun is fired from the other side of the street. In slow motion I watch the center of the sculpture explode. The entire sculpture collapses. Inside the car, I see Dennis's and Virgil's heads tip forward. I scream and run into the street, followed by my dad. Virgil looks up. His face is bleeding. Dennis looks up. I keep running.

Then everyone is shouting and running.

Officer Farley rushes the car from the other side. A man in camo follows him and pulls Dennis out of the car by his coat. I can't tell if the man is trying to protect Dennis or punch him. Officer Smith grabs the man, and the man hits Officer Smith in the stomach. Then everyone starts hitting each other.

Then everyone is shouting and running.

I can't see Virgil in the car anymore.

Someone swings a fist past my head. I duck behind my dad. We keep moving. Then somebody connects with the side of my dad's head and my dad goes down. I drop to the ground to get him, and my hand is immediately crushed under someone's boot. I shove off the person's boot and yell, "Get off me, you cow!"

I look up the leg and find a familiar face. Mr. Muir says, "KJ, my word. Are you all right?"

"Somebody punched my dad," I say.

Mr. Muir grabs Dad's hand and helps him up. "Samuel, you have blood coming out of your ear."

Dad says, "I hit something hard when I landed."

"You need to see someone," says Mr. Muir.

Dad says, "What?"

I yell, "Dad, can you hear me?"

"Stop yelling," he says.

Mr. Muir pats Dad on the back. He leans down to me and says, "Clean it real good, and I'll drive him into Bozeman tomorrow."

The fighting is over almost as quickly as it started. Most

people leave in a hurry. I guess no kids will be sitting on Santa's knee tonight at the pharmacy. I see Sondra, Dennis, and Dennis's parents huddled together. Addie and Kenner are both gone. Kenner's posse of morons is gone, too. I see Officer Farley and Smith cuffing two men and throwing them on the curb. But I see no sign of Virgil, Eloise, or Aunt Jean. I turn to Dad. "Did you see Virgil? I think something happened to his face. I think he was bleeding, too."

Dad stands but tips to one side. He grabs on to me to steady himself. "Virgil will be all right, honey. It was probably just a stray pellet. If they'd been aiming at him he'd have more than a little blood on his face. But I hope the police find that fool with the shotgun before Eloise does. He won't stand a chance."

"I hope Eloise tracks that guy down and peppers him. I hate this whole town."

Dad doesn't seem to hear me. He looks down the dark street where Virgil's car sits empty. The car door on Virgil's side is still open. He covers his ear with his glove to stop the bleeding.

He turns to me. "Don't blame everyone for the actions of one fanatic."

Dad can say what he wants, but we both know there was more than one fanatic here tonight. There was a truck full of men wearing camouflage and a whole town full of people cheering for them. There was a street full of people hitting their neighbors. I feel like I just woke up in a town full of strangers.

Dad staggers again. "Just dizzy," he says.

I put his arm over my shoulders, and we walk home in the broken flashes of Christmas lights that line the streets, mindlessly blinking.

18

SIDE EFFECTS

NO ONE ANSWERS the phone at Aunt Jean's. I help Dad clean and pack his ear. It takes a long time. I get him ibuprofen, beer, two pillows, and seven blankets.

"Are you trying to bury me?" he says.

"You should be fine." He doesn't look fine.

"What was Virgil thinking?" he says, more to himself than to me.

"I don't know. Maybe that he could show people . . . that wolves belong here."

"With an ice sculpture? KJ, people that scratch to make ends meet don't think like that. They don't care about the idea of wolves, they care about their livestock, they care about staying out of debt. And for some folks, hunting is their religion."

"But people do care about the idea of wolves. I mean, last year more sheep got killed by bald eagles than wolves, and you don't see anybody shooting them in parades."

"Honey, the kid's got nerve, but what good did it do? Did he change any minds tonight? Did making a big scene do more harm or good?"

"I thought you liked wolves."

"For crying out loud, I'm not talking about what I *like*." His tone is razor sharp. "I *like* a lot of things. I *like* being able to hear out of both ears. I *like* having you in one piece. I *like* not making enemies of every hunter from here to Chicago. Because I *like* being a guide and paying my bills. This is about reality. And the reality is that wolves make people crazy, including you."

I know better than to prolong an argument with Samuel Manning Carson, especially when he's been on the wrong end of a fist. I go to the kitchen and make him a sandwich. I put the stool under his feet. I turn on the TV. I put my hands in my pockets.

"Oh, get out of here, would you! Tell Virgil I thought his sculpture was . . . well . . . it was beautiful. Stupid as hell, but beautiful."

I know it costs him something to say anything nice about Virgil. Part of him probably wishes he'd been the one shooting. He wouldn't have missed. I hug his shoulders gently. "Thanks, Dad."

He pulls away from me. "Get."

"Don't drink all that beer before I get back, you might have a concussion or something."

He throws me a dirty look and I bolt for the door.

I speed across town in Dad's truck, spinning over the ice. All I can think about is the look on Virgil's face right before and after the shot. The two images flash back and forth appearing to almost blend together in a nightmarish composite. I feel numb.

I knock at the door. No one answers. I lean against the door and yell, "It's KJ."

Eloise's steady voice calls back, "In here, honey."

Virgil and Eloise are at the kitchen table. There is a first aid kit sprawled everywhere. Eloise is cleaning Virgil's blood off his face with gauze. My feet freeze to the floor.

"Virgil," I whisper. "I would have come sooner. My dad got punched in the ear." It sounds funny when I say it, but nobody laughs.

Eloise says sharply, "Town is full of rotten drunks. How's he doing?"

"His ear's torn up. We'll have to see in the morning." I can't stop staring at the holes in Virgil's face. I've seen my dad hurt before. I've seen my own face bloody and bruised. But blood doesn't belong on Virgil's face. "Virgil . . . are you . . . I'm so sorry."

"Could you come stand over here by this kid," says Eloise. "I think he'd like a little distraction."

Virgil smiles at me and I unfreeze. "Hey," he says, and winces.

I stand next to his shoulder. I can see the puncture wounds from the pellets: three swollen pinpricks in the shape of a triangle. Even as I look at the holes, I can't believe Virgil has been shot. By someone I know, in the middle of the Christmas parade. He reaches and grabs my hand.

Eloise puts on a large ugly bandage. "We called his dad, and after he got done telling me I'm a bad mother, he said there isn't anything else we can do tonight. He said to get X-rays of his chest in the morning to make sure nothing's in there we've missed." She glares at Virgil. "I've checked every inch of your parka and there wasn't any sign of a hole. Except the one you must have in your head to enrage a city full of drunk, armed elk hunters and ranchers. Haven't you ever heard of writing your congressman?"

"Does that work?" I say.

"I'm fine," he says.

She nods. "I've got an errand to do now. Can you watch him for me, KJ? And Aunt Jean, if she wakes up? She was pretty shook."

"Where are you going?" I say.

"To the police station," she says.

I think about what my dad said. "What are you going to do?"

She looks at me fiercely. "I don't own any firearms, so don't worry. Of course that doesn't mean I couldn't do it with my bare hands."

"Mom," says Virgil, with a tenderness that startles me. "Be careful."

"Don't worry about me. You just rest now," she says, and walks out of the kitchen without looking back at her injured son.

As soon as Eloise is gone, Virgil slumps in his chair and relaxes. "Weird, huh?" he says.

"It's insane. You look really tough though." My mind goes back to his story about breaking his best friend's nose. "But are you . . . mad? You know?"

He sighs. "No. But I want to lie down."

I pull him up to standing and walk him back to the room I haven't seen since I insulted him. He's added more photos. His blankets are still swirled up with clothes. I shove the clothes onto the floor and organize the blankets. He climbs in the bed. I sit down next to him. His closes his eyes.

"Your dad hates me now," he mumbles.

"He said he thought the sculpture was beautiful."

Virgil opens his eyes. "Does that mean I'm forgiven?"

"I don't know what it means. Not any of it." He smells

like bandages and medicine. He breathes quietly. I say, "That was the most amazing sculpture I've ever seen."

"Did you like it?" he says, drifting.

"I loved it. You're a genius."

"Don't go anywhere for a while, okay?"

I think, in a blurred way, of my dad at home alone, surrounded by old blankets and beer. I wonder if he'll fall asleep with the TV on. I promise myself I will leave as soon as Eloise gets back. "Okay." I put my head down at the foot of the bed. "Just till your mom gets back."

I wake up when I hear the phone ring. Virgil's feet are in my face. The sun is coming through the window. I look up and see Virgil sound asleep, lying crosswise from me, buried in his hair. This might be a romantic moment if I wasn't about to be flayed alive by my father. I can't believe I just fell asleep and then snoozed until morning. I hear another ring. Dead. I am completely dead.

I bolt to the kitchen. I hear Eloise say, "Thank you. He's doing fine. How's your ear?"

Eloise looks up at me and shoos me with her hand. "She's on her way. I asked her to watch Virgil and Jean while I went to the police station. I'm sorry about that."

Eloise's face narrows as she listens to the receiver. Her mouth shrinks to a bitter pucker. Finally she says, "I hated to wake her."

After another ugly pause she says, "Oh, please. You knew exactly where she was."

Eloise waves me toward the door again. I step slowly, unable to turn away from the approaching disaster. Wait for it.

Eloise shouts, "So what if they did sleep in the same room. I gave him enough valium to tranquilize a polar bear."

Eloise is many things but diplomatic isn't one of them.

As I step through the screen door I hear Eloise say, "Hope you get feeling better, Samuel. You might try some valium yourself. And maybe your doctor could prescribe something for being a pain in the ass."

When I get home Dad does not speak to me when I talk to him. He is watching the news. His face has puffed up and the bruises are getting their color. I am overwhelmed with BDG (Bad Daughter Guilt) but I don't know what to do. Feeling guilty makes me mad, and being mad just makes me feel more guilty. I go into the kitchen and bang around some pots and pans while I pretend to clean. Finally I storm into the other room and say, "I fell asleep. It was an accident."

He looks at me in total disgust. He stands up and leans on the chair. Here it comes. "You're not like them, KJ." His voice is low and deliberate. He's been thinking about this. "You don't have a rich dad or a PhD mother. You don't have a ticket to travel around the world. You aren't going to get a free ride to a fancy university. If you piss off the whole town you can't make a phone call and leave. If you get pregnant, or just get your heart ripped out, that'll be your problem, not his. In a few months, he's leaving."

"Dad, nothing happened," I blurt out.

My dad sighs. "Katherine Jean, around here you have to clean up your own messes. And you're making one with him."

He goes to his room with an ice pack and doesn't come out until Mr. Muir calls and offers to drive us into Bozeman to see Mr. Muir's ear doctor.

"No thanks," says Dad. "I'll live."

Mr. Muir shows up about ten minutes later. "Most dads with a teenage daughter might be grateful for a bad ear, but I think you'd better think about the long term here, Samuel. You want to be able to hear her apologize later in life, right, KJ?"

"Yes," I say.

My dad eventually agrees to go, but tells me to stay behind and clean up the house. "I hate a mess on Christmas," he says.

"I'll have it done by the time you get back."

Mr. Muir says, "We'll be gone most the day, so don't worry if we're late."

"She won't," says my dad as he climbs in the truck.

I call Sondra for sympathy. Sondra's mom says that Sondra is "visiting" Dennis.

"Not sure what that's about," says her mom, her voice low and grainy. "He always struck me as a ninny."

"Ninnies don't draw fire in a local parade," I say, trying to keep my voice even.

"Yeah, I guess he's got that going for him. I had a soft spot for outlaws in my youth. All it ever got me was Sondra and a jack squat credit rating."

No wonder Sondra needs a pet.

Finally I call Addie but not for sympathy. From Addie I want answers. I start out fine, but I'm up to rant speed before I can stop myself.

"I mean someone fires shots into a crowd and nobody even cares. Somebody has to know who did it, right?" I hear a baby fussing near the phone.

"It wasn't Kenner or William, if that's what you mean," she says. Her voice is bouncy. The baby stops crying, but I hear gurgling sounds.

"Are you sure? I mean did you see them not shoot at the float?"

"No, but . . ."

"They both hate wolves and Kenner hates Virgil."

Addie's voice gets more shrill. "That doesn't mean he did it."

"Somebody did it. And somebody saw who did it."

"Well, at least you're right about that much. But don't hold your breath for people to turn in someone they know, for someone who doesn't even live here."

"Dennis and Virgil live here."

"You know what I mean."

"I guess I don't," I try to slow down. I know this isn't helping. "Would you tell me if you knew?"

"KJ, you've got an attitude problem. You think everyone is immoral just because they don't agree with you."

"I don't like people who shoot at my friends."

"So you just automatically assume that it's Kenner or William. They're ranchers so they're bad guys." The baby cries into the phone. Addie says, "All right, little guy. Hey, I have to go."

"Whoever shot that gun broke the law."

"There are all kinds of laws, KJ. And around here, taking care of your own is at the top of the list."

I hang up the phone feeling worse that I can remember. I have enough guilt and anger in my veins to boil off my skin. I need to work.

I trudge to the grocery store and try to avoid eye contact with anyone, since I hate my whole town today, even the snowmobilers, who are just cold tourists. I keep my head down in the checkout aisle except to say hello to Harmony, the woman at the register. I wander slowly toward the street but dread going back into the cold. I look up at the bulletin board that Mr. Gardner, the owner, keeps for public announcements. What I see nearly makes me drop my bags.

WOLVES DESTROY LIVES

Join the statewide referendum to remove the "Yellowstone" wolf.

Please help send a message to the bullies in Washington. With enough signatures we can put wolves on the ballot, where they belong. If we stand strong, we can get rid of the wolves once and for all.

Protect yourself!

Sign now!

Fourteen people have signed the petition. Kenner's mom is at the top of the list.

I turn back to Harmony. "How long has this been up?"

"I think somebody put it up this morning. What does it say?"

I walk out of the store into the snow without answering. It says something bad just got worse.

All the way home I tell myself one angry ranching family can't destroy the Wolf Recovery Project. You can't just overturn the Endangered Species Act because it makes some people mad. This case has been argued in courts for years before the wolves were reintroduced. On the other hand, there were fourteen signatures in one morning. Apparently there's a lot more than one angry ranching family. I've read enough to know that history isn't on the side of the wolf.

It takes a skin-peeling shower to heat me back up. I mop the floor, make dinner, wrap our pathetic Christmas presents, including my own, do the dishes and six loads of laundry. Still no dad. I put the dinner in Tupperware and start on the bathroom. The house is silent except for running appliances. I don't call Virgil. He doesn't call me. I go to sleep on the couch, waiting for my dad to come home. Christmas is in two days.

Fa la la la la.

KJ'S CHRISTMAS DINNER JOKES

Q: How do you know a wolf is full?
A: He stops breathing.

Q: How do you know a rancher's full?
A: He stops complaining about wolves. . . .
(He's saving that for dessert.)

Q: How do you know my dad's full?
A: The beer's gone.

19

GIFTS

ON CHRISTMAS MORNING I get hiking boots from Dad and an orange in my stocking that I put in myself. It's goofy, but oranges are one of my favorite traditions. Eating big fruit always makes me feel like the sun is shining somewhere. I make cranberry pancakes. I put on Christmas music. I give Dad books and new gloves. He barely talks.

At noon the doorbell rings. It's Sondra.

"Alleluia," I say. "Come in."

"Can't," she says. "Mom's a psycho on Christmas. Not to be left alone. But I have something for you." She winks.

I don't have anything for her. I run into the house and bring her back my hulking orange. I put it in her hand. "I wrapped it myself."

She winks again. "Good work. I can't even see the tape."

"That's probably because you wink too much."

She gives me a stiff good-bye hug. She stands back and looks at me. "Merry Christmas, KJ."

"How come we weren't friends until this year?" I say. "You're so nice."

"I don't know. I never really noticed you that much, I guess."

I close the door. In a few years, I'll probably think about what Sondra just told me about myself. Right now, I focus on her present. It's in a shirt-size box but it could be anything. She's wrapped it in a paper grocery bag that's been cut to fit perfectly. I didn't know Sondra was so domestic. I shake it. It feels heavy like a book. I don't want to open it right off. I love not knowing what it is. But I want to know what it is. But I don't. Geez.

I walk past Dad into my room and look at my box. Sondra is full of surprises. Finally I can't stand it. When I take off the lid I am very glad I am being surprised in my room.

The first thing I realize about my present is that it's not from Sondra. The second thing I realize is that I'm not breathing. I let some air out manually and sit down on my bed. In the box is a framed picture of me lying on a rock, writing in my journal. The light of the Lamar Valley shimmers behind me, illuminating the tall grass. The robin's-egg sky is layered with clouds. There is a halo around the rock. Even with me in the picture, it's beautiful.

There is a note taped to the glass. It says, "For Wolf Girl. Love, Virgil."

I read the words over and over and over.

WOLF NOTES

Happy New Year, West Enders!

That was certainly a memorable Christmas!

No word yet on who fired their shotgun into a crowd of men, women, and children. Three stray pellets hit Virgil Whitman in the face.

The police don't have any suspects and they don't want to talk about their investigation.

As a result of the fighting that happened after the shooting, one nose, two parkas, one ear, and the town's reputation were messed up pretty badly. Two men were arrested for disorderly conduct, but were later released so they could go home for Christmas.

The other casualty of this parade gone haywire was the magnificent snow sculpture created by Virgil Whitman and Dennis Welch. When asked what he thought about being shot at in a hometown parade, Dennis Welch said, "It was like being in a movie." Virgil Whitman had no comment.

We welcome your comments, if you have any. . . .

LETTERS TO THE EDITOR

Whoever shot at Dennis and Virgil is
totally lame.

Anonymous

Dennis and Virgil don't know anything about ranching. If they'd ever
had to take care of cattle, they
might not think wolves were so *#%!
beautiful.

Anonymous

That was the best Christmas Stroll
I've ever been to.

Clint

20

INVERSIONS

IT'S THE FIRST day back at school since the shooting. We're watching a feature film on sexually transmitted diseases in Health. Virgil is sitting next to me, reading under his desk. Kenner is sitting two seats in front of us, yucking it up as if nothing has happened.

Virgil's face is still red but the swelling is gone. Everybody's been talking about the shooting, like it happened last night, not two weeks ago. Virgil is a celebrity. In typical Virgil fashion, he seems oblivious to all of it.

Me—not so oblivious. I am trying to keep from punching Kenner in the mouth.

Kenner leans over to Road Work and says, "Hey, what do you get when you cross a tree hugger with a wolf?"

Road Work says, "What?"

Kenner says, "The big bad faggot."

Road Work laughs like he gets it.

Virgil keeps reading.

I lean forward and say, "What do you get when you cross a rancher with a sheep?"

Kenner and company glare.

"Two flocking idiots."

"KJ the Retard," says Kenner, "gettin' fierce."

Cue laughter by mental midgets.

Coach Henderson, the health teacher says, "Quiet." Quiet is important to Coach Henderson. In addition to being a teacher, he's also the football coach and a fireman. He needs this class to catch up on his sleep.

Kenner whispers cheerfully at Virgil, "Hey, wolf faggot. Your girlfriend's sticking up for you."

I say, "At least he doesn't double-date with his brother— the same girl."

Kenner stands up. Virgil stands up, too, but he walks out of the room without a word.

"Do you men have a problem?" says Mr. Henderson to Virgil's back. The door swings shut.

I say, "Posttraumatic stress."

"Oh," says Mr. Henderson.

Kenner flips me off and turns around. I'm so mad I nearly miss the romantic moment where the girl tells the boy she has an STD.

On the way out of class Road Work gets up slower than the rest of the mob and bumps into to me with his wall of a body. He says, "Besides, Addie's not dating William anymore. She was only doing it to make Kenner mad." He says this like it somehow proves something.

I say, "Well, shoot. She should have asked me. I'm good at that."

I see Virgil in the hall on his way to English. I don't know what to say.

He says, "Don't do that."

"What?"

"I'm fine."

"Fine," I say.

"Fine," he says.

I walk away, fine as a switchblade.

Virgil walks into the lunch room with Dennis. Dennis is grinning. "Anybody here want my autograph? I just wrote on a third-grader's lunch box."

Virgil says, "It's going to his head."

"As opposed to your face?" says Stewie, laughing.

"Hey," says Virgil, touching his new scar.

"It's totally cool—you're like a war veteran, only younger," says Clint. "Do you score pain meds for that?"

"Please!" wails Addie, slapping her mashed potatoes with her spoon.

"Please what?" I say. Anybody but Addie can tell Virgil and Dennis not to make a big deal of this.

She glares at me. "Look, KJ, I wish it wouldn't have happened as much as you do. I just wish everyone would stop talking about it."

"I thought we're supposed to tell people our true feelings. Don't you love that?"

"Relax, KJ. It's okay," says Virgil.

"How is it okay?" I say.

"Because Addie's right."

The table is silent except for the sound of Virgil pulling his precious homemade salad out of his recycled bag. I dump my tray and head for the library.

In math I get zero out of five on my quiz. Mandy grades my paper. She writes me a note in her fat curly handwriting. "Nice job!" She puts a frowny face inside my zero. It's exactly how I feel.

I try to jog home, but the sidewalk is icy. The town is swallowed in a winter inversion. The trapped air is dirty and bitter. I hope Dad hasn't been busy today. Lifting things up and down is misery for him. And we both know whose fault it is he's miserable. I speed up, but the faster I run, the more I slip.

The store is empty. The register is unattended. I call hello and get no answer. I walk to the office in the back and find Dad lying on the camp cot in the corner, sound asleep.

His face is the color of his sheets and there is blood on the pillow.

"Dad?"

Nothing. I push on his shoulder and he opens his eyes. "Hey, are you okay?" When he finally sits up he clears his throat but doesn't answer.

"Is your ear hurting you?" My BDG is in overdrive.

"I want you to close tonight."

"You're bleeding again."

Dad lies back in the bed and looks up at the ceiling. It scares me.

"How's school?"

"Great."

We sit in silence. Finally he says, "You'll have to do your homework in the shop. I don't want you to use me as an excuse for getting behind in school."

"No problem." What I love about Dad is that he never takes a day off criticizing me. He's committed.

"That's my girl," he says. "Tough like your mom."

I hate it when he compares me to her. Luckily it doesn't happen very often. "Why don't you go home, Dad? Sleep on a real bed."

"I'm serious about this," he says, sitting up awkwardly. "College admission boards don't care what your reasons are. They want results."

"Got it," I say.

"I look at results, too," he says, and hobbles out the door.

By six it's actually busy. People have to wait for help. One man leaves before I can finish answering his questions about pack trips. If Dad were here, he'd be furious.

By seven, the crowd starts to thin and I get my bearings again. I can make eye contact and small talk. Then I look over and see a man lifting a T-shirt. Mid-twenties, raggedy beard, thick arms, and a big puffy coat. I watch him put the shirt inside his coat and keep looking around the store. He circles the store looking at flies and camping gear for a few minutes. It's going to be bad either way but I know what I have to do. He starts for the door. I step from behind the counter. He's a foot taller than I am. The old me would just let it go. Too embarrassing. Too many ways I can screw this up. *Wolf stare*, I think, *come on.*

The store has an audience of fifteen or so people. The red blotches on my neck start before I can even get over to talk to him. I say quietly, "Can I talk to you for a minute?"

"About what?" he says in a tight voice.

I look him in the chest and say, "The shirt in your coat."

"What?" he says loudly.

I look up at his face, "You need to pay for that shirt."

"What shirt?"

Everyone looks.

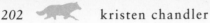

I say, "Under your coat."

He opens up his jacket with his hands still inside the pockets. He has big padded pockets, but the shirt isn't visible. He says, "What shirt?"

I look up at his face. His mouth is puckered. I know he still has it but I don't dare ask to look in his pockets. I flinch. "My mistake."

"It sure is," he says, and walks out of the store with righteous indignation and my dad's shirt.

"My mistake," I say to everyone staring at me.

A gray-haired woman standing close to me leans forward and whispers, "Don't you worry about it, dear."

The shoppers go back to their grazing. I go back to my register.

When work is over, I lock up and run home. My lungs ache from the cold, but I run anyway. I tell myself it's not my fault that creep stole a shirt. Dad is fine and Virgil doesn't know what he's talking about. I'm just running because I'm cold.

Wolves are supremely social animals, and when expelled from their natural pack, they are supremely lonesome.

Thomas McNamee,
The Return of the Wolf to Yellowstone

21

REPERCUSSIONS

WHEN I WALK into the police station, Officer Farley is sitting at his paper-strewn desk rubbing a cigarette into his full ashtray. His face is red and slightly bulging. I was hoping to talk to Officer Smith.

"Hi, Officer Farley. Could I ask you some questions for the school paper?"

"You supposed to be in school, KJ."

"On my way. Do you have a minute?"

"Make it quick."

"I wondered if you had any leads on the shooting." I try to keep my voice respectful and my chin down. I pull my pad of paper and pen and hold it conspicuously in front of me. Officer Smith is nowhere to be seen.

"That is a police matter, young lady, and you are late for school."

"It's for school, for the newspaper. I'm the editor. We're doing a follow-up story on the shooting at the parade."

Officer Farley glares at me. "Well, Miss Editor, I have work to do and it's against the law to miss class."

"No leads on the shooter then?"

"Shooter?"

Farley's eyeball-popping disgust is interrupted by the phone ringing. After a few introductions Officer Farley's eyeballs start popping out again. Oddly enough he looks right at me as he's talking.

"No foolin'. Right out of the ground?" he says into the receiver.

"How many do you have out?"

He pauses, then continues, "I certainly will. I have her right here in fact."

I look around. I'm the only "her" in the room. He scribbles words on paper and hangs up the phone.

I say, "Is something wrong?"

He grinds the cigarette in the tray like a sore. "It seems that someone tore down a fence at Martin's ranch last night. Bunch of their cattle got loose. One got all the way to the highway. You wouldn't know anything about that would you?"

"I was at home last night."

"How 'bout your boyfriend?"

The welts on my neck are erupting. Curse my skin. "He's not my boyfriend."

"Fine . . . the hippie?"

"The hippie was playing bingo with Aunt Jean at the Senior Center last night, late."

Officer Farley gets ugly when he's irritated, and he's not all that nice to look at to begin with. He says, "It's entirely possible that the fence at Martin's was pushed down by the cattle themselves. Cows will do that. But the problem is that Mr. Martin seems to think that it has to do with people in town thinking his son is responsible for the Christmas parade shooting. You have any idea about where that rumor might have gotten started?"

I put my notepad at my side. "All I've done is ask questions."

Officer Farley gets another cigarette out of his pocket and lights it. "Sometimes a question's not a question. Like if you ask someone if they realize what a pain in the keister they are. You get me?"

"I get you."

"Good. Now get."

At school I am greeted by Addie talking nose to nose with Virgil in the hallway. "Did you hear?" says Addie.

"I just came from the police station."

"Who would do something like that?"

"It could have just been cows getting out."

"They're a good family, KJ. With a good reputation."

Virgil pats Addie's shoulder. "Let's go into class and sit down."

Addie walks into the classroom ahead of us.

"What's her problem?" I say. "She's not even dating either one of them now."

"She cares about people. Even people she's not dating."

"Uh-huh," I say. *Sure she does,* I think. *Especially when she has your shoulder to cry on. Give me a break.* "Should we try to write something about this? To be fair?"

"That's probably a good idea."

"The Martins will shoot me if I go out there to interview them."

"We could interview Addie," he says.

"Oh, yes," I say. "You can ask her her true feelings about it."

"What's that supposed to mean?" says Virgil.

"You're the reporter."

"No, you're the reporter," he says. "I'm the photographer."

"Well, take some good pictures then. I'm sure Addie is very photogenic."

I storm into the room and sit next to Sondra. Virgil sits next to Addie and Dennis. After Addie gets done telling the whole class about this monumental event of possible cow undoing, Addie commiserates some more with Virgil. Thankfully Sondra saves me by showing me the poem she's been working on, "Valentine for the Bison." She's even done her own drawings.

"Do bison like valentines?" I say, still steaming. I'd like to give Addie a valentine right now.

"Don't you see how lonely the bulls get in the winter? You can just see it in the way they hang their head in the snow."

"Aren't they just looking for food?"

"Yeah. But even the bison cannot live on grass alone. All animals long to be loved."

"Mammalian defect," I say.

"Yes," says Sondra. "But viva the defect."

We sit looking at her drawing. I correct some spelling on her poem and she lets me, without getting mad. Maybe I could be Sondra's pet. She could teach me to sit, stay, and keep my mouth closed when I want to say territorial, female-dog kinds of things.

VALENTINE FOR THE BISON

By Sondra Bucknell

When winter fields are white as eggs
The buffalo bulls have chilly legs.
They stand and snort in desperation.
Their love lives are in depravation.
They miss their herd, who've gone away
Even if they will return someday.
So here's a wish for all cold bison
Who stand in need of a liaison—
May spring come soon, with heifers hot.
Stay in the park, and don't get shot.

22

SILHOUETTES

EVERYTHING IS WORSE at four in the morning.

I flip back and forth under my quilts. I have a guilt-and-jealousy stomachache. Curiously, drowning my sorrows in a bag of licorice and a quart of Mountain Dew the night before didn't help as much as I thought it would.

Yesterday Virgil interviewed Addie at lunch, off in their own little corner. He barely spoke to me afterward. I'm sure she was the perfect injured heroine. And the whole school was still talking about how awful it was that "environmentalists" were on a "rampage." Kenner didn't come to school for the second day. Give me a break.

I went by the grocery store on the way home from school

to check The List, for the referendum. The first page was completely full of signatures and they had added a second. I've heard that there are now "lists" in Red Lodge, Island Park, and Ennis. Last week Cody had a public meeting about the wolves that nearly ended in a punch-out.

When I started writing about wolves to get people more interested in them, this wasn't what I had in mind.

Of course this isn't all happening because of a few articles in a school newspaper. Or because I've been talking to people about wolves or asking questions. I can't take credit for Virgil getting shot or whatever really happened at the Martins' ranch with their fence. I don't know why other towns are getting riled up all of a sudden. Probably all this "taking sides" would have happened anyway. But the timing of the whole thing sure makes me feel like I threw a rock that's part of an avalanche.

I waste an hour reading wolf reports online, and then I quietly take out my snowshoes and step into the thinning dark. Dad will be asleep until I get back. I walk past the thermometer on the porch. Ten below. Another balmy Saturday in West End.

I head north from town. I get on an old elk trail that I know will be quiet and snowmobile free. I pump my arms and legs. The frozen air hurts my chest. I breathe it back and cough it up. The snow is gray and deep. Before long my thighs and chest burn. I push gracelessly forward into the snow.

212 kristen chandler

Except for my breathing the new snow has silenced every-thing, sucked the noise right out of the air. I want to let the voices in my head be absorbed into the snow, too. I want to be numb on the inside—like I was before I met Virgil, before I cared about wolves, before I tried to be anything but invis-ible. Before I thought I could be like a wolf.

I keep pushing into the snow until sweat beads up under my hat. I go harder. My chest hurts. I go harder. After a few minutes I feel light-headed. I slow down to let my chest recover. I see something gray flash in the trees. I stop mov-ing. I push my heavy breath down in my throat. I tell myself it's nothing. I see the flash again. It's not a bear, it's too fast. It's too big to be a coyote. It seems more than unlikely, but I could swear it's a wolf.

I tell myself to be logical. I just want it to be a wolf. It's must be something else that has gray fur and runs like a giant graceful dog. I search the trees. Why is it here? The Nez Perce pack ranges around in the area, but they always keep far away from town. Maybe it's alone and looking for a mate. What-ever it's doing, if it doesn't have a pack it's in trouble.

I wait. Finally I breathe out, thinking it's gone, and I see one more flash of gray. I run until I find its delicate tracks. I lift my snowshoes and run alongside the giant paw prints, careful not to cover them. I stumble along in the snow until I start to feel light-headed again. I stop and catch my breath and think about how far I am from town. I didn't even tell my dad I was leaving. I take one last look around and head back, in a hurry.

All the way home I feel lit up and brilliant, and it's not just because the sun is out of the trees. The reality of those tracks charges my muscles with energy. Whatever else is screwed up about my life, I love living in a place where accidents like this can happen.

But the other side of my brain eventually intrudes. Why do I care? Why is seeing an animal, any animal, important? It's a wolf. So what? I can walk over and see a caged wolf at the Discovery Station any day of the week.

But seeing a wild wolf surviving in our shared habitat is different.

I walk home in the white emptiness. My breath is steady. I can't wait to tell Virgil.

When I reach the edge of town I see both police trucks parked in front of Mr. Muir's knife shop. This can't be good. It's early, but there's a dozen people gathered around on the sidewalk. As I walk closer to the store I see red words scrawled on the glass facing the street but I can't read them. I see Dad. He's talking to Mr. Muir and to Officer Smith. He looks up and scowls hello. Mr. Muir nods at me, too, but without much interest.

Then I see Virgil. He's taking pictures of the window. I look up at the red words but I have to read them a few times. It doesn't make sense. Next to the words, the adjacent window has been bashed in. Snowdrifts have blown into the store and blended with the glass shards on the red carpet. I listen to Virgil's camera click. In large ugly letters someone has written, "Wolf Faggot."

Virgil walks up to me but doesn't say anything.

"It's like he's daring us," I say.

"We don't know it's Kenner," Virgil says. "It could have been anyone who heard Kenner call me that. Or anyone that talks that way."

"Come on," I say in disgust. "Why do you want to protect him?"

Virgil says, "I don't. People do what they are going to do. Like you."

"What am I doing?"

Virgil puts his camera into his bag. He doesn't look at me. For once I wait, not because I'm trying to give him time to explain, but because I'm too riled up to talk. He takes my arm and we walk over to the corner. The handful of people rubbernecking at the store now stare at us. I glare back until they stop.

Virgil speaks in a low tight voice. "Maybe to figure out who wrote this, we have to know why. You know what I mean?"

"No, I don't."

"Do you think I care if those dicks call me names? Do

you think I want you to get hurt sticking up for me?" he says. He's talking quietly but because it's Virgil it sounds like yelling.

Dad walks up to us. "Where have you been?"

"Snowshoeing," I say. I'm not crazy about everyone yelling at me this morning. I'm not the one that wrecked the store.

"What if one of these whack jobs had found you walking around alone?"

"I've been shoeshoeing by myself a million times."

"Well, there won't be a million and one."

I leave all the fun with Virgil and my dad to talk to Mr. Muir. He has bed head and razor stubble. I say, "I'm sorry."

He nods. "Insurance will cover some of it, but you never get it all back."

"Do you think . . . did they steal anything?"

"No." He looks past me into the store. "I like wolves. So what? It doesn't make sense."

"I don't think this is about making sense."

"What's a wolf faggot, anyway?"

"I've heard the term." Virgil's words stop me from saying more, but that doesn't mean I don't feel guilty about it. This store is Mr. Muir's livelihood. Teaching school is just a public service.

"If somebody doesn't like my opinion on wolves they can just tell me. Whatever happened to civil discourse?"

"Civil discourse?" How can a man who sells knives talk like a philosophy professor? "Do people do that anymore?"

Mr. Muir rubs the end of his face like he's taken a punch. "Well, it beats bashing windows with baseball bats."

I walk home with Dad in silence. Bad silence. I don't tell him that there's a wolf running around on the edge of town. I'm not going to tell anyone, not even Virgil or Eloise. I figure a lone wolf is a long way from being the most dangerous thing around town these days.

Virgil says the question is not who but why someone is hurting people to get rid of the wolves. I don't know if that's true. I think whoever wrecked Mr. Muir's store, as if I didn't know, is about as thoughtful as a guy with a machine gun in a Taco Bell. But I guess if I want to know who, I'm going to have to ask why first.

Civil discourse? I might need to do a little more research.

It's almost impossible to change minds.
People use wolves for all these other values.
The wolves themselves are pretty boring,
but the people are fascinating.

Ed Bangs, Gray Wolf Recovery Coordinator,
U.S. Fish and Wildlife Service

23

THE BUCK STOPS HERE

I TALK TO myself for five minutes before I make the phone call. This is what homework can lead to. Calling Federal employees.

I look at my notes that I've gathered from the Internet and the four other phone calls I have made so far. I'm about to call Ted Buck, the coordinator for the U.S. Fish and Wildlife Service in Washington, D.C.: Mr. Walks-Softly-and-Carries-a-Big-Federal-Stick. He's famous for saying he doesn't give a shit about whether the wolves stay or go or anything else for that matter. On the other hand, he drives all over Wyoming, Montana, and Idaho trying to help people and wildlife get along. Everyone I've talked to says he's the man to call.

I remind myself not to talk like I just sucked helium. I dial slowly.

"Ted Buck."

He answers his own phone? "Oh, hi, Mr. Buck."

"May I help you?" His voice is low, spare, and impatient. He sounds like a rancher. This is funny because he's the man ranchers love to hate.

My brain sputters.

"Ma'am?"

"Yes."

"May I help you?"

"Yes." I look at my notes again, grasping for anything to fill my empty mouth. "I am just wondering if . . . I'm calling because . . ."

"Honey, have you got a question? Because I'm getting a cramp just listening to you spin your wheels."

"Yes. I do have a question," I say as much to myself as to him. "I am a resident of West End, Montana. I'm calling to ask about a public meeting. About the wolves and the referendum."

"Now we're getting somewhere. What can I tell you?"

"Can you come here?"

"You want a meeting, huh?"

"I read about the one you had in Cody, and I think we need one here in West End."

"Let's back up a half step. Would you mind telling me who I'm talking to?"

"Oh, sure." I pause, suddenly getting a view of how this conversation must sound to Mr. Buck. It feels like seeing myself in a public mirror and discovering a gaping hole in my pants. "I'm KJ Carson. I live in West End with my dad. He's a fishing guide. I'm sort of his assistant. But I also write this column for the high school newspaper about wolves, which is where some of the trouble started. But I think the real trouble is that people need to start talking to each other about this, instead of shooting each other."

Mr. Buck's voice goes up a notch. "Shooting each other?"

"Well, a little. I mean, I may have overstated that, considering that my friend didn't die and they were probably aiming at his ice sculpture, not him."

"I assume you mean the shotgun incident where a young man was injured during a parade."

"You know about that?"

"Yeah, I know about that."

That imaginary hole in my pants is getting bigger. "Well, so I just thought if people could hear what you have to say and talk about . . ." In the back of my mind I hear Addie's voice. ". . . their feelings . . . it might help."

"Miss Carson. It's an expensive thing to have a public meeting. Not only do I have to come out, but we have to rent a building and then hire a recorder, a hearing officer, and a secretary. Then we need security people. All that costs money. The government isn't in the business of group therapy."

I don't say anything for a minute. I let my brain catch up to my mouth and what Mr. Buck has just said. Finally I say, "How much does it cost if this initiative against the wolves goes on the ballot? How much does it cost if somebody bashes in another store window? Or takes another shot and doesn't miss?"

Mr. Buck chuckles. "Yes, wolves are expensive little buggers."

"Don't you need to have more meetings anyway? I mean you might as well have it here as anywhere else. At least you know you'll draw a crowd."

"How many would you say?"

"Everybody I know and all their ticked-off cousins, grandmas, and drinking buddies."

"Sounds about right. Can you hold on?" Mr. Buck doesn't say anything for a minute but I can hear him rustling papers. Finally he says, "Two weeks soon enough?"

"Two weeks? You can set it up that fast?" I feel the cheeseburger I had for lunch jiggle in my stomach. Holy smack.

"We like to strike while the iron is hot. And your area's been getting pretty hot."

"Too hot if you ask me."

He clucks his tongue, like he's writing something down. When he finishes he says, "Miss Carson?"

"Yes?"

"How old are you?"

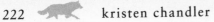

"Seventeen. Almost."

"That's about what I thought."

"Does it matter?"

He chuckles again. "Just to me," he says, and hangs up the phone.

NOTICE OF HEARING

The U.S. Fish and Wildlife Service is holding an open house and public hearing to discuss the management of wolves in Montana, Idaho, and Wyoming. Questions and comments are welcome.

The meeting will be held on Saturday, February 26, in West End, Montana, at the Union Pacific Dining Lodge, starting at 6 p.m.

Guns, knives, and beer should be left in your vehicle.

24

COMMUNICATION BREAKDOWN

I COME EARLY. Everyone else in town has the same idea, and there is a line out of the lodge at five thirty. The Union Pacific railroad built the old dining lodge in the twenties, back when the railroad went through town. The rough bark walls are braced by stone pillars that look like they could withstand the caldera blowing. Might come in handy tonight.

When I get inside I see Virgil, Dennis, and Sondra milling around next to Eloise. I walk toward them and trip on a set of folding chairs propped against the back wall. The chairs clatter to the floor in a loud, explosive way. The whole room, especially me, jumps two feet sideways. At least no one throws a punch.

Dad's coming late so I need to save him a seat: a seat that isn't right next to Eloise and that isn't right next to people who are violent, crazy, or obnoxious. So in other words, outside. I look around. On one side of the room are the environmentalists, on the other side are the ranchers and the hunters. I see Mr. and Mrs. Martin. I see William, too, but he's standing up against the wall by himself. He looks about as comfortable as I do. I unfold the chairs I tripped over and stow away in the back.

I am surprised by all the strangers. There are guys with ponytails holding Buffalo Nation posters, and women in camo, families that have the wind-worn look of ranchers and farmers, Jackson Hole types in fur-lined dress coats, and a whole bunch of women sitting together who look like grown-up Sondras.

Virgil comes through the crowd toward me. He doesn't look mad at me anymore. "What are you doing back here? Are you afraid to sit next to me?" He smiles. After a cold front it's nice to see the sun again.

I laugh. "I like keeping my back to the wall."

"Not a bad idea," he says.

"You aren't going to exhibit any 'artwork' tonight, are you?"

"Um, no . . . I'm here on assignment," he says, pointing to the camera around his neck.

"Me, too," I say. I pull out my pad and pocket tape

recorder. I pluck my pen out of my pocket and drop it.

Virgil picks up my pen and hands it to me. "You dropped your writing utensil."

"Thanks," I say, smiling. It's funny, but having Virgil remember that embarrassing moment relaxes me.

At the front of the room there's a bustle of activity with mikes, chairs, and speakers. I see Mr. Buck.

"Is that him?" Virgil says.

"Yep," I say. "I can't believe he came."

Virgil steps in close. It's the closest he's been to me in a week. For a split second I'm Virgil blind, which is not bad actually. Then I hear one of the Buffalo Nation guys sparring with one of the ranchers across the room. Virgil says lightly, "Better be careful what you ask for I guess, missy."

"I guess," I say, feeling sick.

Virgil takes my hand. "Don't forget to duck."

"You're the one that needs a bodyguard," I say.

"Aunt Jean put some bear spray in her purse."

"That's just what we need," I say. "A room full of blind hunters."

Virgil squeezes my hand and moves back into the crowd.

When Dad comes in he looks tense and miserable. I say, "Do you feel all right?"

"It's been a long day," he says.

"Why don't you go home? I'll catch you up in the morning."

"I hate to miss a good public brawl . . . but I might have to take you up on that."

"Don't worry. There's always another brawl."

Officers Smith and Farley come in and sit down in front, conspicuously armed.

Dad motions up front. "Who are all these people?"

I talk into his good ear. "The lady in the middle is the Federal consultant. She's supposed to take comments and keep the peace."

"Good luck," says Dad.

"The guy next to her is Ed Buck, the U.S. Fish and Wildlife guy. Not sure what I think about him."

"Does he work for the government?"

"Yeah."

"Well, there you go."

"Next to him is the guy who got all the money together to pay ranchers for the livestock the wolves kill."

"Yeah, I've read about him," he says, shaking his head. "Bet he wonders what he got himself into."

"In the front row is the guy who got the petition going in Red Lodge saying that the wolves are killing all the elk and cows and sheep and unless we hurry up and get the wolves back out of Yellowstone we're all going to get brain cancer."

"Really?"

"Not really. He's a state rep."

"How do you know all this?" says Dad, staring at me.

I shrug. "The Internet?"

"Obviously you have too much free time."

I don't say anything to that.

"It's not like they're going to get rid of the wolves by signing a petition. Too much has happened," Dad says.

"I hope you're right," I say.

The Fed lady tries to call the meeting to order with a gavel-banging tantrum. "Tonight we're here to give you some information and to find out what you people think of having the wolves back. Nothing gets decided. Anybody acts out of line we throw him or her out. Clear?"

Civil discourse. Yeah.

Then Buck pulls out the PowerPoint and gives a history lesson.

First he talks about how there were once two million wolves in the United States, and nowhere more plentiful than in the greater Yellowstone area. Then he shows slides of dead wolves strung up in rows, and a few people clap.

He talks about how wolves were killed off in the park by the mid-twenties and how the elk and deer ate the grasslands and mountainsides down to dirt and the stream banks washed away because there were no trees left to hold the soil together. How other species declined in a domino effect and even elk and deer had problems because of diseases caused in part by their overpopulation.

Then he moves on to an overview of the fifty years of

environmental wrangling that resulted in the government bringing fourteen wolves into the park and fourteen into Idaho under the Endangered Species Act. There is a lot of booing and cheering in the audience.

The Yellowstone wolves were kept in pens for a year to make sure they wouldn't just run back to Canada. During that time every news agency in the world showed up to photograph the wolves, and the day they were released into the wild, wolf mania began. People have been streaming into the park hoping to see them ever since.

Now the wolves have dispersed throughout Wyoming, Idaho, and Montana. Other native species have diversified. Forests and streams are recovering. For better or worse, the elk and deer numbers are way down. And livestock and pets have been lost. Ranchers on the edge of bankruptcy have one more battle to fight. It's a compromise of failure and success.

The crowd is restless.

He finishes up by saying, "The wolves can be a pain in the neck, and heaven only knows plenty of you'd like to see them gone, but I think our time would be better spent talking about a way to make this work." He gets a few catcalls. Then he says, "And I'd like to thank the young woman who invited me here tonight. Is KJ Carson here? She promised you'd be a lively bunch."

Holy smack.

Everyone looks around. I freeze. Dad looks down his very long nose at me, and he doesn't look happy. "Katherine Jean, *you* called him?"

"Yes?"

He leans back in his chair and shakes his head. "This is your idea of cooling things off. Didn't you learn anything from Virgil getting shot?"

"Civil discourse, you know."

Some helpful type yells, "She's back here, Buck."

Dad shakes his head. "Stand up. You started this."

I bob up and then melt back into my seat.

Mr. Buck says, "Give her a hand. This is a kid with some spunk."

There is weak spurt of applause.

Sondra yells, "You go, girl! Wolves rock!"

Dad pulls his coat off the back of his chair. "You go, girl. I'm going back to work." He walks into the crowd. I want to follow him but I can't. I'll have to explain when I get home. I didn't lie to him. I just didn't tell him I called Ed Buck.

"Questions?" says Mr. Buck.

A man raises his hand and says, "You ever seen what a wolf does to a herd of sheep?"

"They eat them," says Mr. Buck. A few people laugh. "Next question?"

I sit in my chair, motionless, while my insides redecorate.

A man yells, "Shoot, shovel, and shut up! Shoot, shovel, shut up!"

Others join in and the Fed lady has another gavel tantrum. "Pipe down or I'll cancel the meeting."

The shovel cheerleaders simmer down.

The Fed lady says, "We are now ready for comments. Make a statement, in three minutes or less. Then sit down and shut up."

A line forms to the microphone.

Ben from the garage says, "Wolves are a Washington conspiracy. Take 'em back to Washington where they belong!!"

"Wolves are the heart of this country," says a woman covered in turquoise.

A guy decked out in camo says, "Put 'em on the ballot, and we'll show you where you can put 'em."

"Wolves are returning balance to the ecosystem," says a man with a clipboard.

An old-timer follows him. "You ever try to balance a dead herd of sheep, buddy?"

One of the estrogen set hustles up to the mike. "Which you get paid for . . . without having to kill them yourself."

"Hunters like to eat, too. What rights do we have?"

"What rights do the animals you kill have?"

"The right to remain silent."

Cheering and a gavel tantrum ensue. Virgil appears next to me. "You didn't tell your dad?"

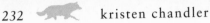

"I thought he'd be mad," I say.

Virgil snaps off a shot of the family in front of us and the parents glare at him. He says, "You were right."

The Federal lady yells, "Quiet down! Or this meeting is over."

"You'll have to forgive us," says Jonathan Daniels, a snowmobile operator, to the Fed lady. "Some of us haven't had this much fun since the Christmas Parade."

Half the crowd sniggers.

Eloise stands up and gets in line behind Daniels. I take a deep breath. Daniels turns, looks at her, and then clears out.

Virgil puts down his camera. "Oh, man . . ."

Eloise's voice cuts across the packed room. "First, I wish I found this topic as amusing as Mr. Daniels. Unfortunately the last time this town had any kind of exchange of opinions about the wolf, someone shot at my son."

"Here she goes," says Virgil.

Eloise continues, "Second, since my son has a souvenir from living here implanted in his face I feel that I am a property owner of sorts. We own a piece of your history. In part, it's a history of courage and idealism but largely it's a history of opportunity squandered. Now your history is that the wolves are back. That's history. You can sign all the petitions you want, that's the law now. And thug violence isn't going to chase the wolves away either. You have a chance here to make a deal with your future, or you can stick your head in your hat and leave. But people who behave like Neanderthals aren't just endangered. They're dead meat."

Loud angry boos fill the air. People are yelling. Mothers are tucking their kids in their laps. Virgil says, "You two . . ."

"What?" I say.

"That's it," yells the Fed lady.

Officer Farley raises his hands. "People! People!"

Suddenly Tom from the Cowboy Hotel store runs in from the back. He is still in his coat. He has snow in his mustache. "Hey. Hey." His eyes are wide open. "Where's the Fire Department? We got a blaze at Sam's shop."

25

A HOT TIME IN
THE OLD TOWN TONIGHT

I SHOVE THROUGH the crowd onto the street. Smoke hits my lungs. Virgil runs next to me. The fire alarm goes off at the volunteer fire station. I've heard that alarm plenty of times, forest fires are a way of life around here, but this time the noise sickens me. The alarm is for our store, my father.

In the heavy air the smoke stays low, choking the streets. I slip on the ice. Virgil grabs my arm. "He's all right," he calls over the noise.

I don't say anything. He has to be all right. I've already lost my mom.

When I reach the store, black smoke is everywhere. Flames leap out of the back of the store while the face of the store is dead and motionless. I gag on the ash in my throat.

Coach Henderson yells for people to get out of the way. I search the rim of people forming in the street. Neighbors are sprinting to the scene with buckets and extinguishers, but I don't see my dad. Every freak from here to Missoula is suddenly here to watch our store burn. I feel Virgil's arm. "Keep looking," he yells, and drags me into the crowd.

I don't see my dad.

Even in the subzero weather the sickening heat is everywhere, burning into our clothes and skin. People are shouting.

"KJ?" says Virgil. He looks at me funny. "Cover your mouth. Let's go around back."

We push through more gawkers and then swing behind the fire truck. Two volunteer firemen yell at each other. Smoke, snow, noise, and flashing orange lights all roil around me. I keep moving without moving. I hear sirens.

Suddenly I don't know where I am. I hear the sirens, popping wood, and shouting, but I disappear in the smoke, even to myself.

"KJ? Hey!" Virgil is pointing.

I look into the smoke and see what I think is Dad's head. It's him. He's standing next to the unmistakable frame of Big Larry from the gift shop next door. The two men are back from the main fire, spraying the huge campfire extinguishers from the store on the smoking bushes. I choke again.

Virgil grabs my shoulder. "Whoa," he says, and then pulls off his shirt. I realize he's still wearing his camera. "Hold this over your face."

I do what he says and walk away, to Dad.

I stand behind him.

He turns. He looks at me and then past me. He looks angry.

I feel Virgil behind me. I hand Virgil his shirt.

"Can I help?" says Virgil.

"Do you ever wear clothes around my daughter?" says Dad.

"What happened?" I feel the ash burn in my throat.

Dad coughs. "We nearly have this contained but you'd better get away from this smoke."

Three men I don't recognize push us out of the way and run another hose into the back door of the store. Maybe it was a good thing we had everybody in three counties here tonight. After a few horrible minutes the flames quiet, but smoke blooms everywhere with the water. I see the guts of the store through an open wall. I can't tell how much they saved. Some of it.

"How did it happen?" I say.

"Someone set a fire in the garbage bin and it jumped," says Larry.

I say, "Could it have been an accident?"

"They cut off the lock on the Dumpster to do it," says Larry. "That doesn't seem like an accident."

Dad gives me the look. The one that says, *Hold onto yourself.* He says, "I was resting in the office with the lights off. I heard a truck in the parking lot. It lurched as it pulled away. Backfired like . . . a fart. I kind of drifted off for a second, wondering about it, until I smelled smoke."

"If you'd fallen asleep . . ."

"I didn't," he says. "And whoever set the fire didn't know I was there. They would have had to be stone stupid to drive right up to the store and park like that if they thought I was here."

"They must have figured you were at the meeting, Samuel," says Eloise, arriving behind Virgil. "Must have thought the whole town would be at the meeting."

Dad squints at both of them. "Apparently a few people missed it."

I say, "I'm so sorry."

"It's a little late for that," says Dad, looking off into the smoke of his shop.

"Don't you dare take credit for this fire, KJ," says Eloise. "We have no idea who or what started this. And if someone did start this because of the wolves . . ." The idea seems to stop her for minute. "It just shows that you must be doing something right to make a person capable of being this mad."

"You know, Eloise," says Dad. "For an educated woman you can be genuinely stupid. I would really appreciate it if you and your son would stop filling my daughter with asinine ideas."

"Dad," I say. "They didn't do this."

"Well, they may not have lit the match . . ." He shakes his head at me and walks through us to talk to the firemen standing at their truck.

Eloise kicks the blackened snow with her boot. "I handled that pretty well. Virgil, will you walk me home?"

"Just a second, Mom," he says. "I'll catch up."

Virgil walks around the scene and takes pictures of everything. True to form, most of his pictures aren't of the fire. He takes a lot of shots of the giant burned-out garbage can and the snow around it. He gets some great close-ups of the tire tracks that lead up to the garbage. Like we could match those?

Larry and I stand watching. Stupid as sticks. Finally Larry says, "Need to feed my dog."

I put my hand on Larry's arm. "Thanks for being here."

He shakes his big shaggy head. "You're dad's a nice guy. Folks sure hate them wolves though."

Virgil walks back to us and takes our picture. "Larry, you have a big cut on your head. Do you want me walk home with you?"

Larry looks out from under his blood-smeared eyebrow and then spits in the snow. "Nah, I'm good."

Looking at Larry I start to make a list in my head of all

the bad things that have happened since I got interested in wolves: Virgil and my dad getting hurt, Mr. Muir's store getting smashed up, maybe the Martins being vandalized. It's possible that someone accidentally lit the Dumpster on fire behind our store after accidentally busting open the lid. But it's hard to imagine on the night of the meeting on wolves that a store that's owned by the father of a wolf lover can catch fire by coincidence. So this is round two, and my dad, who has patiently tried to stay out of this thing, is the big loser again.

I say, "I have to go find my dad."

"Good idea," says Larry, walking off.

My eyes are burning. I look at Virgil. "When I saw that smoke . . . I couldn't have handled tonight without you."

Virgil tips his face to mine. "No way. You're the Wolf Girl, right?"

Wolf Girl? What a joke. The idea that I could be some kind of new, braver version of myself, that I could make a good difference instead of screwing everything up, is an absurd fantasy to me now. A fantasy that could have cost my dad his life.

Virgil touches my shoulder. "But hey, you have some serious repairs to do here. And the less you see of me for a while, the better."

"What does that mean?"

"I'm just saying maybe I should make myself scarce."

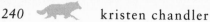

"You didn't do anything. Unless you want to see me less."
I knew I'd screw things up with him. It's me. I screw things
up. And Addie's sweet and pretty enough to sell toothpaste.
Why wouldn't he want to be with Addie instead of me?

"Sometimes it's hard to know who to be mad at. But
people usually find someone." He pauses and looks around
like he's lost something. "You take care of yourself, okay?"

Then he squeezes my hand and disappears into the dark.

TO DO LIST

Don't tick off Dad.

26

THE QUIET GAME

VIRGIL IS ABSENT in journalism. The rest of the class wants to hear about the fire. Dennis compares it to the planet in *Star Wars* that blows up. Addie asks me if I would like to talk about it. Sondra tells her to mind her own business.

Mrs. Baby marches in as the bell rings. She drops her purse in her desk drawer and slams it closed. She points at me and says, "Outside."

Once we're out in the hall she says, "I'm being put on probation."

I didn't see that one coming.

"Apparently the principal has some concerns about me letting the students have too much freedom of expression. I don't even know what his problem is. You haven't said anything . . . what did he call it . . . 'provoking,' have you? I mean you just write your little updates and talk about . . . wolf stuff."

"Some people really hate . . . wolf stuff."

"This is ridiculous. No one reads what you write in the school newspaper. It's not like you started a riot."

"No . . . But I did call the guy with the U.S. Fish and Wildlife and asked him to have the town meeting here."

"What are you talking about? You can barely dress yourself."

"I'm pretty sure I dress myself, Mrs. Bab . . . Brady."

"Oh, I know. I just mean it's all so silly. You're a kid."

"Yeah," I say. "It's pretty silly."

"Anyway you have to cut the wolf thing or I'm fired."

I feel bad for Mrs. Brady. She didn't sign on for trouble. She didn't even really sign on for the newspaper. She just wants to teach people to sift their flour before they mix it with creamed sugar. She wants health insurance and a quiet lunch hour. "Mrs. Brady, I'm going to be busy helping my dad with the repairs on the shop. Would you mind if Dennis takes over as editor?"

"The principal mentioned that to me." She pauses and makes a face like her underwear is too tight.

I say, "Dennis will do a good job."

"You were a fine editor, honey. And you're a spitfire of a writer, too."

Mrs. Baby has no sense of irony.

Virgil makes it to school in time for math. I see him talking to Addie outside of class. When I get close they stop talking. I say "hi" and walk past them.

I find my seat. I don't fall apart.

Joss and Mandy titter when I sit down.

Mr. Muir stops me after class. "Sorry about your store."

"Yeah, it's a bad year for stores around here."

Mr. Muir looks impatient. "The ACT is in June. I'm driving the van to Bozeman with anyone who wants to go to college when they grow up."

"June?" I look at him doubtfully.

"Here's a prep book. You're going to start now."

"I haven't exactly been setting the world on fire in here lately."

Mr. Muir squints at me and smiles. "Don't worry, KJ, you'll burn it up."

Mr. Muir. Holy smokes.

There is no hurry to get home.

Tomorrow and every day after, there will be more work than I can do to repair the shop but today the insurance people are counting the cost of things. I head to the tree house.

I walk on a packed snowmobile trail. I look around for tracks. I know that wolf I saw isn't going to be this close in to town, but I look for signs anyway. With the hysteria in

West End, it would be a disaster if the wolf started poaching people's dogs or showing up on people's porches. But that's not going to happen. I haven't heard anyone mention anything about seeing a wolf in town. So that means that wolf is dead or gone. Probably both.

I only sit in the tree house for a minute—well, a couple of minutes.

It's hard to believe everything that's happened. Last summer I was afraid of not fitting in and of failing algebra. I guess it's like my dad says, the quickest cure for a hangnail is a broken arm.

I look out over the edge of the tree-house platform at the deep crusty snow beneath me. With the snow drift it's only about ten to twelve feet but I'm not crazy about heights, even mini-heights. A squawky raven grazes the tree line and lands not far from my perch. "What are you looking at?"

The raven doesn't answer.

"What do you think?"

The raven tips its head at me and flies away. Show off.

I climb the small handrail and jump.

I get stuck feet first in the snow. After a little scrabbling I pull myself out. Unfortunately one of my boots comes off. I sit on the snow, look up at the tree house, and laugh. I would never have done this last year. I'm just not sure if that is a good or bad thing.

Three weeks can feel like a long time. But three weeks of brutal homework, fixing up the shop, my dad not speaking to me, no trips across the park to see the wolves, and Virgil avoiding me feels more like an ice age. On the upside, I'm getting pretty decent at jumping out of the tree house.

Dennis takes the note from the office for Mrs. Baby. She's late again. Dennis likes being the editor. I like reading the notes he puts on Baby's desk.

It's from Eloise. Virgil has a cold, again. For the last three weeks he's probably made it to half of his classes. And when he's here he just puts his head on his desk and sleeps. I have asked him what's going on but he just says, "Not sleeping well." A girl can only ask a guy what's wrong so many times and then it's nagging.

I'd ask Addie what to do, but she's busy right now. Making Virgil so tired he can't even come to school.

Sondra says, "You want to meet for lunch?"

I nod.

In spite of my attempts to inoculate myself by hurling myself into space, I have come down with the silence flu. A highly contagious form of social dysfunction, spread by my father, who talks less than most rock formations. He doesn't even harass me about school. He eats dinner in front of the news so he doesn't have to look at me. His silence feels like shouting. I am as silent as he is.

Mr. Muir corners me after class. "How're we doing?"

I shrug.

"How's your studying for the ACT?"

I shrug again. I don't have enough words to explain how much I don't want to talk to him right now.

"You know what I've figured out about you?"

I brace myself for a lecture on my poor work ethic, my poor attitude, and the dirt under my fingernails.

"You aren't great at math, KJ. But it's being afraid to fail that kills you. There isn't any room in your head for numbers."

Adults. Sometimes they're less dumb than they look.

I still don't want to talk to him.

He pats me on the back as I walk to his door. "It's a good thing it's a written exam."

At work there is a note from my dad. It begins, "To Be Completed." I've been relegated to the passive voice.

I go to the grocery store to get cleaning supplies. They've added a fourth piece of paper to The List to accommodate all the signatures. People must be making a special trip into town just to sign up. I'm sure glad we had that nice meeting to clear up all the hard feelings.

Darlene's Wolf-Watching Web Site for Women

It seems the alpha male of the Druids is quite the Casanova. He may have bred with not one but three of the Druid gals this time around, including his unforgiving alpha mate Number Forty, and our sweet Cinderella wolf, Number Forty-Two. You have to feel for Cinderella! This is going to get awkward this spring.

Love ya!
Darlene Wolf Watcher

P.S. Pinochle on Thursday. Wolves Forever!!!

27

CAN'T LIVE WITH 'EM.
CAN'T SHOOT 'EM.

MEN. BOYS. BEASTS.

I wish I didn't care what Virgil is doing. I wish I could hate him or blame him or forget him. That would be a lot easier than watching him talk to Addie after school and then disappear into Aunt Jean's Cadillac with no idea where he is going.

"Hey, Addie," I say, after Virgil drives off.

"Yes," she says coyly.

"What are you doing after school today?" I say just as coyly.

"Working. Like usual. Mom has five quilts she's doing for a show in Bozeman so I get to do all the dirty work." Addie's mother makes quilts and then sells them at craft shows all over the state. Addie says she gets her "intuitive side" from her mother. My intuition tells me Addie is not just helping her mom this afternoon.

"That must be really hard," I say.

"Not really," says Addie. "I like housework. It's relaxing." She talks quickly and keeps walking.

I keep pace with her even though I know she wants to get away.

"How's the shop coming?" she says with a dose of perky.

"Oh, you know . . ." I say. "We never stop laughing at our place."

"Really?"

"No, not really."

"Oh," she says with a pout. "Well, just keep sending out those positive feelings to your dad. He'll come around. That's why you're in such pain. . . . you are a warrior for good."

At this point the only warlike thing I want to do is throttle Addie, so I have to leave. I can handle guilty lies, but the pseudo-psychology perky hypocrisy is too much even for a warrior like me. And yes, it's possible I am slightly out of my mind with rampaging jealousy.

I walk to the shop and Dad is talking with a contractor. They are arguing about money, so I don't go in. Dad comes outside and actually speaks to me. "KJ. I need you to drive out to Charlie Dalton's in Ennis and get the wood sample he has for me. Here's the address. I need it yesterday. This guy in here is jacking me all over, saying he can't do the finish the way I want. I'd go myself but I'm waiting for the plumbers."

In spite of my seething over Addie, this is news. I bask in the light of my father's sentence structure, and the fact that he has actually entrusted me with a job that involves me leaving the city limits.

"Sure," I say.

I hop in the truck and head for Ennis. The roads are dry today, so it's only marginally stressful. My job is to get the sample and come home. I make a mental note to myself: *"Whatever you do—don't screw up."*

I roll down the windows and breathe in the cold air. I turn on the radio full blast when I hit Highway 287. Sixty-two miles of nothing but road, music, and gray sky. I have two hours before the store in Ennis closes, so I don't have to speed. I look at the ranch homes as I pass. I look out over at Hebgen's icy shores, wondering if we will get the store put together before the snow melts.

The radio bleats a horrible country song. I know all five words, so I sing along. I pass the dam and the visitor's center for the '88 earthquake. Within minutes I am passing prime stream water on one side and prime ranch property on the other. I see the muddy entrance to the community where Kenner and Addie live. At the front of the entrance, parked next to a dirty snowbank, I see Aunt Jean's Cadillac.

I nearly swerve off the road.

I turn off the radio and concentrate on the lines that keep me from crashing. There is nowhere to pull over. But then again, if I flip the truck it might be good, as long as I don't actually live. I can't remember where I am going. I am overreacting. I am OverReActIng. I AM OVERREACTING.

I roll up the windows. I crank up the heat. It doesn't help. I turn the radio back on. The sound makes my ears ring. I turn it off again. I concentrate on getting to Ennis without wrecking Dad's truck.

When I get into town I find the shop, the man, and the sample. The man asks me if I need a glass of water. I don't make a good impression. I head home. For fifty miles I tell myself that even if the Cadillac is still at the gate I have to keep driving. There isn't anything to do. He's not breaking a law. He's just dumping me.

When I get to the Cadillac I slow down and then I stop. I get out of the truck. I get back in the truck. I promised. I drive every miserable mile back to the store, give Dad the sample, and ask him if I can borrow the truck.

"What for?" he says, impatient to get back to the plumber.

"I need to talk to Addie," I say.

"Can't you call her on the phone?" he says.

"Boy trouble . . . you know, it's better in person," I say sympathetically.

He nods. I walk for the door.

"One hour."

"You got it," I say as calmly as possible when you are a green-eyed lunatic. I can barely get out there and back in one hour. But then, how much time to do you need to confront your worst nightmare?

There is just enough light to see inside the Cadillac. I peer at Virgil's health book on the backseat. Looking at that book sears me with humiliation. Health class. The day I stuck my nose in it with Kenner and embarrassed Virgil. And here I am again. What am I going to say? What am I doing here? I walk back to my car. I stew ten minutes. Dad is expecting me back. I get out of the car and start walking.

I follow the path into the two-family development. When I reach the fork in the road I see truck lights coming toward me from Addie's house. It's Addie.

She pulls up next to me. "Hey. I'm so glad you're here."

"You are?"

"Yeah, I've been telling him for a week that he needs to come clean."

I look at her with as much neutrality as I can muster. I know it's not her fault I drove him away. But I also know she had this in mind all along. "Well, thanks."

"I think they're all up at the house." Then Addie does the darndest thing. She points up the road to Kenner's house.

"You won't believe it. You know, he's not half bad for a city kid."

I stand in the road. This must be what the deer feels like right before the lights from the semi connect. What is Virgil doing at Kenner's? Why isn't he at Addie's house, sucking her face off and eating all her home cooking? I have to catapult from one betrayal to the next, without completely exhibiting my whole inner freak show to Addie. "I . . . I . . . Yeah. Well, thanks," I repeat.

She looks out her truck window with nauseatingly empathy on her face. "Do you want me to go with you? I could drive you up and smooth it over for you like I did for Virgil. I know it must be hard for you since I know you've figured . . . well, you know. This really is so brave of you."

I am so far from brave right now I'm not even the opposite of brave. I look up the road to the Martins' silos. At least there are answers up there. I nod and climb into Addie's truck.

As we bump up the drive Addie keeps peering at me. Finally she says, "I'm glad he called you. I was getting pretty tired of covering for him."

I peer back. Addie has been telling Virgil to be honest with me, while I have been silently hating her for being a conniving backstabber. I hate it when discovering something wonderful about someone else requires me discovering something pathetic about myself. "Thanks for driving me," I say.

"Oh, geez, no. I just hate this whole 'secret' thing, no matter how rude you've been to me. I think what Virgil is doing is so . . . well, you know it probably won't help anything as far as the wolves go, but maybe it will help Kenner and his family. Virgil says it's a lot harder than he imagined it would be. They've both had to let go of their persona. I think it's very empowering."

I look over at Addie, dwarfed by her family's huge truck. "You've been reading a lot of psych stuff this winter, haven't you?"

"Oh, yes! My mother says I'm going to wreck myself."

"No," I say. "I think it's great."

I can see Kenner's mom, Mrs. Martin, in the window of her kitchen doing dishes.

Mrs. Martin comes out front and stands on her porch. She's followed by Kenner's little towheaded sister, Heidi. Heidi is holding a cat so pregnant it hurts me just to look at it. Mrs. Martin looks over me but not at me and rests her irritable gaze on Addie. "Yes, Addie?" she says in clipped succession.

Addie's voice turns to one-hundred-proof honey. "This is KJ Carson."

"I know who she is," says Mrs. Martin.

"She's here to see Virgil, aren't you, KJ?" I can tell Addie wants me to say something, but anything I say is going to betray how little I understand about what is happening.

And this doesn't look like a woman who suffers fools, so I start with the only true thing I know. "Mrs. Martin, I've come to talk to Virgil but I was wondering if I could use your phone first. My dad is expecting me and I don't want him to worry."

Mrs. Martin sighs, as if I'm confirming her worst fears about me. "The phone's in here."

As I step into the small, clean house I hear her say, "I'm not running a hotel here."

Inside the home there is little free space. In one corner, there is an ancient upright piano covered with family photos, a pint-size violin on a stand, a bookshelf, a green couch, and a covered rocker. In the other end of the room is a round dinner table and chairs made of varnished wood. On the wall next to the kitchen sink there is a cross and a calendar. Not exactly the Ponderosa.

I call the shop. No one answers. Not good. I call home. "Hey, Dad? Are you okay?"

"Where are you?" he says, no doubt looking at the caller ID.

"I'm at the Martins' place."

"The Martins'? What in blazes are you doing there?" His voice is more of a threat than a question.

"Can I tell you when I get home? I promise to get up at four and work on the store."

"What are you doing, KJ?"

"Dad, I need to sort some things out."

"Katherine Jean. Those people . . . You can't go into a person's home and accuse them of something."

"I'm not doing that."

"Is this another one of your civil discourse ideas? The last one didn't turn out so good for me."

"Dad . . ." I want to make him happy, but there is no way to do that right now, even if I hang up and walk out of the house with no answers. I can only manage the disaster in front of me. "How about thirty minutes, plus drive time?"

"That's plenty of time to start a mess," he says, and hangs up in my ear.

I turn around to the sound of boots clomping on the wood floor and boys' voices. I hear Virgil laugh. It sends a wave of fear and pleasure through me. I hear Kenner say, "No way. You were off by five feet. You nearly shot a hole in the barn." It's Kenner's voice but without the edge.

Virgil laughs and walks into the kitchen. I feel the red blotches of embarrassment sweep up my throat, and I am grateful for my scarf. He looks up, his eyes startled. I don't know which is more mind-boggling to me though, that I am standing in Kenner's living room watching Virgil pal up with Kenner or that the two of them are holding shotguns.

"KJ?" says Virgil. He looks as confused as I feel.

Kenner just stares at me.

"Hey," I say.

Mrs. Martin walks in after them on her way to the back of the house. "Put those things away now. You two know the rules. You have ten minutes and then I want you boys getting all the animals in. Kenner, go help your sister. That cat of hers is going to go burst. And your dad and William need help with the feedin'. We don't have time for socializing tonight."

"What brings you out here?" says Kenner, the edge back in his voice. "I thought nature boy was keeping this a big secret."

I struggle to keep up with the shifting social terrain. I look at Virgil for help in knowing how to answer but all I see are more questions. Once again I punt with the truth. "Virgil didn't tell me anything. I was driving by and I saw his car here."

"So you're a stalker then," says Kenner. "Well, I believe it. Nothing you do would surprise me."

Addie jumps in, "Oh, hush, Kenner. You mean you didn't tell her after all, Virgil?"

"No," says Virgil, looking at me and then looking at the gun in his hands. "I didn't."

I can see that Dad was right, except it's only taken me thirty seconds to make the mess. "Addie," I say quietly. "I appreciate your help. Will you tell Mrs. Martin thank you for letting me use the phone?"

I step as quietly to the door as I can and slip into the cold air. A young border collie mix looks up from its place under the swing on the porch. It wasn't here when I came so I'm guessing it must be Kenner's dog, his replacement for the one the wolves killed. It jumps to attention and barks at me but doesn't come closer. I walk quickly down the path and then onto the road that leads to my car. I am nearly to the highway when I hear someone running behind me.

"Wait."

I turn and see Virgil hurtling toward me. If I was a good daughter I would jump in my car and drive away.

"Wait! KJ!" His words make thin clouds between us. "What are you doing here?"

I am too confused to make anything up. "Just what I said. I had to go to Ennis and I saw your car. I thought . . . I wondered what you were doing."

"Okay," he says, still breathing hard. "What did you think I was doing here?"

"I don't know."

"I think you thought," he says, stepping closer, "I've been avoiding you."

I step back. "I've got to go."

"Because of your dad?"

"This has nothing to do with my dad, Virgil. And don't you pretend . . ."

"But it does."

I'm not cold anymore. I'm seething. "How many times are

you going to blame everything on my dad? For three weeks I had nothing but . . ."

"Could you shut up so I can tell you something?"

We glare at each other in the dark.

"Sorry," he says softly.

I say nothing.

"This is going to take a minute. Do you want to go sit in your truck?"

"Are you sure the Martins will let you back in the house?"

"No," he says flatly. "Mrs. Martin feels like you have bad-mouthed her boys to the town."

"That would require me to have someone to talk to, wouldn't it?"

"Let's get in your truck."

I start the engine. He leans back against his seat. I watch him in the half-light. His mouth puckers as he blows heat into his fingers. I remind myself that he is a big fat liar that has been ignoring me for weeks. He says, "I'm trying to help."

I fold my arms across my chest. He clears his throat.

"When your dad's place burned it scared me. I kept thinking what I would do if something happened to you. Then I realized that was the problem. . . . The whole town was scared, that was what was driving everything."

"So you decided to take shooting lessons from the Martin brothers?"

"No," he says impatiently. "I decided to come out here and talk to the Martins. Put a face to what I was afraid of. Hear their side of the story."

"Must have been an amazing story."

"It really is, KJ. These people aren't what you think."

"How would you know what I think?"

"I don't," he says. "But I know what I thought. I didn't have any idea how hard it is for them."

"What *did* you think? Hard is what ranchers *do*. That's their *specialty*. They do hard like photographers do . . . weddings. That doesn't make it okay for someone to shoot at people or burn down their store."

Virgil raises his voice again. "Would you stop being so mad and listen to what I'm trying to tell you?"

"I can't stop being mad just because you tell me to."

Virgil reaches across the air to touch me but I pull back. He scoots back on the seat. "Okay. Be mad. But I need to explain. At first I just wanted to talk to them. Addie came and made sure they didn't kill me. It was tense. Then we all sort of got to be friends, after a while. So I wanted to be useful. I volunteered to sleep with the herd."

"You what?" I stare at him. Even for Virgil this is bizarre.

"They laughed at me, too. Eloise thinks I have a death wish."

"You sleep outside with the cattle?"

"It's still way too cold to sleep outside. I stay in the bunk-house. During the day I fix fences and scout for tracks. At night I get up at intervals and walk around, checking on things, making a little noise, and make man smell on every-thing, if you know what I mean. I read about it in book about cattle drives."

"How do you watch them all? Do the Martins keep all their cattle here in the winter?"

"No, they can't afford to. But the ones that are here were being harassed. They've had the Madison pack right on the place. So I'm a walking deterrent."

"You're a freaking cow babysitter, is what you are."

"I figured if my scent scared off the wolves, they wouldn't be shot, the cattle wouldn't be eaten, and the people would settle down."

Virgil never stops surprising me. Never.

"Is it working?" I say.

"We haven't had an incident since we started doing it."

"Kenner helps?"

"He and William spell me a little each night. It's pretty cool of them really."

"What are you talking about? You're guarding their cattle for free."

"Well, they pay me in kind. William taught me to shoot soda cans, and Kenner taught me to pee my name in the snow."

"Can't beat that."

"And Mrs. Martin feeds me. . . ."

I try to imagine this. "Does she make you vegetarian dinners?"

"No."

"So what do you eat?"

"Are you my mother?"

"But, these people . . ."

Virgil throws up his hands. "These people are your neighbors, KJ. And before I moved here they liked you or at least they didn't hate you. They liked your dad. Now they feel as persecuted as you do. They feel that in addition to having wolves forced on them, they have half the town looking down on them for something they didn't even do."

"They are good storytellers."

"Do you really think the Martins are stupid enough to set fire to your dad's store?"

It's a good question. Not one I've considered much lately because I've been busy thinking that Kenner is stupid enough to do anything. Finally I say, "What about the words on Mr. Muir's store? Who else but Kenner would write something like that?"

"I don't know. But I don't think it was him."

I look out the window. The highway is silent. I'm late.

Then, maybe just because it's been a very long three weeks for both of us, we stop talking. That's the thing about kissing. You don't have to talk. You can spend hours not talking. Entire eons not talking. Unless of course you are me and your dad is waiting to incarcerate you when you get home. I look at my watch. "I'm in so much trouble."

"Yeah," he says, drawing a smile on the fogged-up window.

I turn on the defroster. It's going to take a minute.

"Will I see you tomorrow?" I say.

"I hope so."

"Where?"

"Can you come back here?"

"Oh, the Martins will love that."

"I'll talk to them. I'll call you after school tomorrow."

"You can't just quit going to school, Virgil. Even in Montana, we have laws about that. And you weren't doing so hot to begin with."

"I know. If you and I could trade off it would be better."

"Trade off?"

"Yeah. But I'll bet Addie's family would let her do it with you. And maybe even Sondra and Dennis would help. We could maybe even get school credit for it. Call it research for the paper or health or something."

"I sort of lost my spot . . . remember? Wait, you are serious?"

"I have to keep it going to show that it works."

"And what if it doesn't?"

"Then at least I've learned how to shoot and piss with greater accuracy."

"You've got it made."

"I need a girl. These cows are starting to look good."

Just as Virgil says this, a semi barrels by and sprays a wall of mud all the way from the road to my dad's truck. I turn on my wipers. "Have you ever noticed how bad things seem to happen when we're together?"

"It's occurred to me."

"And that right when we're getting along, for some reason we stop getting along?"

"Yeah. Why is that?" says Virgil.

"I don't know. Maybe we're cursed or something."

Virgil smiles. "I guess there's one way to find out."

"You sure you want me to come out here with you?"

"Are you sure you want to come out here with me?"

I kiss him one last time for bad luck and drive my dad's mud-splattered, fogged-up truck home.

Poem Composed While Driving Home in the Dark

My entry there was not auspicious
But Virgil's kisses were delicious

28

OCCUPATIONAL HAZARDS

THE GOOD NEWS is that when I get home Dad is asleep on the couch with the TV on, snoring like a bear with a head cold. The bad news is that he had sauerkraut for dinner, and I nearly pass out from the smell. Sauerkraut: German for pickled barf.

I sit on the floor next to Dad. I wonder what he will say when he wakes up. I wonder what I will say. How can I tell him? I replay the night, slowing down for the part where I am kissing Virgil, and then speeding up for the part where he tells me that he wants me to help him babysit cows. I try to think of something about tonight that won't make my dad furious. At least I got the wood sample.

I realize with disgust that I am in Virgil-induced denial. If I tell Dad that I want to go camp out at the Martins' a few times a week, he will disown me. If I go out there, Kenner will probably tie me up with bailing wire and pee his name on me. If I don't go, Virgil will have to do this amazing thing on his own. If I do help him, I will probably flunk out of school and end up as a waitress at a greasy bar where men pay their tips in gold teeth. If I do go, and Virgil can prove that the wolves can be dealt with in other ways besides killing them, then maybe the town could get over all this wolf insanity and get back to the business of being overworked and underpaid like the good old days.

I grab a pillow from the floor. Even the pillow smells like sauerkraut. I watch the shapes on the television: death, destruction, doom, and a new baby hippo at the Denver Zoo. I'm smiling again and it's not because of the hippo.

Dad's face is tucked into his coffee cup. I might as well be telling him I am running away to become a professional mime.

"So we'd be kind of like old-fashioned shepherds, but with cows," I say for the third time. "The girls and I could go on the same nights, I guess, if the other girls get permission."

"So you think this is going to make ranchers stop killing wolves?"

"If it works . . . I mean maybe it could at least show killing wolves isn't the only answer, and that pro-wolf isn't anti-ranching. Maybe people would stop signing that stupid petition."

"You're planning on becoming a permanent resident at the Martins'?"

"No."

"So what do they do when you leave?"

"Maybe if it works we could get some grants or something. . . ."

"That's your solution? Grants for sleepovers?"

"It's a start."

"Then everyone is going to live happily ever after?"

"Dad, I'm asking . . . your permission."

He looks at me coldly. "I'll put an ad in the paper for shop help." Then he lifts himself from his chair and leaves me alone in the kitchen with a BDG knife through the heart.

I make a few phone calls. It seems that Sondra's mother would love to have her out of the house and Dennis's parents think it would look good on his résumé for all the freakish tech schools he's applying to next year. Addie says she might not have much time but she will "do her best to be supportive of her friends in their journey toward self-actualization and healing." I think that if the wolves spoke English we could just play some tapes of Addie talking, and they wouldn't come anywhere near the Martins' place.

I race to the shop, where my dad is sorting new supplies

in the back room. I don't actually try to talk to him. I just get to work. We work like that for about four hours before I leave to get some food. When I come back he is on the phone and the words floating in the dry air seem to calm things down a little. I know I can do the store and the night shift a few times a week. I can study a little when I'm out there, too, just like I do here. And the season is so slow this time of year—even if the shop was all finished, the town's basically shut down anyway.

I get up the nerve to ask my dad where he wants the new set of fire extinguishers. He frowns. "Well, with all this good will you're spreading around, you better put one at each door and then order another set."

"Dad. I can work the shop and keep up my grades. I can miss a little sleep. Everyone else said they'd help, too. So it will only be a few nights a week."

"I'm sure it will be delightful," he says.

"Come on, Dad. Why is it so bad to try?"

"Might want to sell a few of those fire extinguishers to the Martins."

"You aren't really going to put an ad in the paper, are you?"

He doesn't answer.

At three o'clock the phone rings. It's Virgil.

"What's the plan?" he says.

"Everyone is on board if the Martins will have us. I think

we should try to make it girls with girls if we can, and some-body probably needs to, you know . . . train us."

"You want to learn to shoot?"

"I can handle a shotgun, but I don't know much about cattle."

"You know how to shoot?"

"Occupational hazard."

"Your dad speaking to you?"

"Is it my birthday or Christmas?"

"No."

"Then I guess not. I won't be able to keep this up once the tourist season starts."

"Got it. I'll tell the Martins. This is so great. I don't think I could keep doing this on my own. Plus I miss you."

I look over at my dad, eavesdropping on me with his good ear. "We'll make a schedule at school, where you will be at-tending, and not flunking out, right?"

"Yeah. Yeah. And, KJ, I know . . . I should have trusted you."

I say, "I hope you're right."

For the strength of the Pack is the Wolf,
and the strength of the Wolf is the Pack.

Rudyard Kipling, "The Law of the Jungle"

29

THE RUINS

THE BUNKHOUSE SMELLS like cedar, dust, and old mattresses. Hooks on the wall hold every contraption known to man. Shelves are filled with bottles and gadgets neatly organized. Some shelves are actually labeled. It's like a laboratory.

I put my gear on the cot and get my shotgun out of its case. Time to go to work.

The door squeaks and Kenner walks in.

I flinch. "Oh, hi." I haven't gotten used to fraternizing with Kenner yet.

Kenner looks irritated. "Addie just called. She has to babysit. Typical of her."

"She's not coming?" I try to sound calm. "Sondra called

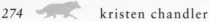

me right before I came. She's not coming either . . . has the flu."

"Yeah, this is going to work. . . ." he says.

"Just give it some time. They'll come when they can." Excessive optimism isn't really my thing, but somebody has to pretend this will work.

Kenner stands in the corner by the stove looking uncomfortable. "So you're alone on your first night? Good thing you have that shotgun."

"Yeah," I say. "Good thing."

"You know how to use it?"

"I can kill cans. I'm just going to use bird-shot shells though."

Kenner smirks, "You can go home if you want, KJ. It's kind of scary around here at night."

"I think I'll be all right."

He tips his hat back on his head. "Do you want me to bring you a night-light?"

Wouldn't be Kenner if he wasn't giving me grief.

"I brought my own," I say, hauling out the head lamp and the spotlight I brought from the store.

"You've got to be kiddin' me," he says. "Did you bring a blankie, too?"

I pull out a wool blanket I brought from the store's back room. It has a few holes but it's thick, and it blends nicely with the dust bowl decor of the bunkhouse.

"Sweet Mary." He laughs. "I can't wait till you see one of

those beasts. You're going to run all the way home."

As if I've never seen a wolf. I smile demurely. "I guess I better get out there and look around, if I'm going to get eaten by sunup."

Kenner pauses at the door. "You're really going to try do this alone . . . on your first night?"

"Guess so."

Kenner shakes his head. "That takes some nuts."

"You already know I'm nuts."

Kenner laughs. Not in his typically rude way, but in the way I've heard him laugh when he's with Virgil. "Listen," he says, "I've got a midterm in history but I guess I could come out here for a while."

I pick my shotgun off the bed. "I'll be okay."

Kenner kicks at the bare wood floor. He's not so bad when he stops being a jerk for five seconds.

I say, "What's all this stuff in here for? On the walls."

"That's Will's stuff. He's a fix-it genius."

"What does he fix?"

"On a ranch you have to fix everything yourself and everything breaks. Especially when you need it."

"He's organized," I say.

"Yep," says Kenner. "He put his own truck together from scrap."

"That thing in the yard?"

"Calls it Frankenstein. And he has a boat, too."

"I've seen that."

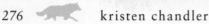

"Yep."

We stand looking at each other. I wish Addie and Sondra were here.

He says, "You're going to freeze your butt off out there, you know. We could just make a run-through and then you could go out again first thing in the morning."

"Gortex is my friend," I say, modeling my new red tundra coat. I may not have friends in high places but I'm in retail, which is almost as good.

"You're still going to freeze," says Kenner.

I smile at him. "I'll come get you if I have a problem."

"Sure, but don't walk around the whole night. Take some breaks. The stock will be fine," he says. His voice is soft, virtually friendly. "And I'll be up late."

"Thanks," I say.

He nods. "No problem."

There's a knock at the door. Will walks in wearing his rubber work boots, looking serious. When he and Kenner stand so close together I can see the family resemblance, but Will is like the concentrated version of Kenner. Smaller and all about business. "Dad needs you to finish checking all the gates," he says to Kenner. He looks at me. "We don't want any open gates," he says, and walks out.

Kenner stays put until Will is gone. "I know you think that me and Will are connected to what's been going on. But we'd never do that stuff. We just hate wolves."

"Okay." I don't want to talk about it.

Kenner points to the stove. "If you need to crank that thing up, go ahead. My parents would hate it if you froze in your sleep."

"I don't think I'm going to sleep much tonight."

"You aren't," he says. "But take some breaks."

"Got it."

"Who'd be scared of you anyway?" says Kenner.

"Hey, the hood is scary," I say pulling my hood up over my head and pointing my fingers like guns.

"Yep," he says.

The seven pastures hold one hundred cows apiece. I walk between the pastures flashing lights, spreading my human scent, listening for weird "I'm-being-eaten" noises, with my shotgun slung across my back like a soldier of misfortune. I wander around the pens they have for other animals, too—the chicken coop and the bum lamb pen that Mrs. Martin keeps as a hobby. Exactly as Kenner predicted, I'm cold, alone, and scared out of my wits. Luckily I'm so worried about messing things up that I'm not sleepy. But it's only midnight, so there's time for that, too.

The cattle smell like hay and ammonia. They bawl to each other in the cold, bumping around to keep warm. They don't seem to mind my spotlight. They don't seem to care about anything really. I make a mental note that cattle are not the most intelligent of God's creatures.

My mind wanders. I see Virgil sprawled over his desk in

Health and know that will be me tomorrow. I see my dad huffing and puffing around the immaculately clean shop, asking me about school, looking for a reason to complain. Then I see the wolf in the woods, that beautiful lone wolf and wonder what I will do if that wolf, or any predator, shows up looking for dinner.

For the last week I have frantically prepared for this night—I've done everything I can to be on top of school and work. I have begged, borrowed, and purchased the warmest gear I could find. And I have dutifully, thoughtfully, practiced my marksmanship. But that sure doesn't mean I'm ready for what I'm doing.

Suddenly I hear a noise by the barn. A bucket falling. Two cows bawl loudly. Then another. I yell, "Hello?" My voice disappears into the dark. I put on my spotlight but can't see anything except cattle moving in their shadows.

I lift my gun up and walk fast. I know it could be anything, and I sure don't want to spray bird shot before I know what I'm pointing at. My mind races through the possibilities; wolf, coyote, cougar, and human. The cows keep bawling. I can relate.

I finally get to the pasture with noisy cows and frantically swing my light. If I lose one of these animals . . . the idea nearly shuts me down. And what if whoever or whatever is out there isn't stalking cattle? I keep walking the fence line, flashing my light. I see nothing but cow butts. Then out of nowhere I see a shadow flying across the light. I send my light flooding toward the barn and find my predator. Virgil.

He waves with one hand and puts his finger to his lips with the other.

"Very funny. I could have shot you!" I say. But I'm too relieved to be mad.

He jogs over to me. "Kenner called and told me the other girls stiffed you. He said you wouldn't go home."

"I'm just glad you aren't a wolf," I say. I feel a trickle of sweat on my back.

"How do you know I'm not?" he says, raising his arms over his head and howling softly. "You should take me to the bunkhouse and examine me. . . ."

"The bunkhouse sounds good. Is it okay to leave the cattle?"

"Of course. Have you been out here all night?"

"Yeah."

Virgil wraps his arms around my giant coat. "You've got to pace yourself, KJ. Didn't Kenner tell you to take breaks?"

"But what if something happens on my break?"

"Nothing's going to happen. I've been here for three weeks. I take full-fledged snoozes and we've been fine."

"That was you. . . . I'm cursed."

Virgil lets go and we walk to the bunkhouse. "I killed a few chickens before you came. We're good."

"I didn't know you did voodoo in Minnesota."

"Obviously you've never been to a butcher's shop in the Midwest."

Once we get into the bunkhouse I realize how cold I am. It hurts to thaw. Virgil helps me out of my coat because my hands are too stiff to work the zipper.

"You need to sleep," he says. "I'll take the next shift."

"This is your night off."

"I've had hours of sleep. And I drank a thermos full of tea on the way over," he says, shoving me toward my sleeping bag.

"You drink tea?"

"I'll get you up at five so I can get out of here before Mrs. Martin sees me. She doesn't believe in coed housing."

I climb into the bag. Everything burns and aches but especially my fingers and toes. I'm used to long days guiding with my dad, but this cold sucked the life out of me. I close my eyes. It's hard work to freeze to death.

He says, "I can't believe you did this alone on your first night. Weren't you scared?"

I open my eyes. "I was too cold to be scared."

He laughs. He puts my blanket over the top of the bag and sits down next to me on the cot. "So tell me, Wolf Girl, what are you afraid of?"

"Everything," I mumble. "It's my superpower."

"Everything? You can't be more specific than that?"

I consider my choices. "I don't like people touching my head."

He puts his hands in my hair. "I touch your head all the time. It's connected to your mouth."

"You don't count. I let you hug me, too."

"You're afraid of being hugged?" His eyes are wide. "Suddenly things are making more sense to me."

I'm too tired to care. "Shut up. I'm just cautious . . . and slightly repressed."

"Slightly? I've never been with anyone like you. It's like taking a vow of anticipation. Girls usually . . . I mean, being with you is like when I became a vegetarian, only worse."

"Worse?"

"Way worse."

I want to talk but my mouth is calcifying in exhaustion. "I didn't mean to cramp your style."

His voice comes closer to my ear. "There are cramps involved. But you're worth it."

"Thanks." I feel like I'm floating, and at any moment I could spin off into some weightless point of no return. I try to burrow into my mattress. I've slept on thicker newspaper. Virgil traces my face with his finger. I manage to say, "So you know what I'm afraid of. What are you afraid of?"

He makes a basset-hound face. "Me? Not much, I guess. Turning into my parents. Global warming. Ruining your life."

I'm too punchy to know if he's kidding. I'm also distracted by the sensation that my toes are falling off. "Why are you afraid of that? I mean . . . you won't ruin my life."

"What if I fall in love with you? You know, over time and everything."

I sit back up. He's smiling so I know he's kidding. At least I think so.

He laughs. "See?"

"We're juniors. I'd ruin your life, too."

"Probably. But I like ruins, they're photogenic." He stands up and puts his coat on.

"Virgil," my voice is dopey. I feel awake but I'm not clear. Maybe I'm dreaming this whole conversation. "Did you just say you love me?"

"I said I'm going to take the first shift and wake you up at five. You'd better get some sleep. You're delirious."

"That's what I thought."

Virgil turns out the light.

"Virgil?"

No one answers. I close my eyes. I open them. "Virgil?" It's dark and I'm alone. I don't know what just happened. I think I may have dreamed the whole beautiful, terrifying thing.

Addie and Sondra both come on my second night. It's like a sleepover but we watch cows instead of videos. Sondra brings licorice. At least I don't have to do the whole night by myself. We stand rubbing our hands over a fire in a barrel outside the hay barn for a few minutes before we split into shifts. The fire throws our shadows up on the barn wall.

"So did you see anything your first night?" asks Sondra, scooting close to me.

I tie my licorice in a knot in my mouth. "Virgil."

"Virgil came out here with you?" says Addie, shaking her licorice at me. "Oh, the Martins will be scandalized."

"Whatever," I say. "What about you? You've rolled in your share of Martin hay. You're like the family heartbreaker."

Addie says, "That's not funny, KJ. And there wasn't any hay involved. At least not with Will."

"What was involved with Will?" says Sondra. "Because that was weird."

Addie looks at us for few seconds like she's deciding if she can trust us. Then she stares back into the fire. "I made a huge mess of things. As if they weren't bad enough for Will already."

I say, "What's wrong with Will? His leg?"

"No. Yes. Well, you remember how he was before. That whole 'Sure Shot' thing. He was so dedicated. When he lost his scholarship it nearly killed him. One bad rip in his knee and everything he'd worked for was gone. I mean I don't think he even really wants to take over the ranch, and college was his way out. Now the ranch is doing worse than ever and he's like a cornered animal. Just mad at everybody. Having me stir the pot with his brother and then run for cover was a stupid selfish thing to do."

Sondra says, "No offense, Addie. But it seems like William was part of this, too. Didn't he ask you out?"

"Yes. But I'm pretty," says Addie.

Somehow Sondra and I don't laugh out loud.

"Now we all just have our feelings hurt. I guess the heart is a lonely hunter," Addie says with a sigh.

Sondra chomps on her candy. "You know, Addie, that's way too deep for me."

"Me, too," I say. I grab a piece of licorice from Sondra's mitten and put it in my mouth.

Addie says, "Oh, both of you shut up. I'm serious, Will's worse. A lot worse."

"I'm serious, too," says Sondra. "How about we go in the bunkhouse and prevent permanent keister damage?"

I say, "I'll take the first shift. They had some tracks over at the Dennings' place last night and I just want to make sure . . . you know."

"Wake me up when it's spring," says Sondra.

Addie says, "I take back what I said about you, KJ. You're not hostile. You're passionate."

"But not in the hay," I say. "That would be scandalous."

RULES FOR BEING
A RANCHER

Work too hard,
Sleep too little,
Make next to nothing,
Repeat.

30

CAMP DAYS

ON THE SECOND week of being at the Martins' I have a
Friday night shift, so I don't have to go to school the next
morning. Kenner's little sister, Heidi, gets me up for prayer
and coffee at five anyway. I'm starting to like the Martins,
but I could live without their schedule.

"William says I'm a baby," says Heidi while I throw my
clothes on. Heidi is only six, so she likes to follow me around
and tell me things. Even at five in the morning I find her entertaining. "Why does he say that?"

We walk out of the bunkhouse, holding hands. Her hand
is still soft like a baby's. "He says all I do is play with the cats,
and Kenner plays basketball, and Virgil plays with you."

"So we're all babies?"

"He says you're the princess."

"He called me a princess?" This hits a sore spot. I've been covering shifts for everyone since I got here.

"I wish he'd just go back to school like he was going to."

"Why doesn't he?"

She takes her hand away and wipes her nose with the back of her wrist. There's a bruise on her arm the size of a cucumber.

"Where'd you get that, sweetie?"

She looks at it absently, like she's never seen it before. Maybe she's as accident prone as I am, poor thing. The light flickers in the kitchen window, "Oh, shoot, stop talking, KJ! We're going to be late for breakfast."

The Martins are religious about more things than religion. They have a schedule and everybody follows it, even the pagans living in the bunkhouse. That schedule includes sitting around the table, drinking black coffee, and planning the day.

This morning "the menfolk" are all red faced from the cold. They've been up working a while. We sit around the glossy table, and no one talks but Mrs. Martin.

"You see anything last night, Katherine Jean?" says Mrs. Martin.

"Nothing," I say happily.

"Doesn't mean they weren't there," she says. "William

says they're having all kinds of trouble over at the Dennings'. Tracks right up to the back of the house." She hums around the table, pouring and putting things on everyone's plate. I swear she never stops moving, even when she's sitting down.

"Maybe it's working." Quickly I add, "I'd love to learn how you make these cinnamon rolls. My dad would flip if I made them for him."

"Can't think what father would let his pretty young daughter stay alone on a ranch with strange men, but I suppose we all have a different way."

"My dad says your boys are hard workers, Mrs. Martin. He's more worried I'll fall in a hole and shoot myself than anything else."

She lets a smile escape. The she turns back to the menfolk. "You boys fixin' the south fence today?"

Mr. Martin and William nod. William's hair is jumping off his head in eight directions. His eyes are dark on the lids. Kenner's blond head is buried in his arms on the table. Butch and Sundance. I've always been partial to Butch.

"You get your letter for school off yesterday, Will?" says Mrs. Martin.

Will's mild face tightens. "Not much point in that is there. . . ."

She says, "We'll discuss this at dinner."

"You will," he says. His voice is sharp, like the day I heard him smack Kenner by the tree house. Will's a mystery to me. One that keeps getting more interesting.

"Leave it be," says Mr. Martin. He finishes his coffee and looks at me as if it's just occurred to him I exist. "What does your father think about you walking around in the middle of the night freezing to death to save vermin?"

"He's not wild about it."

"Makes about as much sense as leaving grain out for mice."

"I don't like mice much," I say.

"That's a start," says William. He face is mild again and he smiles politely.

I turn to Mrs. Martin and say, "Is there anything I could do to help around here for an hour or two before I go to work? I can do dishes or shovel stalls. I'm not great with mending fences."

Virgil walks through the door without knocking. A gust of cold follows him into the tiny kitchen. He looks as happy as I've ever seen him. He plunks down on the chair next to Heidi and tears into a cinnamon roll.

"What's on the list for today?"

Mrs. Martin smiles at Virgil and sits down to drink her coffee. "You could get Virgil to show you how to do the fences, Katherine Jean. He's a whiz at mending fences."

William bristles and gets up from the table. "Yeah, he's a whiz. Maybe he should show Kenner how to mend them. I'll go warm up the truck."

"Sure," says Mr. Martin. "Be right there."

Virgil hits Kenner to rouse him.

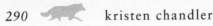

Kenner lifts his head and smacks Virgil back. "Don't they feed you at home anymore?"

"Mom's been over on the other side of the park for three days."

"Who's feeding Jean?" says Mrs. Martin.

"She hasn't finished the soup you sent Monday."

"Three days? I swear," says Mrs. Martin.

"How come you get to swear?" says Heidi.

"Because I've earned it, honey," says Mrs. Martin.

That afternoon I see Will sweeping out his boat. It's early April, not exactly boating weather in Montana. It's a fourteen-foot aluminum clunker he's amped up with a refurbished motor. My dad calls this kind of rig a muscle car on water. But I'll say this for Will: he keeps his boat nicer than most people keep their living room.

"A little early for that, isn't it?" I say. "Unless you're going to park it on the ice."

"You gonna teach me all those secret places your dad stows away his fish this summer?"

"You wish," I say. "Maybe when you teach those calves to stop feeling up us girls with their noses. They're worse than Kenner."

For the first time since I've started working there I hear Will laugh.

By my feet is a bucket full of sponges and sprays. "Can I help you with this?" I say, handing them up.

"All right," he says. He reaches down to get the bucket, but has to twist over the seat to reach it. Suddenly his knee seems to torque in the wrong direction and he pikes forward. He falls down right in front of me but he doesn't make a sound. I jump into the boat.

"Will."

He sits up and drags his legs under him. His face is white.

"Holy smack, Will. Can I help you get out? Or go get someone?"

He pushes himself to standing and puts his weight on his other leg. Then he glowers at me like I pushed him. "Does it make you feel good to feel sorry for me?"

"No," I say.

"Well, that makes two of us. Now could you please get the hell off my boat."

I'm climbing out of the boat as fast as my legs will carry me when Virgil walks into the yard. He says, "You two going fishing?"

"Going home is more like it," I say, walking away. I'm working on four hours of sleep a night, trying to do my homework by lamplight, make my dad happy on top of that, and I'm not in the mood for this anymore.

Virgil walks me to my truck. "Don't let Will get to you. He's having a hard time."

"I know he is," I say. "But you and I haven't slept in weeks. And it's not like I'm sitting around when I'm here. He treats me like I'm a nuisance."

"Would you like Will coming into your store, doing your work?" says Virgil.

I hear Will getting out of his boat. How is he getting out of that boat? He could barely stand up. He'll probably work a full day on that worthless knee.

Virgil says, "Think about what we're doing here. If we can make it through spring without calves getting killed and wolves getting shot, and if we make enough goodwill to keep a few names off that stupid petition, isn't it worth it?"

I tap my foot in the mud. "I'm in for the long haul." What else can I say?

By the third week the group thing starts to fall apart. Sondra gets an ear infection and her mother curtails her camping-out privileges. Addie and Will are not speaking, plus her family needs her at home, so she comes about half the time. Dennis makes three shifts, but the cold gives him nosebleeds. Kenner takes his turn, too, but William now refuses to be part of the whole thing because "it's environmentalist crap." So mostly it is me and Virgil, sometimes secretly together, mostly alone. We don't have any more talks about ruins, and I never get the nerve to ask him about it. We get through a month. I keep up at the store. No one fails school. There are no more fires or broken store windows. There are no wolves in the Martins' pastures.

◇　　◇　　◇

And then something happens. The word gets around. Most of the ranchers in the Madison Valley are reporting sightings; two have lost stock. But the Martins are wolf free. The town paper writes a paragraph about us in the community news, right next to the paragraph about the Bushnells repairing dry rot at their Laundromat. Even Mrs. Baby asks me about our "project." She says she was going to mention it to the principal "on my behalf."

I check the grocery store. The List isn't getting any longer. But the best part is that Mrs. Martin has put a big black line through her name.

JOKE TO TELL WHEN EATING
WITH THE MARTINS AND VIRGIL

Two rabbits were being chased by a pack of
wolves. The wolves chased the rabbits into
a thicket. After a few minutes, one rabbit
turned to the other and said, "Well, do you
want to make a run for it or stay here a few
days and outnumber them?"

JOKE TO TELL TO VIRGIL
THE NEXT DAY AT SCHOOL

Q: How many vegans does it take
to change a lightbulb?
A: Two, one to change it and one to
check for animal ingredients.

31

HUMAN INTERESTS

MRS. BABY COMES in at half past. We all do a double take. She smiles at us nonchalantly. She's wearing makeup, a suit coat, and double wide high heels. "Class, I have someone I'd like you to meet."

In walks a guy I swear I've seen before. He grins at us all and I realize he has a smile just like Baby's. "It's a pleasure," he says in a baritone voice.

"Class," says Mrs. Baby. "This is my brother, David Sand-castle. Maybe you've seen him on the ten o'clock news."

Stewie and Bret stop talking to each other.

"Wow," says Clint. "It's the Sandman."

He says, "And which of you lucky kids are Virgil and KJ?"

Mrs. Baby says, "I know this is a big surprise, but I mentioned your wolf experiment to my brother, and he would like to interview you, you know about the success you've had out at the Martins'."

"I've been following the wolf referendum for the station. Your experiment is a great human interest story."

Virgil isn't here yet. Addie, Dennis, and Sondra are all looking at me.

"Mrs. Brady," I say as politely as I can. "May I see you outside?"

Once we are in the hall I say, "Aren't you going to get in trouble for this?"

"Actually the principal is thrilled. He says it will be an honor to have our school represented by such enterprising students."

"What about Addie, Sondra, and Dennis? They helped."

"He can't interview everyone."

"Have you talked to our parents? And the Martins?"

"Spoke with everyone just minutes ago. Your dad wasn't very excited. But I knew you'd be glad. This is a great way to show people that they shouldn't vote against the wolves. That there are ways to live with them nonviolently."

"But you weren't even paying attention to this a few weeks ago. Who have you been talking to?" I say.

"A journalist never reveals her sources."

"You're a home ec teacher."

"I beg your pardon."

"I'm sorry. I don't want to cause trouble again."

"No trouble. We're just going to meet everyone out at the Martins right now. Where's Virgil? His mom said he was on his way."

"Virgil isn't going to like it."

"Nonsense," says Mrs. Brady.

"Exactly."

Virgil shows up at the Martins' with Eloise. He looks like he hasn't had his tea. "Whose idea was this?" he snaps.

I say, "Don't look at me. I was ambushed."

Mr. and Mrs. Martin actually seem kind of happy, in a nervous sort of way. They show the TV crew around the ranch. Mr. Sandcastle assures the Martins that this interview is going to be good for the town, tourism, and the ranching industry. Just hearing him say that makes my skin crawl.

Mr. Sandcastle seems to be particularly fond of putting me in the middle of Virgil and Kenner, then siccing a camera on us. I'm particularly fond of the moment when a cow blows snot on Mr. Sandcastle.

After it's over I ask Heidi where Will is. She says, "He told Dad letting that guy take pictures for the news was like making a commercial for wolves. Dad didn't like that very much, so Will left."

The spot goes on the evening news that night. It lasts less than a minute. I have a piece of hair blowing up in the wind the whole time. Afterward the anchor says, "It's great to see kids making a difference."

Dad stands up from the couch and pats me on the shoulder. "That ought to generate some discourse."

He goes into the kitchen and starts moving things around under the sink.

"What are you doing?" I say.

He pulls out a fire extinguisher. "Nothing."

A wolf is fed by its feet.

Russian Proverb

32

COWBOY SONGS

MRS. MARTIN INVITES us all to take marshmallows and popcorn out to the barbecue pit and have a little celebration for six weeks with no wolves. They've had a phone call from just about every person they have ever known to say they saw them on TV. My dad's had a flood of phone calls, too, which is great for business because more than a few book a guide trip. But my favorite call was the Wyoming soap company that asked my dad if I wanted to be in their Milk Face commercials. He told them no.

The whole thing is completely ridiculous, except the part where people hear that there are ways to make this work. Even kids can do it . . . if they don't mind going without heat and sleep. Maybe it will make people think twice before they sign a petition to get rid of the wolves if they think they can have their wolves and the cattle won't be eaten, too. A commercial for wolves, just like Will said.

Will isn't speaking to anyone in his family, not even the dog.

Kenner holds the popcorn over the fire with a clamp they use to tag the stock. We all sit close to each other because it's freezing and we like to. Kenner sits next to Addie but he doesn't push the issue, which is nice. Someone makes the obligatory joke about smoke following beauty. If that were true Virgil would never get a break, especially not tonight.

I doze to the blending sounds of the fire, Sondra's bad guitar, and Dennis's recital about the stars being in alignment for something. Everything that happens in this moment is real and gone as quickly as it happens, except for Virgil. For me, time moves around him like the smoke.

I listen to the cattle, too. I guess they're lowing. It's a warm, comforting sound. The sky is bitter cold but clear. So many stars. On a night like tonight it's good to be irrelevant to the universe and still a piece of it. Maybe that's the magic of the Martins' place. You start to think you belong here.

Virgil puts his arm around me. "You look beautiful tonight," he says. Everyone hears him.

"Geez, Virgil, I just ate," says Kenner.

Sondra keeps strumming the chorus to "Sweet Baby James."

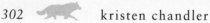

"What else do you play?" says Addie. "How about 'Streets of Laredo'? My dad sings that when we make a fire."

"I don't sing songs that glorify violence," says Sondra.

"Well, that cuts out about every cowboy song ever written," says Kenner.

"How about 'This Land Is Your Land,'" says Sondra. "I know most of that."

"That's not a cowboy song," says Kenner.

Dennis says, "How about 'Wanted Dead or Alive' by Bon Jovi."

Kenner takes the guitar from Sondra and strums. I think he's faking. Then he says, "This is one my dad taught me.

"The range's filled up with farmers and there's fences
ev'rywhere.
A painted house 'most ev'ry quarter mile.
They're raisin' blooded cattle and plantin' sorted seed
And puttin' on a painful lot o' style.

There hain't no grass to speak of and the water holes
are gone.
The wire of the farmer holds 'em tight.
There's little use to law 'em and little use to kick
And mighty sight less use there is to fight.

There's them coughin' separators and their dirty,
dusty crews

And wagons runnin' over with the grain
With smoke a-driftin' upward and writin' on the air
A story that to me is mighty plain.

The wolves have left the country and the longhorns
are no more
And all the game worth shootin' at is gone.
And it's time for me to foller, 'cause I'm only in the way
And I've got to be a-movin'—movin' on."

His voice dips to the last note and then disappears. No one says anything. Kenner laughs and hands Sondra back her guitar. "That's a cowboy song."

"Geez, Kenner, I just ate," says Virgil.

Those Martin boys. They're full of surprises.

33

CRYING WOLF

IT'S ONE O'CLOCK and Virgil isn't here. It's the end of April and all the teachers are binge testing. We both have a math test in the morning and I threatened Virgil with his life if he didn't get some sleep. I'll be tired tomorrow, too, but at least I've studied. For the last two days he's barely stayed awake long enough to answer the roll.

The snow is muddy tonight. We've had a warm snap. It's almost warm enough to be pleasant. I stand at the gate by the barn and listen to the sloshing of the cattle. I'm ready for a snooze, but I'm too tired to walk across the yard to go inside. I lean against the fence post and close my eyes.

I wake up when I hear cows bawling in the far pasture.

I listen for Virgil's voice but hear only cows complaining. I am about to turn on my flashlight when I decide it's time for a little payback. I wonder how I can get out there and get behind him without him hearing my feet.

I stand perfectly still, trying to see into the dark. The bawling is loud. They sound like they're moving around a lot. I start walking.

My boots splash in the mud so I give up trying to be sneaky. "Virgil," I call as I walk. I can't believe Virgil came out here after I told him not to. I look through the darkness. All I hear is moving cows. I wonder absently, *Why are they moving so much?* Then suddenly my brain wakes up.

I run.

When I get to the pasture all the cows are on one side of the pen. I shine the spotlight out and catch the three shadows on the opposite side of the pasture. I see their long, thin haunches in a circle. One turns and I see teeth. Teeth and reflecting eyes. I also see the carcasses at their feet.

I yell, "No! No!" The wolves go back to eating. They aren't even bothered by me. I pull around my shotgun. I try to aim. I can't hold my arm steady. I lift my gun and fire up into the empty sky three times, one for each wolf. The wolves disappear like smoke.

I turn around, soundless. I can see the lights come on in the Martins' kitchen. I turn the light back on the two dead cows. They're torn to pieces. Everything is torn to pieces.

34

COLLATERAL DAMAGE

I ANSWER A lot of questions, for a lot of people. The Fish and Wildlife people grill me in front of the Martins like I'm an ecoterrorist. The answers boil down to this: I fell asleep, the cows were already dead when I got there, and, no, I didn't let the wolves kill the cows on purpose.

That afternoon I go back to school and take my math test. I know if I fail this test I'm failing his class. Mr. Muir asks me if I want to stick around after all the other kids leave. I can't tell him too much because I'll start to bawl. He grades my test but doesn't give it back to me. "Go home. We'll figure this out tomorrow."

The next day Ed Buck's men come in. The three wolves are tracked down and shot. There are two pups with them that are also "accidentally" shot.

Now we're the real news. Papers in Montana, Wyoming, and Idaho run pictures of Virgil, Kenner, and me. The Billings and Bozeman papers both run editorials talking about the wolf referendum and the management crisis. They describe the shooting, the vandalism, the fire, and last, but not least, some young people's "naive, misguided, idealism" in pursuit of a "feel-good solution."

The Internet picks the story up. Pro-wolf and anti-wolf Web sites. Liberal and conservative Web sites. People-with-nothing-better-to-do Web sites. Joss and Mandy forward a link to an inventive picture of me holding bleeding wolf pups, with the caption "Blood on Her Hands." I unplug my computer.

I'm an example of all that's wrong with the environmental movement, teenagers, and America. Maybe I can get a recording contract.

Mr. Martin calls Virgil. We're not invited to come back.

Virgil and I sit next to each other in every class, but we don't talk. Addie, Sondra, and Dennis don't talk much either. Kenner ignores us. His friends aren't so quiet. They chuck notes in class, and Road Work asks me if I'd like go hunting with him and his friends after school. Joss and Mandy offer to buy me a new flashlight. I see Virgil getting shoved at lunch. A girl I barely know bumps me in the hall, completely by accident of course, and knocks my books out of my arms. Addie's old friends won't speak to her. The typical shunning. I wouldn't care, except it reminds me of what I have done.

My friends stick together. But we walk around with an invisible boundary between us and the other kids at school. We tried to do something a different way. We wrote the paper and then we made the paper. Now we are like the United States of Failure.

At home Dad doesn't say a thing.

He doesn't put away the fire extinguisher either.

Wolves and livestock don't mix. That's the reason they were eradicated back when. It's nice to say that maybe they will learn to coexist. And that can happen for a day or two, or a year, whatever. Wolves mean dead livestock. And that means out of our pocket when you have dead livestock.

Martin Davis, fourth-generation rancher,
Paradise Valley

35

SEEING IN THE DARK

WHEN I WALK into Dad's room he rolls over and looks at me wide-eyed. I say, "I can't sleep."

"Why not?" he says.

"I need some fresh air."

"Open a window."

"I need to walk."

"I need to sleep."

"So sleep," I say.

"Wait," he says. "Do you want to talk?"

"Not really."

"Don't be gone too long. . . ." he says, and rolls back over in bed.

I grab some things and head out in the dark. It's early May so it's still freezing at night, even though the snow has melted in the valleys. I start for the tree house. When I get there I keep going. I have to keep moving.

The petition vote is a week away. If it passes, the wolves' presence will be weighed in the balance again. The voters will decide if they think the Wolf Reintroduction Project is working and then Washington will decide if they agree.

If wolves are taken off the Endangered Species Act the states will be in charge of what happens. The states will have the option to let people hunt wolves everywhere outside the park. Maybe even inside the park. If wolves can be shot on sight they won't last long. Weapons have improved a lot since the wolves were wiped out last time.

My feet are heavy. I walk into the park along the river. The steam from the black water hangs at the banks. I listen for life but I can hear only the river, gorged with winter runoff.

I start thinking of all the ways there are to die of stupidity in Yellowstone. Certainly walking alone at night when winter-starved bears, buffalo, and moose are knocking about has got to be up there in the top ten. My problems ought to be solved within an hour or two.

I wonder about the lone wolf I saw this winter. I know she or he has to be dead or gone, yet I can't help but hope that I could catch a glimpse or hear this wolf one last time. I leave

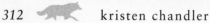

the river path and head into the foothills, then veer toward the mountain ridge. It feels good just to walk.

My bearings get less dependable, and when I see a stray dirt road below me I walk toward it. The night is diluting into gray. The returning birds chatter in the pines. I can smell the boggy grass in the marshes below me. Despite my best efforts, no animal gores, gouges, or gobbles me up.

Then I see the truck, William's Frankenstein truck, idling in the middle of the dirt road with the driver's door swinging open. This is a long way from the ranch and an unlikely hour to be working, even for William.

The hair on my arm stands up. I step softly as I make my way toward the truck.

First I see Will's black work jacket and beanie. As I get closer I see his breath floating upward. He's breathing hard. He half buries something in the ground that looks like game and then hunches over three different bushes doing something with his hands. Something horrible.

He's setting snares.

Does he know what those things do? *Of course he does,* I tell myself. *That's why he's doing it.* So the wolf, coyote, or dog that comes for that meat will stick its head into one of those snares and then slowly, painfully choke itself to death in piano wire.

The smart thing to do would be to wait until he's gone and take down the snares. "Hey, Will," I call casually.

He startles. "Hey, what's up, KJ?"

"Yeah, what's up?"

"Not much," he says picking up his shovel.

I feel the blood in my face. I say, "You can go to jail for that."

He shakes the dirt off his shovel. "Wolves are out of style, haven't you heard?"

I walk to one of the bushes and pull the line with my hand. It's woven into the sticks of the bush, ready for a fight. "These . . . it takes up to an hour for an animal to suffocate." I can't find words I'm so angry.

"Yep," he says. His eyes narrow in on me.

"It's also illegal."

"What are you going to do about it? Tell your friend at Fish and Wildlife? He actually liked blowing those wolves away. Get your newscaster buddy out here? I don't think he's interviewing screwups today."

I grab the snare out of the bush by pulling up instead of back. It comes loose but leaves a red line on my hand. I make a fist and shake the line at Will. "You are setting snares *inside* the park. No matter what happens with the petition, it's still going to be against the law to trap wolves in the park."

He voice rattles. "Whose law? Is it anything I have any vote about?"

"Will. What are you talking about?" I know Will hates the wolves, but this is crazy. You just never think someone who has passed you the butter would set up animal torture devices.

He stands with his arms crossed against his chest. "Don't I have the right to protect my home, to stop these creatures from spreading into my territory?"

"Not like this. It's against the law."

He reaches down and picks up his shovel. He says, "Sometimes the laws are wrong. I have the right to keep my family safe."

"Strangling wolves isn't taking care of your family, it's sadistic." Then something ugly occurs to me, and it's out of my mouth like bad milk. "What else have you done?"

He taps the shovel lightly in his hands. He says, "You're a self-righteous baby, KJ. You play games that hurt people and sometimes people will hurt you back."

"Will, you aren't like this."

"What am I like, KJ? You and Addie figure that out?"

Will gracefully lifts the shovel to his shoulder like a bat. I feel my stomach come up in my throat. He says, "Swing, batter-batter." He swings the shovel and I jump. The shovel doesn't even come close to me, especially since I've jumped about ten feet in the other direction. He laughs. I'm ridiculous.

"What's wrong with you?" I say, shaking all over.

He says, "Turns out, that's a pretty long list." Then he walks over to the bait he's put out for the wolves. He digs it out of the ground. "But there are some advantages to being me. I know there are things a lot scarier than getting hurt. Like watching your family's business die. Like watching someone you care about get hurt. You got the stomach for that?"

"What's that supposed to mean?" I say. Is he talking about his family or mine?

He carries the bait back to the truck and drops it into the bed. It lands with a wet thud. He says, "Have a nice day, princess." He climbs into his crappy old truck and drives away. The engine lags and then pops. Just like a fart. Just the way Dad described it.

As surely as any pullet in the yard, I was a target,
and I had better respect what had me in its sights.

Wallace Stegner, *Where the Bluebird Sings*
to the Lemonade Springs

36

RIGHTS OF SPRING

"WHERE HAVE YOU been?" Dad says to me when I walk in the door.

"On a walk. I woke you up and told you when I left."

"You did?"

"Yes, I did," I say, dropping into a chair.

"How long you been gone?" Dad has felt sorry for me since I got the cattle and wolves killed at the Martins' but he's still nursing a bad ear, a business in the red, and a grudge against Virgil. I can't say as I blame him.

"I don't know," I say. I walk past him into the bathroom and close the door. I wash the cuts in my hands. It was hard to get the three snares out without tools, especially since I was so mad I couldn't think straight after Will left.

I go out to the table and hand Dad a roll of adhesive bandage. "Can you wrap them?"

He looks at my hands and then at me. "What happened?"

"You aren't going to like it."

He inspects the front and back of each hand. "So what else is new?"

"Tell me again what the backfire sounded like on the truck you heard the night of the fire."

Dad's face tightens. "You're right. I'm not going to like it."

"Tell me," I say.

"It had a chug delay and then a backfire. A lot of trucks have that."

"I ran into Will setting snares with bait, inside the park."

"Snares?" Dad isn't in love with wolves right now but I know what he thinks about snares. And the kind of people who set them. Then he catches up to what I'm getting at. He grimaces. "What does this have to do with the fire?"

"You should have seen him, Dad. He said he was protecting his family, that he had the right to protect them any way he needed to." I leave out the part about Will swinging a shovel to scare me and then threatening to hurt "someone I care about."

"It's wrong but it still doesn't light a match," says Dad, the attorney.

"He was driving that old truck of his. I've never heard it before. But it's distinctive."

"So you just assume that because he's illegally setting snares and he has an old truck that backfires he's the one. KJ, I've taught you better than that."

"You *have* taught me, Dad. You've taught me to listen to my instincts. You've taught me never to back off when you know you're right. This time I'm right. And I'm not backing down."

"You have nothing, KJ. A hunch. From the look of your hands you don't even have the snares anymore."

"But you could identify the sound of his truck, right? It doesn't sound like other trucks."

"Of course not. KJ, listen to yourself. You have nothing but wounded pride. And if you start spreading it around without proof . . ."

"This has nothing to do with my pride."

Dad keeps wrapping, tighter and tighter. He says, "I think it does. And your obsession with Virgil."

I yank my hand back and the tape tears. "Dad! You aren't listening to me! Will started the fire, and even if he didn't mean for you to be there, you could have died. He's dangerous."

Dad throws the adhesive tape on the countertop and

walks in a half circle. He comes back to me with his finger shaking in my face. "I have listened. I have listened until I'm blue in the face. You are going to listen to me for a change. This is so far over the line. . . . You are to say nothing about this to anyone, least of all Virgil and Eloise. You are going to stay in this house, do your homework, work at the store, and keep out of the Martins' way."

I shove his wagging finger away from me. "And when this petition passes? When it's legal for people like Will to start blasting wolves all over kingdom come?"

"They are animals, KJ! Grow up," he yells.

"You won't let me, Dad." I walk to my room and close the door.

I wait until I hear the front door slam and then I call Virgil.

He says, "The road opened through the park today."

"How soon can you be here?" I say.

"What should I bring?"

"A sleeping bag."

Virgil pauses and then says, "I thought you'd never ask."

I don't pack much. I can't think that far ahead.

I should clean myself up. But all I can think about is how furious I am. I stumble around my room and find a hair-brush. I take off my shirt and put on a less dirty sweatshirt over the top of a bra that my aunt gave me before I actually had breasts. I stare into the mirror. I have bags under my eyes so dark I look like a prize fighter.

I check the Internet for wolf activity. Pups have been sighted for numbers Forty, Forty-Two, and one other beta female. For Forty-Two's sake this is bad news. This might be the end of Cinderella. And it's not the happy ending either. If I let myself think about it my head will fall off.

Virgil gets to my house in a hurry. He acts nervous when he comes to the door. His hair's a mess. The collar on his T-shirt is frayed. He stands sideways and keeps his hands in his pockets, squinting in the harsh spring sunshine. "Ready?"

"Ready," I say, throwing on my pack.

He smiles and lights up the doorway. He says, "Did you know that you're beautiful?"

We take Jean's Cadillac. We don't talk much until we get to Madison Junction. I don't tell him about William. I just want to drive and be with Virgil for a while.

There are migrating bison all over the roads. Little orange babies wriggling along after their mothers. Prehistoric papas block traffic as if it didn't exist. Canada geese squawk along the river's banks preening in the new grass while a brace of ducks float tails-up down the river. It's America's best spring parade.

"Is your dad okay with this?" Virgil says lightly.

"No."

Virgil slows for a stray calf. "So I'm going to get arrested?"

"Do you mind?"

Virgil doesn't smile. "Tell me what's going on, when you're ready."

As we weave up past Gibbon Falls, I watch the mountain fall away from my side of the road. I feel carsick. Dad will be coming home soon for lunch and when he sees I'm gone Eloise is going to get a phone call.

We stop in Mammoth for gas. Elk are everywhere, feeding on the Forest Services' domestic grass buffet. I call my house and leave a message. "I'm with Virgil. No hanky-panky, I just need some time. I'll call in the morning."

When I get back to the car Virgil grins. "Have I ever told you how much I enjoy getting in trouble with you?"

"This ought to be your kind of weekend then."

We don't hurry. We stop with three other vehicles to see a black bear yearling digging around near the Petrified Tree. A coyote jogs along a hill just before the Tower-Roosevelt turn-off. I drive for a while. Virgil takes pictures of everything but seems obsessed with wildflowers. He kisses my arm. Everything is waking up, including me.

"Virgil," I say. "What if you know something horrible about a person who isn't always horrible?"

"Your dad is a pain in the butt, KJ, but I wouldn't call him horrible."

"Not my dad. What if you are going to cause bad stuff in order to stop that person from being so awful . . . but if you don't other people might . . ."

"I'm not so good at hypothetical."

I say, "Can I have the licorice your mom sent?"

My mind circles back to Cinderella. I tell Virgil about what I read on the Internet.

"Maybe they'll just kick her out," Virgil says.

"That's how it works, I guess." I say. "Payback's an alpha female."

At last we drive into the Lamar Valley. I roll down the window and let the cold air blow my foggy thoughts out of the truck. The smell of pine fills the car. In spite of everything, the space in this open range makes space in me, for things that are still possible. The snow blankets the higher ground, but the plain is sprouting life. The buffalo are here en masse, gorging on the new grass while their calves charge in all directions. Elk lounge in the lodgepole. Eagles and ospreys perch in groups. Cranes and herons crisscross the sky while pronghorn dart in the meadows. The Serengeti of the West is in full swing.

When we turn at Slough Creek I feel the old excitement. We drive up to the campground on the gravel road. A solitary man stands on Dave's Hill as we pass. We recognize him and stop to ask what he's seen.

"Didn't see it myself but I just heard that mean old

Number Forty kicked the stuffing out of Number Forty-Two tonight. Getting too hard to see anything now, but I heard it was a bad one."

"Did Cinderella, I mean number Forty-Two, get up?"

"Yeah she got up, but she crawled off to her den on her belly. Getting ugly up there, ain't it?"

I thank him politely. I wonder if the wolves have any idea how entertaining their misery is to our species.

As we're leaving the man says, "Hey, did I see you two on the news the other day?"

Virgil says, "Must have been somebody else."

By the time we set up camp and eat it's nearly dark. Slough Creek is bear central so we don't cook anything, and we put everything edible—but us—in the car. We sit close to the fire and each other to stay warm. I can't stop my brain from looping around about William and my dad. What if William tries something again when I'm not there? What if I'm exaggerating this whole thing? Who did he mean by "someone I care about"?

Virgil says, "So are you going to tell me or what?"

I take a deep breath. "I saw William setting snares inside the park. When he drove off, his truck made a noise like the one my dad described the night of the fire."

"It backfired?" says Virgil. "Huh. I never thought of that." He looks like I just told him Will has a bad haircut.

"Did you get the part about the snares? Choking wolves to

death inside the park? I've had this conversation with my dad already. It's not just the backfire, which, by the way, sounds disgustingly distinctive. It's the way William acted. The way he talked about his 'rights' . . . and the way he wields his trusty shovel."

"His shovel? Did he hurt you?" says Virgil.

I explain about batting practice and Will's threats. Then I tell him about my dad, and how he thinks the solution to everything is to stick me in a pumpkin shell and there he'll keep me very well. I say, "William wants to hurt things. Even Heidi said she wished he'd go back to school."

"That's why he can't go back to school, KJ. He's got problems. And it's not his knee. He's made up his mind that the wolves are the reason the ranch is losing money and he's stuck there."

"Exactly. And the worst part is I've helped him do it. I've made the wolves a scapegoat for the whole town. Every time I screwed up I gave normal people a reason to hate everything wolves stand for. I'm the perfect diversion."

"West End can be a mean little town. Why do you blame yourself for that?"

"Because it's *my* mean little town."

Virgil blows into his hands, then holds them over the fire. "You could leave."

I stir my stick in the embers. The ashes flutter up and make my eyes blur. "Right. And go where?"

"Minnesota has a hog festival in June."

I laugh like I'm choking. "A hog festival?"

"In the fall you could finish up at my school. They'd love you on the newspaper back there."

I stop stirring. "Minnesota? And what about my dad?"

"You're leaving in a year anyway. Your dad would probably be relieved to have you far away from all this junk."

The idea of leaving all this trouble behind . . . I know it's impossible but it sounds so good right now. Of course my dad won't go for me shacking up with Virgil. He's liable to come shoot Virgil in his sleep just for tonight.

Virgil goes to his sleeping bag. He takes off his boots and then his shirt and then his pants. His boxers are taxi yellow. Everything about his body is real and beautiful.

"What are you doing?" I say.

"I'm cold." He shrugs and climbs inside his bag. "You should try it."

"My dad warned me all you wanted to do was take my shirt off."

"I took *my* shirt off." Virgil props up on his elbow. "Is that what you think?"

"I think you're not a big fan of clothes, on anyone."

"True. But you're not anyone to me. I want you to come with me to Minnesota. With or without your shirt."

I take off my shoes and then climb into my bag. I unzip my jeans. I writhe inside my bag like a pubescent caterpillar. My head pounds. Minnesota. I'd start to eat pig's knuckles and talk like Virgil. Could I really leave? Could I do that? By the time my jeans are off I'm nearly sweating. I put my head out. "Yeah, I'm warmer."

"It works better if our bags are right next to each other," he says. "Well, it actually works best if you're in my bag, but I don't think that's a good idea tonight. You might take advantage of me."

I scoot closer to Virgil and then lie on my back and look up at the sky. There are a lot of other places to live besides this postage stamp in the middle of nowhere. Of course my dad won't let me. But I'm more trouble than I'm worth now. He gets new guides in a week. He could just hire one extra. I could finish high school without the scarlet W on my chest. And I'd be living with Virgil. We could get into the same college and then be this amazing wildlife team that travels all over the world. We could have our own television show and action figures. "This summer?"

"I don't think we should wait until summer." Virgil rolls around in his bag. He looks nervous again. "I should have told you."

Not words I want to hear. "Told me what?"

Virgil pulls his bag up under his arms like a towel. I can see his goose-bumpy shoulders in the light of the fire. "A few weeks ago Kenner told me that he thinks that Will shot at the ice sculpture in the parade. Kenner said he felt bad because he was the one that told William about the rumor that Dennis and I were making a float. William volunteered to work at the staging area and he would have seen the Cadillac and had time to get up on a rooftop. The Steak House has a ladder that would have made it easy. Kenner said he asked Will about it after. Will said, 'Freedom of expression goes both ways.'"

"Freedom of expression?"

"Yeah. Exactly. The next morning I went out and took pictures of the tires on the old truck Will keeps behind the barn."

"Frankenstein? Let me guess, they match the pictures you took by the Dumpster at the fire."

"They're a little skinnier than usual and they make a funny tread. I looked them up. Ford made 'em like that in the early thirties but then they changed them after the war. So it's pretty convincing."

"Convincing! I can't believe you!" I say. "You knew Will nearly killed my dad and you kept working there?"

"That's why I worked there, sort of. After the fire, I thought the best way to deal with all the hysteria in town was to spend time with the people who were the most angry, and the Martins seemed like they were at the top of the list—literally. I didn't figure out that Will set the fire until Kenner told me about the parade. But by then Will seemed to be doing so much better. I thought if I told you, you'd flip out."

Good guess.

Virgil shakes his head. "This has gotten completely out of hand. We've pushed him off the deep end."

"Now who's taking someone else's blame? Will's cuckoo all by himself."

"Sure he's messed up, but don't you see how we've helped? His family trusted us and we got their stock killed and made them the joke of every ranch from here to North Dakota. Do you think people will run their cattle on their pastures now?"

"Are you serious? You think this is all our fault?"

He talks faster. "I think it's time to leave."

"You're leaving? School's not even over."

"I don't care about school. Everyone needs some time to cool off."

"Come on, Virgil. Will needs a whole lot more than a time-out."

"Eloise will be fine with you coming to Saint Paul if your dad says yes."

"Does she know . . . about Will?"

Virgil shakes his head. "Are you kidding?"

We're excruciatingly silent. I close my eyes but I can still see the pinpricks of stars inside my lids. Across the air comes the sound of howling. Three short yips and a long call. It's close.

The sound calls something back to me. I sit up. "I can't just leave. You can't leave either. We have to go back and tell the police."

Virgil looks up at me. "Tell them what? No one will believe *us*. It will just make a bigger wedge between you and your dad and the town. And the Martins will be torn apart."

I try not to raise my voice but I can't help it. "So what? Will did it!"

He shoves his hand through his hair. "Nobody wins if you go after Will."

"Nobody wins if I don't. I saw a bruise, Virgil . . . on Heidi's arm."

"Stop it, KJ. In all the things that Will's done he's never intentionally hurt anybody. Kids get bruises."

"Sometimes they do," I say.

A wolf yips and howls again.

I listen and then I try to listen to myself. "And sometimes . . . sometimes you have to bust some heads."

A solitary howl floats across the valley.

"What do you do with the heads once they're busted?" says Virgil.

My voice raises again. "You can't yoga your way out of everything."

"Is that what you think of me?"

"What do you think of me? What kind of a person can leave her dad and just hope he doesn't get nailed by the local whack job? What kind of person looks the other way while people go around torturing animals? And maybe kids?"

Another wolf returns the call, with a long deep howl.

"I'll take you back in the morning," he says. "Then I'm out of here."

"You have to tell the police."

He says, "I should never have told you."

I roll over and close my eyes until they leak.

A while later I drift off. I have my old dream about wolves. A pack of seven or eight. I'm human so I kick at them and throw my fists. They rip and swallow whole pieces of me but I don't die and I can't escape. I just keep fighting.

I wake up to the sound of a wolf whining.

"Hey, knock it off," says Virgil.

"What?" I whisper.

"You kicked me."

"Sorry."

The whining comes again but fainter. There are no corresponding calls like last night. Something's wrong. I look at my watch. It's four thirty.

"Let's go," I say, nudging him.

"Go where?" Virgil says.

I reach around for my two-way radio and turn it on to the station Eloise uses. If there's something going on with the wolves the Wolf Mafia will be talking about it. Virgil stays in his bag. I listen while I pull on my clothes and roll up my stuff. I hear static and people jabbering with excited voices. Then I hear Eloise's voice. ". . . Specimen Ridge."

Virgil sits up. He grabs the radio and adjusts the dial.

From the speaker a man's voice says, "Wounded wolf. It's

staggering. I can't see who it is. We need somebody fast."

There is flurry of people trying to cut in and then we hear Eloise again. "Wolf down. Collared. Not sure which . . . Right off the road, in the ditch off by Specimen. It's not moving."

Voices clamor over the radio to identify the wolf. Each collared wolf has an individual frequency it emits when its mortality signs indicate death.

A voice on the radio says, "Maybe Number Thirty-Four, sounds like his signal."

Eloise says, "It's not Thirty-Four. Too far from home."

Another voice says, "Has to be a Druid. As far as we know, they were the only pack in this area last night."

I feel sick. "It's Cinderella. Forty's killed her."

Over the radio Eloise says, "Forty was spotted at Forty-Two's den last night. Forty-Two had One Hundred Three and One Hundred Six with her, but it doesn't sound good."

"It's her." I kick dirt on the fire.

"I'll start the car," says Virgil.

After driving a few long painful minutes, we pull into the gathering congestion and hike down the road to the ditch. The sun's starting to come up. In the center of the crowd is a man I recognize as Mitch Tanner, the head biologist in charge of the reintroduction. He waves his arm across the crowd and it hushes instantly. "Everybody, we've got an injured animal down here. Could we get you to stand back?"

Someone yells, "Who is it, Mitch?"

Smith pauses. The dread inside of me makes it hard to hear. He says, "I'm afraid it's number Forty and she's in bad shape."

There is a communal gasp.

Number Forty? Not Forty-Two, but Forty.

"Well, what do you know?" says Eloise. "Cinderella grew some teeth."

I follow Eloise and Virgil into the coats and bodies, but I can't keep up. I am buried in parkas. I keep moving forward, pushing through the crowd. I fight the panic that is swelling up inside me. When I reach the front, I see Mitch Tanner, Eloise, and two rangers, inspecting the body. The ranger's hands are covered in blood.

A ranger has been posted to keep everyone else back. I wait until his back is turned and then get close enough to see giant gouges on the wolf's shoulder and stomach. Parts of her head and face are ripped wide-open.

An olive sleeve grabs my shoulder. "We need you to move back, miss. For your own safety."

I glare at him. "She's not going to hurt anybody. She's dead."

He tips back his green hat with the perky tassel. "Nobody said that."

"What are they doing?"

"I'm afraid you're going to have to step back now."

"If she's not dead, why don't they take her in?"

"Miss. They're doing everything they can. In most cases we just let nature take its course."

Something loud is ringing in my brain but the sound is too loud for me to hear. I feel Virgil standing next to me. I notice that people are staring not at the wolf but at me. Eloise looks over. Virgil takes my hand and pulls me close. "Let's get out of here."

The ranger gives him a sympathetic nod, like I'm having a seizure.

Tanner and his crew slide a small tarp under the wolf and wrap up her body. The cleanup is quick and efficient.

Tanner carries Forty to his truck, and gently places her on the front seat, as if she's alive, and then gets in with one of his olive sidekicks. He gives the crowd a pacifying wave. The truck pulls out fast with a siren twisting on its roof, winding past the mess of cars parked in the road.

Virgil and I walk through the crowd. Phrases float around me.

"Did you see how they gutted her?"

"Do you think she'll make it?"

"Not a prayer."

"Hey, aren't those the kids on the news?"

I want to yell at these people. This isn't a television show; it's real life. Virgil grips my hand so tight I can't feel it. He practically shoves me in the car.

"Are you okay?" he says.

"They ripped her face off."

"Wolves are thorough."

"She was the alpha, with pups. Wolves don't do that."

Virgil starts the car, "I've never seen it before. But the pack probably just got sick of Forty's abuse. When she came to Cinderella's den, Cinderella and the others had a chance and they took it. They busted some heads."

"And what if they hadn't?" I shoot back.

The scar on Virgil's perfect cheek is red. "They're wolves. Do you get that? That's how wolves are. *You* don't have to be like that."

"I'm not."

Virgil pulls the car over sharply to the side of road and nearly hits a fat man coming out of his Winnebago. Virgil grabs my arm hard. He's not Gandhi now. "I'm not kidding. It will only make it worse. Why don't you get that?"

He puts both arms around me, crowding out everything but him. Everything is jerking and spinning inside of me. I pull away and stare him in the face. It's like when I looked at the wolf, only different. I see him and I see myself. I see that I'm wrong and so is he. In that moment I know there is a place between fighting and backing away, a place that transcends fear and creates the possibility of change. It's the very same place in me where I love Virgil. I bury my head in Virgil's coat. I stop spinning. I am perfectly quiet in his arms.

I'm not afraid to love Virgil anymore. But I can't let that be my reason for what I do next.

Fear makes the wolf bigger than he is.

German Proverb

37

THE BIG BAD WOLF

WE DRIVE WITHOUT talking for three hours. I don't believe he can leave. I've lived in this town all of my life, and now after nine months I can't imagine West End without Virgil.

I ask him to drop me in the street in case my dad is inside, waiting with a Smith & Wesson. Virgil parks by the curb and we roll the windows down. I don't know why. Down the street a tour bus rolls past. The tourists are starting to come back. I hear a dog barking. It's only mid-morning but it feels like this day has lasted my whole life.

Finally I say, "It'll probably be good to get back to Minnesota."

"Not really."

"So stay."

He turns his head away from me. "I'm going to miss you, Wolf Girl."

If I say good-bye to Virgil my face will melt.

I get my bag out of the back and put it by the side of the road. He gets out of the car and stands next to me. He takes my hand and rubs it. Honestly those hands should be registered as lethal weapons with intent to brainwash. I take my hand back.

We stand in the street. Both of our faces start melting.

"Sometimes the bravest thing you can do is walk away," he says.

I say, "Sometimes it isn't."

He gets in his car and drives away.

I need to go in my room and collapse until next spring. But I don't.

My dad isn't home, the car is, and he's left the keys hanging on the ring. The odds of this suggest I've used up all my good luck for the day. I leave my dad a note. "Gone to Martins. Be back soon." I hope I'm telling the truth.

I try to sound natural. "Hey, Kenner."

"Hey," says Kenner. For some reason he smiles at me.

Heidi is jumping all over me. The kittens came in a big way and Heidi has brought me three of them to hold at once. Mrs. Martin looks happy to see me, too, in spite of everything. I say to Kenner, "I know you're busy with work and all but can I talk to you about something?"

"Why don't you two run out to the bunkhouse and get out of my hair?" says Mrs. Martin.

"What about me?" says Heidi.

"You better get those kittens out of here before your dad comes home, or we're going to be having kitten soup for dinner."

We walk out to the bunkhouse in awkward silence. I see Frankenstein and the boat are both gone. When we get inside, Kenner plunks down on a chair and stares up at me. "So get it over with."

"What?"

"Your speech. You telling me how sorry you are about the cattle. But you want to work out here during the summer 'cause you heard that our weights are still better than everybody else's. My mom's been pecking at my dad about it all morning."

"Your weights are better?"

"Yeah. Doesn't mean they're fat as they'd be if there were no wolves. But we did okay. Probably just a fluke."

"That's amazing."

"You skipped the 'I'm so sorry about everything part.'"

"I am sorry about everything."

"I've been making your life hell since third grade. We'll call it square."

I walk over to the cabinet and look it over carefully. I

wonder how much more wire Will has behind the door. I don't want to get Kenner into this. But he is. We all are. Now I have to use a small bluff. "How soon until William gets home from the lake?"

He looks surprised but doesn't ask how I know. "Depends on the fish, I guess. Why?"

"I found Will putting up snares. He threatened me."

Kenner doesn't say anything at first. His eyes wander around the shed. "Why are you telling me?"

"He also threatened to do something to 'someone else.' Who do you think that would be?"

"How should I know?"

"Because you know everything he does."

"I don't. I really don't."

"The parade, the stores, the snares. What's next?"

"What? Just because he hates wolves doesn't mean he did those things."

"What's it going to take? Shooting somebody? He needs help and he won't get it if everyone keeps pretending this is about wolves."

Kenner glares at me. "Yeah, I know what kind of help you'll be. The same kind of help Virgil is, not keeping his big mouth shut. Can't even come out here and face me."

"This isn't Virgil's problem."

"It isn't yours either."

"Will's made it my problem. "

"Well, then I guess you'll have to deal with it."

"Turns out Will's not a very sneaky arsonist. He left something next to the fire at our store."

Kenner stands up and kicks at the chair. It skitters across the floor and falls to the ground. "Haven't you ruined my family enough?"

I say, "I care about your family. But he started the store on fire. Yesterday he was talking about hurting someone. He's out of control."

Kenner glares at me. I'm sure he wants to pound me flat, but he doesn't. I walk over and pick up the chair and sit down in it.

He says, "So you're going to turn him in, is that what you came out here to tell me?"

"It can go that way. But if he admits to the fire and the shooting, things are going to be a lot different for everybody. He might not even go to jail."

"You do believe in fairy tales."

"Anything else you want to tell me before I head to Holiday Point?"

His eyes tell me I've guessed right again. He says, "Get out of here."

"I am sorry about everything," I say.

I sneak out so Heidi won't see me leaving without petting her kittens.

Will usually launches his fourteen-footer from the same place Dad keeps his small drift boat in a slip, Holiday Point, but not always, so it was good to get that out of Kenner. With a little luck I should be able to find him. If the weather holds. Then I'm going to need a lot of luck.

Normally with clouds on the mountain like they are today, I might wait a few minutes before I launch, watching the wind. But I don't have that kind of time. Once Will knows that Virgil is gone, it's going to be harder to be persuasive. A lot depends on me being persuasive.

I row out into the choppy water. My hands are still tender from the snares incident, but I stretch out my legs and row hard. The lake is cluttered with runoff debris. I navigate a group of floating logs being visited by mergansers. I watch a bald eagle searching for fish. I wish I was doing this for fun. I wish I had gloves.

I row west toward the dam. I steer clear of another group of logs even bigger than the last. I keep going. The fishing is impossible for novices in this part of the lake, which is why I think I'll find Will here. Like me, he's always doing things the hard way.

I get lucky. Within forty minutes of leaving the pier I see him. He sees me, too, and he stays put.

By the time I row up near his boat my heart is pounding a hole in my chest, and I'm reciting lines to myself about accidents and destiny. Mainly I hope it's not my destiny to be one of William's accidents.

"Look who's here," says William. "Miss Random Acts of Irritation."

"How ya doing, Will?" I come in parallel to Will's boat. Close enough to talk, but far enough away to row backward if I need to.

Will says, "I *was* pretty good until about one minute ago. You come to give me another lecture about wolves?"

"No. But I want to talk to you."

"That's funny, because I want to fish." His lips smack when he talks, and his eyes are watery. He's drunk.

"You have a lot of empties," I say, looking at the beer cans he's stacked on the other seat.

"What else is there to do around here but drink, fish, and hunt? I guess there's one other thing but you're not my type. Are you my type, KJ?"

This isn't going to work. Isn't that what Virgil said? I didn't count on William being drunk. I feel the panic rising in my throat but I ignore it and focus on the next step. My dad says the fastest way to sober up a client is to give them a bill.

Will says, "Did you come out here to stare me to death?"

A gust of wind raises white tips around our boats. I know I can't dance around this but I'm afraid. Finally I say, "Your truck left tracks in the snow at the fire."

"What?"

"You left tire tracks when you set fire to the Dumpster outside of our store. You were probably in such a hurry to

get out of there you didn't think about it. But Virgil took pictures. A lot of pictures. Those are unusual tires. And so is the noise your truck makes. Which my dad heard loud and clear that night and described in detail to the police."

Will squeezes his beer can and throws it into the water. The white caps tip it back and forth and carry it away. "You think I started that fire?"

"Yes, I do. And I think you shot at the ice statue from the Steak House rooftop."

"Oh, yeah?" Will's not much of poker player. His face twists up. "You think too much."

"Accidents happen. It's what we do next that matters."

"You been working on that?"

"Kinda."

"Keep working."

I row closer to him. I can smell the beer from my boat. "You can't keep snaring, shooting, and setting fire to everything that pisses you off."

He spits over his boat. "I can try."

"I don't think you started out to hurt people."

"I started out to get rid of wolves that aren't supposed to be here. And pretty soon that will be legal."

"I saw the bruise on Heidi's arm. Did you mean to do that?"

Will is sloppy from drinking but I've hit the nerve I was looking for. "I've never touched Heidi."

"The college should have given you a second chance. Your parents dumped on you. The ranch is bleeding money no matter what you do. It's enough to get to anybody."

Will's says, "I hate to break it to you Dr. KJ, but hating wolves doesn't mean I'm crazy."

"I don't think you're crazy. I think you need help."

"What kind of *help*? Someone to make my knee better? To do all my crappy chores? To get my parents off my back? Someone to get rid of all the people like you who make it impossible to make a living anymore? You got that kind of help, sign me up."

Far away I hear thunder. I look up and cold rain drops hit my face. I've already waited too long to get off the water.

His voice is livid. "What did you come out here for?"

"I want you to turn yourself in."

He laughs, but he looks at me with something besides total dismissal.

"If you turn yourself in for arson and the parade you might be able to plea it down to a misdemeanor. You could get a fine or probation. But you wouldn't have to hide this for the rest of your life."

"Turn myself in? After what you've done to *my* family?" he says, swinging his arms. The empty beer cans on his seat clatter to the floor of the boat. He stammers, "What the hell are you talking about?"

Between Will and the weather I'm scared out of my skin

but I can't quit now. I've got to make this stick. I say, "Will, I'm talking about a second chance. That's what I came here to tell you. Even though this sounds awful, coming clean is a second chance."

"Jail time? That's your idea of a second chance?"

Our boats rock together, hitting each other in the gray water. "If I turn you in it's all different. You'll do five years just for the fire. And a lot more if they try to prove you knew my dad was inside, or claim the store as a residence. If you add that to Virgil getting hurt and the potential for harm in the parade, you're talking about most of your life. But if you turn yourself in, you might not go to jail at all."

Will folds his arms across his chest like he's getting ready to spring. "How do you know that? You go to law school in your spare time?"

"No, but my dad did." I don't have to tell Will this probably wouldn't hold up in court. I've learned that from my dad, too. It's better to be lucky than good.

He takes out his oar and rows on one side to keep us close. "You would spread these lies about me just to stop me from protecting my family? After my parents took you in and treated you better than they treat their own? After they let you live in their house and eat their food. After you let wolves kill their cattle? You want to send *me* to jail?"

"No." I row backward.

He rows toward me. "Like you say, accidents happen."

Before I can get my oars in the water twice, he's next to

me. All his sloppiness is gone. He swings up with one of his oars and connects with my shoulder. I jump back to get away and fall out of my boat.

The water is so cold I can barely breathe. My head is spinning and I swallow enough water to sink a Boston whaler. When I come up for air, Will's driving away in a spray of water, his boat hitting full speed on the deep waves. The *chug chug chug* of his boat smacking the wake fills my ears as I drag myself into my boat.

The rain is turning to sleet. My sweatshirt and jeans aren't exactly keeping me warm anymore. What I need is a sleeping bag with Virgil in it. I look in the utility box and find an emergency blanket. It'll have to do.

I can still hear the *chug chug chug* of Will's boat. I grab my oars and try to get my bearings. The clouds are low but I'm sure of it. He's heading straight for those logs I saw coming in. Almost as quickly as I think this I hear a cracking sound and the *chug chug chug* stops.

"Will?" I shout, but I'm too far away.

It's not that it doesn't cross my mind to go in the opposite direction. That's the smart thing to do. For all I know, he's fine. But I wouldn't have come out here in the first place if I gave a hang about doing the smart thing.

I dig in my oars but it turns out that it's hard to row very fast in white caps when you're freezing to death and you've just been knocked out of your boat with an oar. On the other hand, I'm motivated.

Within a few minutes I am in the logs. The sleet is turning to heavy snow and a cloud has settled on the water but I see the outline of Will's boat. "Will," I call.

Nothing.

"Will, answer me!"

"Here," he calls.

I row to his voice and find him hanging on the far side of his boat with one arm. He looks like a Halloween decoration.

"What are you doing?" I say.

"I got tossed . . . over the front."

He nods his chin to the chunk of propeller floating between us. I see the front of his boat is taking on water. I row to his side "Can you get in here?"

"Arm's busted." His face is pale and his mouth is bleeding.

"Use your other arm."

He looks up at me like he's not sure where my voice is coming from and then stares off into space. Maybe something besides his boat is cracked.

I lean out of the boat and put my arms underneath his. "On three."

He doesn't move.

"Stop trying to be a hero," he says. "You hate me."

"I don't hate you. And you're the hero, right? Let's see what you got, Sure Shot."

I pull at him but I'm at a bad angle. "Come on, Will!" I yell.

"Won't work," he says.

Holy smack, I'm sick of pessimistic men.

"Don't be such a pansy, Will. Drop down in the water and spin around. Put your good hand on my boat and I'll pull you in."

"You'll never be able to get us both back in this storm. You're already blue."

Part of me, the cold, scared, chicken part of me, hears what he's saying. But I'm not taking orders from my inner chicken anymore. I reach over and pull hard at Will's waist, ripping him from his boat and dropping him into the icy water between us.

Now he's in the water there's no more discussion. He reaches his good arm over the side of my boat, nearly tipping us. I lean out and grab the back of his pants. "On three."

Will growls in pain. I yell. "One. Two. Three."

Will pulls and I yank. It doesn't work.

"Come on, Sure Shot. Let's go."

I lean out farther and count again. Will lets out another pain-filled grunt and together we yank him onto the lip of the boat. The boat starts to flip. I throw myself back to stabilize and feel myself falling backward. All the way backward.

My second trip into the water is paralyzing. I'm too mad to even swear at myself.

I swim and reach up for the rim of my boat but I'm spent. I hang for a second and try to pull myself in when I feel Will's

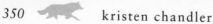

hand on mine. He doesn't say anything, but his hand is steady. I pull up again. We rock badly but somehow with his help I roll into the boat.

Will falls back to the bench and slumps into a heap. I know the beer in Will's system means he's even worse off than I am. I find the emergency blanket and wrap it around both of us. His eyes are half open but he doesn't look at me. "Will? Will, you got me in," I say, hugging him. We're both shaking.

He looks like a ghost. He says, "I didn't mean for the store to catch on fire."

"I know. Did you hit your head?"

I prop him between the life jackets and tuck the emergency blanket over him. Not first aid by the book, but there isn't anything as important as getting us off the water.

I grab my oars. I tell myself I'm going to warm up once I get going. I try to lock my hands around the oars but they don't bend right.

"I can do this," I say through banging teeth.

Will doesn't look up.

I want to climb under the blanket with him and go to sleep. I want my teeth to stop chattering out of my head. I want to stop shaking. I look around. All I can see is snow. I can't just row anywhere. I have to find the dock, or some-place else that we can get into shelter fast. At least the wind has slowed down.

What if I can't do this? I have never done anything this hard. I've failed at hard things all my life. We could die. It happens all the time up here. What if we die because I can't do this?

I see my dad holding that horrid shirt, saying, "A pattern is only a pattern if you follow it." Change the pattern.

I concentrate on the shape of the lake and where I need to go. I tell myself it's like walking in my house at night. The May snow falls in wet lumps from the sky. I close my eyes, lock my hands to the oars, and start rowing.

After about a minute the oars burn the cuts in my hands. I get out the first aid kit and try to wrap them. I'm too cold to pinch the tape.

The rest of me is stiffening, too. My arms and shoulders are locked up. My neck is a giant charley horse. I know what's happening to me. I pull off my four-hundred-pound ice block sweatshirt. My skin is corpse color and I'm falling out of an old training bra that looks like two wet Kleenexes. It's so like me to die in bad underwear.

I'm shaking so much it's hard to stay on the bench. I grab the oars to steady myself and I start rowing. I concentrate on the movement of my arms and legs. The only sound is of my breathing, the oars slapping, and the water hitting the side of the boat.

After a few minutes more I look around. My breath is shortening. I'm shaking like I'm in an earthquake. I'm running out of time. I try to see anything that would tell me where I am but all I see is a cloud of snow. I'm lost. My hands are useless. I might as well be rowing with my elbows. I've never been in this much pain, not even close.

Will's head is tipped forward and covered with snow.

"Will?" I say. "You hanging in there?"

No response.

I can't do this.

I imagine my dad yelling, *Stop rowing like a girl.*

I yell to the snow, "I am a girl!" I give my hands a good shake and keep rowing.

I think about sitting around the campfire at Kenner's place. Virgil's next to me. Dennis is explaining that stars can be dead by the time we see them. Kenner's making fun of Dennis to Addie. Sondra's feeding a chipmunk her dinner. Everyone is warm.

I can't remember how to make the oars work together. My arms are shaking too hard. The oar handles are red. Should've brought the gloves. Should've brought a whole lot more than gloves. I keep rowing.

I want to quit. I want to lie down. I want to disappear. I put my oars together. My eyes close.

I see my bedroom. I see Dad drinking an elk shake. I see Virgil smiling. Then I think I *hear* Virgil. "KJ!"

I open my eyes. I'm dreaming. Am I dreaming?

"KJ!"

He must be within a quarter mile. I call back, "Out here!"

"Row to my voice!"

He didn't leave. He's here. "Keep yelling!"

"Come on, Wolf Girl. You're nearly in."

I put my back to his voice and close my eyes again, but this time I row with everything.

"You comin'?" he yells.

"Yep. I've got Will."

"Of course you do."

"His arm's busted."

"Keep rowing!"

I keep rowing.

"Keep coming!"

I keep coming.

"Almost there."

I look behind me and I see the dock. I see Virgil jogging along the pier. He's waving his gorgeous arms. I keep rowing. I row to the nearest slip and crawl out of the boat. I drag my rope and tie up. Will's still not moving. He'd better just be passed out. He was hard to row in. "Will, we made it."

The snow is quiet. All I see is the boat and the cloud and the pier.

I sit down on the dock and look around. No one.

"Virgil?"

I'm not shaking anymore.

"Virgil?"

Everything stops hurting.

I go to sleep.

38

GOING TO HEAVEN

I KNOW I'M dead and in heaven because I am in my father's truck, sitting in the backseat next to Virgil. He has both his arms wrapped around my shoulders but he's not looking at me. I am rolled in a fluffy blanket. My dad is driving, with Eloise riding next to him. We are heading through the trees toward town. Dad's lights are shining on the road. The old men trees are watching over me. I close my eyes. Dying is perfect.

When I wake up again I am not dead, or perfect. I am alive and in pain in places I never knew existed. I'm wearing mittens so heavy I can't pick up my hands. The faces from my heaven are here though: Dad, Virgil, Eloise, Aunt Jean,

Officer Smith, Mr. Muir, and my entire obnoxious journalism class. My heaven is crowded. But it's warm. I go back to sleep.

The next time I wake up, Dad is standing over me, and he says, "You've milked this long enough."

I sit up. I'm in my own bed but I'm wearing somebody else's blue silk nightgown. My mittens are actually giant gauze bandages. My head is sweaty. The crowd's gone, but Virgil is in the corner with his head against the wall, asleep. I look at Dad. "Whose clothes are these?"

Dad takes my hand, which hurts. "Eloise thought you needed some new things."

Virgil startles awake. He looks at me and jumps out of his chair. "Hey! Oh, hey, you're back." Virgil's smile glides over his face. His eyes are swollen and bloodshot, but his smile is all sunshine. As quick as that, I'm warm.

Dad lets go of my hand. I fumble it back. I say, "Did you come get me?"

Dad cracks a smile, too. "Virgil and I showed up first. Will's family came right after. And then Officer Smith and Eloise."

"I remember being in the truck. Kind of. How did you find me?"

Dad says, "I'm a guide, remember?"

Virgil says, "Kenner called him."

Eloise waltzes in. "Look who's awake. How's our little hero?"

My mind wakes up a little more. "Where's Will?"

"They had to Life Flight him to Idaho Falls," Dad says.

"Is he okay?"

"He alive," Dad says. "But he's in bad shape. Inside and out."

My mind scrambles backward. "Has he said anything?"

Dad says, "Mr. Martin called today. We'll get the police involved when Will's out of the woods. Guess you were right, KJ."

I lie still thinking how hard this is for Will and his family. How hard it's going to be for a long time. I would have loved to have been wrong about Will.

Finally Virgil says, "You looked like a Popsicle when we found you."

"It was so cold. . . ." I replay the last few minutes before I got to the dock. Suddenly my face feels more than warm. "Who found me?"

Dad shakes his head. "Here it comes."

Virgil's smile hyperextends.

"My shirt," I whimper. Unconscious in a training bra. I feel red welts forming over my whole body. "Holy smack."

Dad tries to frown, but he can't. "I'll let it slide this one time."

Eloise shakes her head at me, "Tried to tell you girl. Underwear. It makes a statement."

Few things are more illustrative of the intellectual and emotional struggles we've endured than are the wolves.

Paul Schullery, *The Yellowstone Wolf*

39

NO NEWS IS GOOD NEWS

I GET A FEVER and don't go to school for three days. I read Jane Austen and eat bear claws with Eloise and Aunt Jean. The second afternoon Eloise, Jean, and Dad even go get coffee together and leave me alone with Virgil. Maybe there are some advantages to having our parents be friends after all.

The traveling doc at the clinic says my hands will heal as long as I wear the mittens and keep them plastered with antibiotic cream. "You are lucky to be alive. A few scars on your hands will just make you look outdoorsy."

On Thursday my dad threatens to make me some sauerkraut and I decide to go back to school. I wear a hoodie with a big pocket to hide my mittens. Everybody knows about what happened but nobody talks about it, at least not to me. Will's picture still hangs in the main hall with the award for Most Valuable Player three years in a row. Some things about small towns don't change, they just stop being talked about in polite conversation.

It's ironic to me that I started writing the column about wolves so everyone would get the real story. Now I know a real story about wolves, and I'm not talking. But if someone asked me, I'd tell them that Cinderella doesn't have a fairy-tale ending and if you want to be a princess you'd better be ready to take a royal beating.

The good news is that my teachers, including Mr. Muir, are going to let me make up my work. He's says if we hit it hard for two weeks I might not fail his class or the college entrance exam. He's not making any promises though.

The best news at school is that Mrs. Baby has a brand-new baby boy and she named him Robert Virgil Brady. Baby, what a woman.

We have a baby shower in her bedroom. Addie gives her a quilt. Sondra gives her a certificate that says baby Robert has a star named after him. I give her a fleece baby coat and a subscription to *Better Homes and Gardens*. All the boys go in on a set of miniature lightsabers. Dennis's idea, I'm thinking. Virgil takes her picture surrounded by her family, and everyone smiles at the same time.

◇   ◇   ◇

I get the call while I'm in the shop. Dad hands it to me with his eyebrows raised. "It's for you."

I grab the phone with my mittens. "Hello?"

"Ms. Carson?"

"Yes," I say cautiously to the deep voice on the other end.

"This is Ed Buck."

"Mr. Buck? Oh, hi!" I say, steadying myself.

"I heard a rumor about you. You seem to have a knack for becoming the news instead of writing it."

"It's a bad habit. I'm trying to overcome it."

"Well, I just thought you'd like to know. I've been on the phone with some folks this morning at the capitol. Their feeling is that Montana, Idaho, and Wyoming aren't going to have enough signatures to put the referendum on any of their ballots this year."

I fumble with the phone. "Can you say that again?"

"They won't be shooting non-aggressing wolves legally this year."

I lean backward just a fraction, just for a little support in my time of happiness, but the wall I'm leaning on turns out to be a nylon tent. I fall into it and drop the phone. I scramble for the phone as quickly as I can with bandages. "Mr. Buck, are you there?"

"Yeah. I'm here. Where are you?"

"Sorry. I dropped something."

I hear a dry, salty laugh in the receiver. "Well, just thought you'd like to know."

"Thank you so much. For everything."

"Listen, Miss Carson, this isn't the part of the story where I'm telling you that we all live happily ever after. This is a victory for the wolves and you were part it. Maybe bigger than you realize. But eventually the states are going to have to manage this situation themselves. And when that time comes we're going to have to have a plan that keeps a reasonable amount of wolves and cattle and elk alive."

"Okay," I say.

"You be good now."

The phone clicks. I lie still in the fallen tent. There are a million shiny stars on the shop ceiling and I want to count them.

Dad comes over "You okay?"

I grin from one happy ear to the other. I say, "I've never been better in my life."

KJ'S WOLF JOURNAL

Cinderella surprised everyone. Twice. First she fought off her sister to save her pups. Then she saved her pack, by gathering all twenty-freaking-one pups, including her sister's, into a single den. And they all survived. The scientists just scratched their beards, except Eloise, who doesn't have a beard and who thinks Cinderella is going to rewrite a few more books before she's done.

Not bad for a princess.

40

WOLF DREAMS

AFTER THE LAST day of school I go to the tree house. It snowed this afternoon so all the lovely mud and wildflowers have been covered back up with a white blanket, but it won't last. At least the mud will be back, sooner or later. Blankets cover things, but they don't change them.

I use my arms to climb up. I'm taking good care of my hands these days. As soon as they're healed my dad says he's going to teach me how to solo guide on the river. He says I only need about four hundred fishing hours and I'll be ready to go.

I lie still. The snow has stopped and the sky is clear and blue. It's almost warm.

Virgil and Eloise are moving home to Minnesota tomorrow.

Virgil says he'll come back in August to visit. He wants to learn how to row. And he doesn't know if he can live without seeing Kenner's cows every couple of months.

We joke about it, but I don't want him to go. The hard cold truth is that he might not come back. People change. Things happen. I try to imagine a future where we are together, but there are so many things ahead that I can't see anything but this afternoon's sky. Maybe the future is like rowing for shore. Your only choice is to try or give up.

The wind blows the snow off the tree and it touches my face. The air smells clean and crisp. I hear dogs barking in town and it reminds me I haven't heard anything about the wolf I saw in the woods. Not a single reported sighting. I guess anything could have happened to it. I think about the other wolves I've met this year, and it makes me feel lonesome all the way through. I curl up in a ball and take a nap.

I dream about wolves. I see them running in perfect coordination and I follow them, but I'm not a wolf. I'm not prey. I'm nothing but myself.

I wake up to the sound of someone climbing up the tree house ladder. It's Virgil.

He sits next to me. "What are you doing up here?"

"Dreaming," I say, rubbing my face. "How did you find me?"

"I'm good at that," says Virgil. "Did you notice it's freezing again?"

I look at the sun. It's in a different position from when I fell asleep.

Virgil says, "It's a lot of work keeping you alive, you know that?"

"That's what you're for."

"Hardly."

"What do you mean? I couldn't have survived this year without you."

"You wouldn't have had to survive if I hadn't come along and made such a mess of everything."

"Give me some credit, Virgil. I was a mess a long time before you got here."

"Well, now I'm the mess." He taps his foot in the snow. He shakes his hair over his face. "I don't want to go."

"People always say that. Right before they go."

"What if I don't? Would it ruin your life?"

I stare at him. Carbonated blood rushes to my head. "Virgil . . . have we had this conversation before?"

He looks away.

I pull him back to face me. "I thought I dreamed you saying those things. I never got to say I feel the same way."

He puts his hand on my arm. "This is a lot harder than I thought it would be. I'm not as tough as you are."

"Are you kidding? You're so stoic you don't even get mad when people shoot you."

"That was easy. This totally sucks."

"So we'll figure something out," I say. "Where's midway between Saint Paul and West End?"

Virgil beams. "Well . . . there's a gas station in Medora, North Dakota, called the Turquoise Turtle. They sell carrot juice slushies." He pulls out a piece of paper from his pocket and hands it to me. He's written me the directions. Like I can drive to North Dakota.

He smiles and pulls me backward against his chest. He wraps his arms around me. I'm completely warm.

I say, "We'll ruin each other, okay?"

"Okay," he says.

We sit quietly.

Virgil says, "What were you dreaming about?"

"Wolves."

"You need a new hobby."

I look off into the trees. "You know what makes wolves magnificent?"

"Good teeth?"

"They're great killers."

Virgil rubs his chin. "Twisted . . . but interesting."

"Lots of animals are stronger, faster, smarter, or more exotic than wolves, but the way they hunt . . . that's what makes us hate and love them."

Virgil doesn't talk for a while. I love that about him. I love listening to him think, especially when he's thinking about something I said. I lie back in the snow, so I can see him. I want to remember everything about how he looks right now. The scar on his cheek is an asymmetric dimple. Like everything else about him, it's beautiful to me. Finally he says, "That's because we're killers, too."

"Some of us are. But we get to decide. A wolf just is."

He lies down next to me. "KJ, you're beautiful when you're obsessing, but I'm freezing."

"I think I'm finally getting it."

"Pneumonia?"

"I mean that I don't want to be a wolf."

He says, "I kind of like you as Wolf Girl."

I kiss him. Not a dweebie high school kiss, but a Montana spring kiss. "Do you want to go now?"

"No," he says, kissing me back.

We lie next to each other and watch the clouds pass. They're white clouds in a wide-open sky. Not a storm in sight. But you can never tell what the weather's going to do next around here. I guess we'll have to wait and see. Whatever is coming, right now it feels pretty good.

Epilogue

THE BIG ONE

I SIT WITH Dad in the middle of Wade Lake. The ice is finally off, but it's still cold enough for coats. Dad won't let me row even though my hands are fine. He says he wants me to save my strength for the fish I'm going to land, but I know he just has a case of BDG (Bad Dad Guilt). I let him row.

We fish with nymphs. The fish are hungry, but they're feeding on the bottom because of the cold. When it gets warmer in a week we'll be into the season full on and won't have a day to fish for ourselves until September.

Out of nowhere Dad says, "Do you miss him?"

I look up mid-cast and pile my line like a five-year-old. I reel in and start detangling. "Yeah," I say.

He says, "He's going to have a lot on his plate this summer."

I cast again and mend my line. The secret to lake fishing is patience. You can't rush lake trout, but you can sucker them with a good drop. "I know," I say. "He'll be back."

"His mom's probably got him traveling. I guess. Probably going all over the world this summer."

I look up before I cast out again, "He's in Saint Paul. In summer school."

"Or he's in Saint Paul."

"But I do miss him."

We fish without talking for a time. The fish don't seem interested in what we're selling. My dad switches to a Woolly Bugger. After another five minutes he pops out a brown trout that looks about half starved. "Hungry and dumb," says Dad, as he releases the brown back into the water.

He takes a break and eats an apple. "It's a good thing you did with the wolves."

"You aren't mad?"

"It turned out all right."

"Didn't do you any favors."

"Or you either, I guess."

"I guess," I say.

Dad sits back and watches me cast. I'm stiff but I'm getting my line out there anyway. He doesn't correct me. I feel good. I touch the water with my fingers and think of wolves:

wild wolves, bad wolves, great wolves, dead wolves, fierce wolves.

"How did you do it?" he says. His voice is taut but not unhappy.

"Do what?"

"How did you make it back to shore? You were so blue when we found you, I thought you were dead."

I don't make a joke to change the subject. I don't say anything. I just cast while I think about what I will tell him, and how much of it I need to save for myself. I know he's been saving this question, carrying it around like his last sandwich. When I don't answer he pulls the brim of his hat down and goes back to casting.

Suddenly my line disappears and my reel explodes with the gorgeous sound of spinning gears. I nearly lose my grip, but I manage to recover and keep my tip up. This is a monster.

My dad shouts, "Whoa! Can you hold him?"

I shout back, "If the leader holds."

"He must be as big as the boat. Give him the whole reel if you have to."

I give this brute the reel but I have to fight to keep him from going under the boat. My dad says, "Don't hurt yourself now. I can take him."

"I'm fine," I sing out. The music of the reel fills my ears. He dives and then I reel and then he dives and then I reel. My hands ache. Suddenly the line stops and holds. There is no movement, just pressure. My dad says, "Are you sure that's not a log? No use hurting yourself over a log."

"Dad," I say with a fat greedy smile, "I'm not letting go."

He spits over the side of the boat. "They're your hands."

After one hundred and eight minutes the biggest fish I may ever hook in my life, a fish so big Dad says it would have set a record for Wade, runs hard under the boat and snaps off. I don't curse, but my dad does, mostly at me for holding on so long.

I toss some bread in the water and sit down in the boat. The breeze cools my sweating head. I drink some water and watch a grebe land a few feet from the boat to eat the bread. The air smells like mud and fish. The pines murmur with wind.

I say, "I imagined you chewing me out."

Dad nods.

"When I kept going I felt brave or something and I just kept going. Then, at the end, I heard Virgil's voice. It helped me find the shore."

Dad says, "You were ashore when we got there. You couldn't have heard him."

"I know." I have said more than I planned, and less, but it's not bad. I don't mind if my dad knows how I feel.

He rows. We watch the water together.

Finally he says, "Sorry you lost that big one."

"That's fine," I say. I smile at my father. "It's just good to get out."

kristen chandler has spent summers in Yellowstone at her family's cabin since she was a young girl. She is a fisherwoman, a marathoner, a writing instructor, and the mother of four children. She and her family live outside Salt Lake City, Utah. This is her first novel.